VIOLET SKY
SECOND CHANCES

VIOLET SKY SECOND CHANCES

EVE MARIAN

Paige Publishing

September 2021 First Edition

The characters and events portrayed in this book are fictitious. Any similarity to real persons, living or dead, is coincidental and not intended by the author.

Designations used by companies to distinguish their products are often claimed as trademarks. All brand names and product names used in this book and on its cover are trade names, service marks, trademarks and registered trademarks of their respective owners. The publishers and the book are not associated with any product or vendor mentioned in this book. None of the companies referenced within the book have endorsed the book.

ISBN-eBook: 978-1-7778013-3-5
ISBN-paperback: 978-1-7778013-4-2
ISBN – hardcover: 978-1-7778013-7-3

To my children, Patricia and Gabriel,
Thank you for your patience while mommy held her head in her hands in front of her laptop.
Your love and enthusiasm raised my head up high.

One

Michaela

I hated the heat. There was no breeze, no shade, no end in sight of this suffocating heatwave. It was the end of September, so I wasn't prepared for it. The dry, white, long-sleeved T-shirt I'd put on this morning was now damp and sticking to my body. I tied my curly brown hair into a ponytail and ran my finger underneath my eye to clean my makeup. I was not in a pleasant mood by the time I arrived at the café.

Nicholas had asked me to meet him back in Calabria, Italy. It was no easy feat to coordinate more time off from work, but I gave Suzanne, my boss, no choice. I had to come. I had to know exactly who I was.

When I stepped inside the café, it was busier than I thought it would be at ten o'clock on a weekday morning. A number of men and women sat and chatted in groups, and I scanned the room, waiting for one of them to wave me over.

A shiver of unease ran down my spine. I turned my head to the left. Three men sat at a table by the bar and all eyes were on me.

This must be my table.

An older gentleman, probably in his fifties, sat with one leg crossed over the other and two younger men flanking him. They were all dressed in long pants and jackets, and my temperature rose just looking at them. As I got nearer, I recognized one of the younger men. I had met him at another bar in this town just a few short weeks ago. He'd offered to buy me a drink that night, but I was with Hunter and thought it best to decline. I should have expected him to be here. Nicholas did mention one of his men had spotted me in this very town that night. Now I knew who it was.

"Buongiorno," I said when I arrived at their table. They all stood up, and the younger man—the one I didn't recognize—pulled out a chair for me.

"*Grazie*," I said.

"*Prego*," he responded.

"We can speak English if you prefer, Michaela," said the older gentleman.

"Yes, thank you." I was relieved. Most of my Italian had been exhausted by those two words.

"My God, it is so wonderful to see you," said the older gentleman.

"Nicholas Giannis, I presume?" I asked him.

"Yes, I apologize. Let me introduce everyone. As you've guessed, I'm Nicholas and this is Marco, whom you met the last time you were here."

I gave Marco a nod, but I held back my smile. In addition to declining his drink, I was nearly killed at the airport because of his intel.

"And this is my son, Adam," said Nicholas as he gestured toward the man who'd pulled out my chair.

Adam didn't smile. Instead, he stared and watched my face. I kept it blank for now. I planned to tread carefully at this meeting. I noticed while Nicholas, Marco and I perspired, Adam's tanned skin looked cool and unbothered—much like the rest of him. I disliked him instantly.

"It's very nice to meet you," I said and made a childish point of looking only at Nicholas when I said this. Marco cleared his throat and shifted in his seat, but Adam didn't flinch. Then, I remembered something Nicholas had said during that life-changing phone call.

He had mentioned Adam before; he'd said that Adam... "You were the assassin at the airport?" I asked, stunned by the recollection.

"Keep your voice down," Adam whispered, but there was no softness in his tone.

"You nearly killed me and that's all you have to say to me?" I asked incredulously.

"I wasn't aiming for you," he said simply.

Unbelievable! "Well, it's a good thing you have terrible aim, otherwise you would have killed my..."

He stared at me with his eyebrows raised, waiting. "Your what?"

"My boyfriend...ex-boyfriend...my friend—regardless, you nearly killed him!"

"Yes, he would be dead if I hadn't misjudged his quick reflexes. I won't make that mistake the next time," Adam said.

"There won't be a next time," I warned him. I kept my voice steady despite the emotions battling in my heart.

He didn't respond, but he tilted his head and I read the "we'll see" response in his eyes.

"Are you staying with Anna Maria Tassone?" asked Nicholas, bringing his hands together in a single clap. I turned my attention back to him.

"Yes, she's been kind enough to give me a room while I'm in town for the week."

"I'm glad to hear it. Signora Tassone has been a friend to your family for many years and many generations," he said.

"Yes, she has. And speaking of my family, tell me, what do you know about my parents' death?"

Nicholas rubbed the back of his neck. I should have given him more time, but I couldn't wait any longer. I'd traveled more than seven thousand kilometres, taken an eight-hour flight from Toronto, to ask him this question in person.

A little over a week ago, I received a phone call from a man I'd never heard of before but who claimed to know me. It was Nicholas, and I've replayed his words in my head over and over again. He told me that my boyfriend was a manticore, my mother and I were Sheds—descendants of an ancient Egyptian god and the natural-born enemies to manticores—and that my parents' death was not accidental. In fact, they were killed by a manticore. Hunter didn't immediately deny any of this and I no longer wanted to hear his explanation. I wanted to hear it from Nicholas.

"Are you sure you want to discuss that—"

"Yes," I interrupted him. "I traveled all this way because I need to know why you said their death was not an accident."

When he glanced at my face, he must have read the stubborn resolve in my jaw. "All right, I'll tell you," he said and casually looked around, ensuring no one was listening before he continued. "I met your mother, Lucia, when she was only nineteen. I met her here in Italy at Signora Tassone's house. She knew about her lineage. Her mother had told her everything about The Sheds."

I nodded but my stomach sank. Her mother had told her everything. I couldn't believe my mother had kept it from me. I knew nothing until that fateful phone call from Nicholas a few days ago.

"Your mother was ready to take on the kingdom of manticores. She worked relentlessly on investigating news reports on extraordinary feats of strength or strange animal attacks. She would follow the culprit until she was satisfied that no manticores were involved."

"And if they were?" I prodded.

"If they were, she would fearlessly pursue them," said Nicholas.

"Pursue them for what purpose?"

Nicholas didn't respond, so Adam interjected for him.

"To assassinate them."

My mouth hung open. I don't know why his bluntness shocked me. I should have expected something like this when Nicholas called me a warrior on the phone. But I wasn't ready to hear my mother described as a killer.

"Don't look so stricken, Michaela," said Nicholas. "These manticores she killed...they were killers too. Well, all except for the last one. That was the one your mother never could get over."

Nicholas's voice changed from sombre to frantic. "I told her it wasn't her fault—she had made a mistake—but she couldn't get over it. She swore she'd stop hunting manticores from that day on. But it was too late. She paid for her mistake with her life."

"I don't understand. What are you saying?" I shook my head as I tried to make sense of Nicholas's words.

"They killed her for it," he explained. "Manticores killed your mother because she had killed their queen."

Two

Hunter

I hated waiting. I tried to be patient with him, but I couldn't hold off any longer.

"Father, we need to talk," I said.

I approached him in the breakfast room. I took a chair at the table in front of my father, and Aunt Olympia sat on his left. They both had the newspaper in their hands, but only Aunt Olympia put hers down when I'd walked into the room. "I need to speak to you about a photograph of a woman with violet eyes that was in your study."

He didn't put the newspaper down even after I said this. It still covered his face so I couldn't read his expression.

"Yes, Hunter. But not today. I do not feel up to a long conversation today," he said as he finally put his newspaper down and rose from his seat. "I think I will lie down for a little while in my room. Please see that I am not disturbed."

I choked back an exasperated breath while I tried to regain my patience. Aunt Olympia and I watched him leave the room and walk off toward the stairs.

"Give him some more time," she said to me.

"It's been two weeks. He is taking kingdom business meetings but avoiding any conversation with me," I argued.

"He looked visibly upset the first time you mentioned this to him last week. It may have been too soon in his recovery." She tried to soothe me, but her words were no balm for my frustration.

"He definitely knows something," I said, thinking back to his reaction a few minutes ago. "He did not seem confused by my question, just reluctant to answer it. He knows something, Aunt Olympia, but he's not willing to talk to me about it. That doesn't bode well for me and Michaela. If he truly did kill her mother, I need to understand why. Otherwise Michaela and I can never get past this."

The thought made my insides churn with frustration. I was furious this had happened and even more so to be the one facing the consequences of another's actions.

"Give him time, Hunter. The king is a very reasonable man. Perhaps the photo was of Michaela's mother, but we do not know for sure he had anything to do with her parents' death. I am sure he will explain everything to you when he's ready," said Aunt Olympia.

She truly had a kind soul. To think kindly of another, and see only good in them, was a virtue. I never claimed to be virtuous.

"I'll give him some time," I said. However, I knew this would only appease us both for a little while. I would not be patient for much longer.

As expected, Aunt Olympia smiled at my reassurance. She rose and placed a kiss on my forehead before leaving the room. I remained seated and once again considered the possibilities for my father's involvement with Michaela's mother. Perhaps my father had only run surveillance on Lucia. Perhaps she was an informant and had worked with my father. Perhaps—

"He will never tell you the truth," a voice said from the doorway.

I turned my head toward the entrance and watched Aunt Elenora, my father's twin, walk into the room.

"I couldn't help but overhear your conversation with the king, and afterward the one with my sister. I know you'll not let this go so

I might as well say it. Your father will never tell you the truth," she said.

"Why are you so sure? What do you know of it?" I kept my voice low, but I was tempted to shout and demand she tell me everything she knew. However, I had grown up watching my aunt Elenora, and she preferred to be the one making demands, the one in control, so I told myself to stay calm and let her talk.

She took the bait and seated herself at the head of the table where my father sat earlier. She would not be rushed. She removed the white napkin she'd found on his chair and dropped it on the floor. Moved his discarded plate aside and placed her folded hands on top of the table. Her movements were slow and deliberate. She tried to demonstrate her power over me, in this situation, with her subtle movements. But I could not allow her to overstep my boundaries. Manticores had the instinct to dominate, and Aunt Elenora was not one I would let my guard down around. So, I exerted a little dominance of my own by lacing my question with a command.

"What do you know of the photograph of the woman with violet eyes?" I asked. Even though I'd said it softly, she detected the authority in my voice, and I saw the moment she decided to rescind power back to me. For now.

"Her name was Lucia Shedly Morrone," she said, and I exhaled the breath I held. Finally, someone was telling me the truth.

"Go on."

"We first received intel on Lucia several years before her death. We were hunting a rogue manticore in London for months. We had set a trap for him and we were ready to pounce. However, the night before our planned attack, our team discovered the rogue had already been killed. We were told by those following the manticore that Lucia Shedly had killed him. We didn't know what to make of this, so we began to follow her. When it became clear she was not a manticore herself—or a homicidal maniac—we left it to the human authorities to deal with her crime. But they never did."

I nodded, and my breathing quickened when Aunt Elenora stopped talking.

"Continue," I said, and Aunt Elenora nodded slowly. I did not mistake the movement for a nod of obedience. Instead, she looked annoyed I had interrupted her monologue. She was an actor on a stage, and I was her captivated audience.

"The crime scene was cleaned up and the murder left unsolved. We didn't think more of it until it happened again." She paused for effect.

"A few years later, Lucia managed to get to another rogue manticore before us. There was a series of animal attacks near the French Alps one winter that our kingdom spent months investigating. We finally figured out it was a manticore from Norway who had fled his region, not wanting to control his baser instincts when the magistrate there had given him a warning. But again, Lucia managed to get to him before we did."

I raised my eyebrows at this information, both impressed and perplexed at how one woman had outsmarted an entire kingdom of manticores. But then I shook the thought away. I knew without a doubt that Michaela would be capable of it, too, if she had been in her mother's position.

"While the kingdom's elite service was in an uproar because a human was interfering with manticore justice, your father was far more intrigued than upset by this woman. He arranged to have her followed again, this time for nearly a year before he finally sent a message to her. He requested a meeting with her in Toronto, but she refused to invite a manticore to her city. She was fiercely protective of her family. She insisted on meeting in our city. Your father agreed to meet her here in New York."

Aunt Elenora pushed a strand of her wavy dark hair behind her ear. "Now, I know your father is king, but I vehemently disagreed with that woman coming to our city. We, too, had to protect our own kind, and she had proven herself quite capable of taking down manticores. However, the king said he needed to allow this concession in order to gain her trust and find out who she really was, and what she wanted with manticores."

Elenora leaned back and waited for me to do the same before she continued.

"Lucia did not agree to the meeting right away. She wanted to make sure it was not a trap for her. Smart woman. The king and Lucia spoke on the phone for several months. He would update those of us on the council of his conversations with Lucia. He said there had been misunderstandings on both sides and he was making headway with her. He explained that she'd been taught manticores were soulless beasts who could not control their killer instincts but she now questioned this. In light of the changes our kingdom was making, Lucia wondered if this was still the case. You know how strongly your father feels about manticore reform and teaching us how to control our instincts. He has always wanted us to assimilate and live peacefully with humans."

I nodded, as that had been my father's and grandfather's mission for more than two centuries.

"Your father told us that Lucia was coming around. She had even admitted she may have been wrong to assume all manticores could not control their instincts. She was surprised to hear how many of us already lived and worked within society. He reassured us that she had spoken to members of her team and informed them she would no longer hunt manticores and would explain more when she saw them in person. A few months later, Lucia agreed to meet your father, here in New York."

"It sounds like you're saying my father and Lucia had become friends, or at least friendly. He could not have been responsible for her death."

A sense of relief washed over me, only to be snuffed out by Elenora softly shaking her head.

"Tell me what happened next," I said.

"This is the part where the details have only been assumed, since no one entirely knows why your mother decided to fly to Toronto on her own to meet with Lucia that day. Lucia could not have written to your mother, as she did not know where the king and queen lived, and she did not speak on the phone with her, as we couldn't trace back any phone call coming in from Toronto. It is still a mystery how Lucia got in touch and what she said to get your mother to arrive on her doorstep. Lucia denied it, of course. She said your mother arrived unannounced and uninvited. Shocked to find a manticore at her door, Lucia shouted at her and told her to back away, but your mother insisted that she needed to speak with her. She said the queen was frantic and forced herself inside. She was screaming at Lucia and acting out of control. Afraid the manticore would hurt her teenage daughter, who was upstairs in her room, Lucia said she panicked. She instinctively grabbed your mother and tried to hold her down, not thinking how that would elicit a manticore's instincts."

"If my mother were riled up, holding her down like that would have triggered her survival instinct. She would have lashed back," I said, as I imagined the encounter clearly in my head.

"Yes. Your mother lashed back, and her claws came out. She thrashed and scratched Lucia in the arm. Terrified of being unable to control your mother, Lucia said she tried to contain the situation. She repeated a chant she hoped would only slow the queen down, but it killed her instead. In Lucia's defense, she was probably never trained to contain a manticore, only destroy one."

My head spun and my heart raced. I didn't want to accept it. I was told my mother was killed by an enemy soldier. I'd assumed it was another manticore. "Why didn't Lucia explain what happened to the king?" I said, but even I knew the answer to that. My father loved my mother deeply. He would not have wanted to hear any explanation.

"He was in a terrible state of grief. He couldn't believe what had happened. He didn't even know what Lucia looked like, only those who had followed her did. When a team was sent out to extrapolate her and bring her to the kingdom for justice, they discovered it was too late. She had left with her husband for the airport. The team continued to follow her and send pictures back to your father. I think it was too much to see the photos of a vibrant young woman boarding a plane, while his wife's body had been returned to him in a casket. We received word Lucia was to board another plane, this time with only her husband and a pilot. When my husband Davis asked the king if he would give his permission to take the plane down, your father agreed and said he never wanted to hear the name Lucia Shedly again."

"Who knows about the order?"

"Only the three of us. Your father, me, and Davis. Davis took care of it on his own."

"My God," I whispered.

My life was tied to Michaela's, but those ties were choking us now. My father would never get over what had happened to my mother, and truthfully, I didn't know if I could either.

Three

Michaela

The weeds were a meter high and reached my hip. Tiny needles covered their stems. I brushed my hand over them to feel if they were soft— *Ouch*. Definitely not soft.

I glanced down at my shorts and cringed. I cursed the thought of crossing that weed-infested field to reach the house. I turned in a circle, checking if I had walked in the wrong direction. No, this was it. It was the only home that stood directly behind Signora Tassone's house.

It was my great-grandmother's house, the one my mother stayed in when she met with Nicholas and his father in Italy. It was obvious no one had taken care of it since my parents died nearly ten years ago. The house resembled most of the other homes in the village: grey stone, dark wood shutters, very few windows.

"Come this way," a male voice said from behind the house.

I cupped my hand over my eyes to shield them from the sun's glare. Adam stood behind the house, waving me over. I knew there was a possibility he'd be here, but I was still annoyed when I saw him.

"I don't want to walk through the weeds," I told him.

"Go back to the road and follow it all the way around the house toward the back," he shouted. "I've cut a path there."

I mumbled something about a path being more sensible in front of the house, but I managed to keep my opinion to myself.

"We didn't want to encourage any trespassers with a path directly to the front door," he told me when I reached the front steps. He waited there with his arms crossed over his white T-shirt. I glanced up at him, surprised he had read my thoughts.

"Can you read minds?" I asked him, wanting to know what I was up against.

He shook his head and said without a smile to soften his remark, "No, you just have a terrible poker face. I can read your thoughts like an open book."

I frowned. Then softened my mouth and widened my narrowed eyes to form a blank expression. He stared at me and shook his head again. What a condescending ass.

When I stepped inside, I noticed the home was similar to Signora Tassone's except with a lot less furniture. There was only a kitchen table with three chairs, one couch, and a bookshelf. I also noticed the absence of other people. "Where's Nicholas?"

"He went to retrieve the tomes you had shipped from Toronto. He will be here shortly."

My face must have spoken to him again because he added, "Why? Are you afraid of being alone with me?"

"Absolutely not," I said, and it was the truth. I was tired of this man being rude to me. "In fact, I think you need to be careful how you speak to me, Adam, because while I may look weaker than you, looks can be deceiving."

He walked up to me, hands on his hips, and stared at me hard. His face revealed no emotions, but his voice was as cold as steel. "I know what you are, Michaela, and what you are capable of, remember? What you may not know yet, is that your powers are strongest against beasts not humans. And I am no beast."

That's debatable. But I kept that thought to myself. I held my breath, stared back, and waited for him to read my thoughts. He just glared back at me. He ended the staring match first and surprised me when he raised his arms to assume a fighting stance.

He crooked his index finger and said, "Come on. Show me what you got. Hit me."

"What?"

"You heard me. Hit me."

"I am not going to hit you, Adam. This is ridiculous."

"My father told me you killed a manticore. You can definitely hit me."

"That wasn't on purpose, and I was trying to save Hunter's life."

"Did that manticore have any family? Did they threaten you?"

"Yes...but—"

"You need to learn to defend yourself, Michaela. If manticores learn that your powers are not as immediate with humans, they will use it against you. My job is to teach you how to fight and defend yourself from an attack."

His words motivated me to move. I stepped forward and mimicked his fighting stance: one leg in front of the other, arms up and hands in front of my face.

"Good. Now try to hit me."

I curled my right hand into a fist, thumb out, and punched toward his face. He easily blocked it with his arm.

"Again," he said.

I curled both my hands this time and rained my fists down on him, but he blocked each and every blow.

"Again," he repeated.

I tried the same fury of fists but didn't land a single punch. Exhausted, I said, "I could have just told you that I don't know how to fight instead of this pointless and painful exercise." I panted and squeezed the cramp at my side.

"Yes. But I wanted to see what kind of instincts you have and if there's any natural talent I can work with."

"And?"

"Your instincts are terrible. You pull your punches and not once did you try to use your leg, your most powerful body part."

"Look, I didn't come here to learn to fight. I came to learn who I am and how to control my powers," I said and turned to walk outside. I'd rather wait for Nicholas in the scorching heat than listen to anymore of what Adam had to say.

"A warrior is who you are, Michaela, and learning to fight is how you control your enemies. Now start acting like the warrior you are meant to be!"

The way he shouted at me heated my blood. I barely recalled my hand curling into a fist but it did, and I punched him right in the face. He didn't expect it and neither did I.

I didn't think before I hit him. I just reacted. I had never hit anyone in my whole life. And while my hand throbbed and hurt like the devil, I had to admit it also felt really good.

He tilted his face down to look me in the eye. I could already see a bruise forming just above his cheek. I fought my emotions and stuffed them back down into my chest. I stared right back at him. Truthfully, I didn't know how to feel—happy that I'd hit him or angry that I'd hit anybody.

"Finally," he said. Neither his face nor his voice revealed whether he was angry or proud. Perhaps relieved? "Let's get to work."

This time, I didn't hold any of my punches. I looked for openings, but there weren't any. He blocked every single one of my hits. Then, I noticed he left his abdomen unprotected and I kicked it before I could think twice about it. My foot landed on his stomach, but I didn't pull it back fast enough. He grabbed onto my ankle and took me down with him. I landed with a thud on top of him and honestly didn't even try to break my fall with my hands. Adam breathed out a large exhale. I thought I'd knocked the wind out of him, until he said, "Again."

He had raised himself into his fighting stance when the front door opened.

"Ah, you've already started your training," said Nicholas, his smile stretching from one ear to the other. "Adam is our best fighter. He's never lost a fight in his life."

I caught a glimpse of Adam's jaw twitch, probably from grinding his teeth. While I knew my earlier hit could be described as a sucker punch, I felt immense joy knowing I'd caught one of their best off guard.

"Were you able to retrieve the tomes I shipped?" I asked Nicholas, even though I recognized the box he held as the one I'd used to ship the books.

"Yes. Except it seems that one is missing. I've checked three times, but the first book is not here."

"I should have mentioned it earlier. I'm sorry, but Hunter has that one," I explained.

"Oh," said Nicholas. His eyes shot a concerned look in Adam's direction.

"Is that a problem?" I asked.

"Well, it might prove to be," he said.

"What do you mean?"

"The first book explains the origins of The Sheds—the union of the Egyptian god, Shed, with Ra's daughter," he said.

"Yes, Hunter's professor was able to get that much from the book," I told him.

"Mmm, that's what I was afraid of. If manticores are able to translate the text, then they will understand how you can control them."

"Control them?"

"Yes, as you saw with John, you could control a manticore's heart -- stop it, make it stronger, and not just his heart. You could even..." He stopped, seeming to consider his next words.

"Yes? I can even...?"

"You can even neutralize their venom."

Nicholas must have noticed my confusion because he expanded to say, "You can defeat a manticore without killing him, by rendering his greatest weapon—his venom—useless."

"But Hunter and his family already know I have powers. They saw what I did to John," I said, not understanding why Nicholas looked so worried.

"Hunter could have convinced people it was just a coincidence. He could say that John was so angry, he gave himself a heart attack. Or that Hunter inflicted a wound on John that no one realized was fatal until he dropped dead. But the text is proof that The Sheds exist and they are capable of destroying a manticore. And not only can you destroy them with just your mind, but you can also suppress their greatest, most fatal weapon."

I started to understand why Nicholas was concerned.

"So, what do we do now?" I asked.

"We come up with a plan to get the book back," said Nicholas.

For a quick second, I held my breath and then let out a sigh. I didn't like how this sounded. Nicholas wanted me to get the book back directly from Hunter, but I wasn't ready to see him yet. Especially not after learning what my mother had done. I was no closer to understanding my history now than I was that night in my kitchen when I'd told Hunter to leave. I needed more time and I needed more answers.

"First, you tell me what's in the rest of those books and everything I need to know about being a Shed," I said to Nicholas, and lent no softness to my voice. I wanted no argument from either man right now.

"You're right. I promised to tell you everything," Nicholas said as he pulled out a chair by the kitchen table. He motioned for me to join him. I took the chair directly across from him, leaving the one between Nicholas and me for Adam. When Adam sat down, Nicholas began.

"My father taught me everything I know about The Sheds, and he learned it from his father," Nicholas said and looked over at his son. Adam gave him a nod. "We consider ourselves The Sheds' protectors."

"Is it just you, Adam and Marco? Are there others?" I asked.

"There are others, but not many. There's my wife, Victoria; my father, Alexander; and my niece, Olivia. We've had to recruit a few mercenary soldiers to help hunt manticores since your mother's death, but that's all of us."

"So, it was quite the stroke of luck when Marco saw me a few weeks ago. Since there are so few of you."

"We recruited Marco about nine years ago. He was from this town and was a skilled soldier. We never knew if another Shed would appear, but I had a feeling that if she existed, she would return to this town. Besides, there was still hope that your grandmother would return one day."

I had never met my grandmother. She and my mother had been estranged before I was born. My grandmother had run away from an engagement with Nicholas's father. But that did not stop her daughter, my mother, from seeking that same man out years later behind my grandmother's back.

"I understand why you'd keep an eye out for my grandmother's return to her hometown, but why would any other Shed come here?"

"Just a few kilometres from here there is a hotel called La Porta del Sole."

I said the name in my head a few times, trying to translate it properly.

"The sun's door?" I asked.

"Close. It means gateway to the sun. It is a clever name, no? I wanted the name to signal to any Shed looking for us exactly where we are. My family owns this hotel and lives there. We keep our eyes open for any new tourists in the surrounding villages. Your ancestors laid down roots in this area after leaving Egypt. Any lost Shed who knew this would come here and find our gateway to the sun."

"Why would there be any lost Sheds?" I asked.

"Shed women have always had to live in secret. They've had no choice. In the past when they've revealed their powers to humans, they were forced to tend to the injured. If the injury was too far gone and they could not heal them, the women were accused of causing the injury and then imprisoned for it. If she showed her powers and a manticore caught wind of it, she would be hunted down and killed." Nicholas opened his hands and made a gesture to show the two undesirable outcomes. "So, it was best to keep her powers to herself."

I nodded understanding the predicament.

"As far as we know, there have not been many Shed women born in the last century. Our family has only been able to trace the lineage back to your family, but it's not like we can take an ad out in the paper looking for Sheds. Instead, we keep our ear to the ground and if one needs us, we are here for her. To answer your question, we don't think there are any lost Sheds out there, but if any are in hiding it is our duty to find them and protect them."

"Besides my mother and me, have you met any other Sheds?" A crazy thought crossed my mind. What if I had a long-lost aunt or cousin out there wandering aimlessly around?

"We have not met any Sheds since your mother. Except you."

I was disappointed by his response. It would have been nice to have someone who understood what I was going through, someone to confide in. I brushed off the crumbs of my latest hope and directed the conversation back to my family's past.

"Why did your father want to marry my grandmother?"

"My father was obsessed with The Sheds. His father had taught him everything about them. He told him it was their family's mission to protect The Sheds and help them fulfill their mission to kill any ungodly beasts that roamed the earth. My father thought the best way to protect your grandmother was to marry her. He wanted them to be an extraordinarily powerful couple that would hunt down manticores and start a legacy the world had never seen. Unfortunately, he was more enthusiastic about the partnership than the woman. Your grandmother was smart enough to see it. She wanted love, not a legacy."

"Why was she afraid to come back? Afraid for my mother to reveal herself in public?"

"She didn't really know my grandfather very well. But she knew how obsessed he was about his son marrying a Shed. She probably thought that if he discovered she had a daughter born with the power of the violet eyes, then he would take his revenge and kidnap her daughter."

"And when my mother revealed herself to your father, Nicholas? Why not come out of hiding then?"

"I don't know. Your mother said she had an awful argument with your grandmother about her joining us and hunting manticores. Your grandmother believed we don't get to decide who lives and who dies. Manticores have their own justice system and we should leave them to it."

"And you?" I asked, looking at Nicholas and then at Adam. "What do you believe?"

"We've only hunted rogue manticores. Those who have hurt humans."

"Every beast your mother killed deserved to die," said Adam.

"Even the queen?" I asked.

Nicholas shook his head. "That was a terrible mistake. I am sure any one of us would have done what your mother did if we were in her shoes."

"But if you had not taught her how to kill, the queen would still be alive today," I countered.

"Yes, and your mother would be dead," replied Adam. "And maybe you would be too."

I didn't respond because I couldn't say for sure what the queen was thinking at that moment. Why had she come to our home that day? Had she truly wanted to hurt me? Were Hunter and his family bloodthirsty beasts that only wanted to dominate humans, like John had? I couldn't reconcile this with Hunter's behavior. Yes, he'd lied to me; he'd never told me he was a manticore. He'd practically begged me to take him to my aunt Julie's house to look for clues on my supposed powers. He was loving but never wanted to love me fully. I thought it was to protect me, but maybe it was really to protect himself. Was it all just a ruse? I shook my head to shake off these wayward thoughts.

"Let's change the subject, shall we?" I turned to Nicholas, determined to learn more. "Tell me how my powers work?"

A smile crept onto Adam's face, the first one I'd seen since I met him.

"Well, fortunately, the books you did ship have all the answers that you need," Nicholas said with a smile of his own. "Sheds use chants and meditation to channel their powers. You will need to memorize them and know which ones to use in particular situations."

"I think my meditating next to the king's bedside saved him, but I wasn't chanting or meditating when John died." I still couldn't bring myself to say the words *when I killed John*. "I just imagined his heart stopping and then he dropped to the ground."

"That's incredible," said Nicholas, his hands together as though in prayer. "Without any knowledge of your power or any chant, you were able to do that. Imagine what you can do when you are equipped with the right words?"

"Show me," I said. Nicholas wasted no time grabbing the tomes.

I remembered the texts were written in old Italian, and I could barely read regular Italian. I explained this to Nicholas, but he reassured me that he would teach me.

"It is not very different from today's Italian once you get the hang of the nuances," he said. I placed my head down, next to his, and listened to his instructions.

Four

Michaela

I was never an early riser, but the beauty of the sunrise in this little Italian village had catapulted me out of bed each morning for the past six days. That, and knowing Adam would break down Signora Tassone's door if I didn't meet him out front by 5:45 a.m. The sky gleamed a crisp indigo blue, and the clouds were an iridescent pink that reminded me of cotton candy. The tableau painted a beautiful backdrop to the small homes built along this mountainside.

Adam and I jogged side by side. We'd been running for about thirty minutes, silent except for the whooshes of my breath and the pounding of my heart.

The town near the ocean, where I'd stayed with Hunter a few weeks ago, hummed with people walking up and down the streets. But up here on the mountainside, it was quiet. There were several hundred villagers in the mountains, but they usually kept to their own homes. Veronica told me there was a day in mid-August, called "Ferragosto," when the people from town traveled to spend a day in the mountains, and the people from the mountains spent their day in town. I liked the idea of spending time in someone else's town, understanding them better, but I didn't think one day would be enough. I had spent six days in this village and I wasn't ready to leave tomorrow.

We jogged the perimeter of the village until I spotted Signora Tassone's home a few metres away. I slowed down to a walk and caught my breath. Adam turned to see what'd happened and walked back to me.

"Are you all right?" he asked.

"Yes." I covered my eyes with my hand and gazed at the home where my grandmother had lived, and which I now studied in. I had learned so much in the last six days about who I was and what I was capable of doing.

"I'm great," I said and meant it. I didn't know what to expect when I arrived, but for the first time in a long time, I belonged somewhere. I belonged to something. It felt good. It felt fortifying. It felt like being in love.

"I have to say, Michaela, I wasn't exactly convinced you would fulfill your role as a Shed, but you have impressed me this week," Adam said in his usual deceptively calm voice—the one that gave no hint of what he truly felt.

"What do you mean?" I asked.

"Only that you have learned the language and memorized the chants faster than I thought you would. You've even managed to knock me to the ground again with a leg swipe," he said, and I thought I saw a smile creep up on his face. But it was gone by the time I took a second look.

"Why did you think I wouldn't fulfill my role as a Shed?"

He looked a little uncomfortable. He walked beside me but stared up into the clouds. They had lost their sugary appeal and were plain white again.

"Signora Tassone said something to my father that made me believe you couldn't possibly be a Shed, or at least you didn't have it in you to be one," he said.

"What did she say?"

"She said that you and Hunter looked to be in... Well, you looked like you were together," he said.

"We were, but I'm not sure if we are anymore," I said, and he shook his head.

"Whom I choose to be with is none of your concern, Adam," I told him, although I tried to soften my voice.

"That's what you don't understand. It is my concern," he said and, finally, emotion flashed on his face—it was anger. "It is my family's and my responsibility to protect you, especially from manticores like him." He spat the last part out like even the word tasted dirty in his mouth.

"You don't know him. He would never hurt me," I said with conviction.

"Maybe not intentionally. But he has the strength and the instinct to do it." He turned around to look me in the eye. He placed both his hands on my shoulders and squeezed gently.

"I know you feel it," he continued, and I was alarmed by what he meant by that. "I know you feel your strength and your purpose here on this land, in this village, with me...and my father."

I released the breath I held and nodded.

"It's because your heart already knows who you are, but your mind was never given the tools to express it, to meet its true purpose."

Tears welled up in my eyes because that sense of belonging and purpose was something I had sought for nearly ten years. He was right, I finally felt it now. Adam didn't glance away, and I blinked to hold back the tears but one escaped. He rubbed his thumb across my cheek and wiped it away. He leaned in closer to me, his warm breath tickled my ear. I shivered but didn't move or say anything, and neither did he. I closed my eyes and waited for him to make the next move. He turned on his heels and jogged past Signora Tassone's house.

I stood there alone for a few minutes, trying to gather my

thoughts. When I was sure my legs would hold me up, I walked into Signora's home and straight to Veronica's smiling face.

"*Buon giorno, Michaela,*" she said in a sing-song voice. "*Tutto a posto?*" she asked.

"Yes, everything's fine," I responded. My Italian had improved, and Veronica often spoke both languages to me.

"Yes, it does look like everything is fine—perhaps really fine," she said.

"What are you talking about?" I asked but looked away, hoping she hadn't caught a glimpse of what happened two minutes ago.

"You know what I'm talking about. I saw a spark between you and Adam out there. Be careful or you'll set the whole village on fire the next time." She laughed.

"You're exaggerating, Veronica. We were arguing, actually. He had the audacity to tell me who I can and cannot be with," I explained.

"Of course, he did. It's because he wants to be with you himself."

"That's ridiculous. He's been nothing but a jerk since I've met him. He never smiles at me and he just told me he didn't think at first that I would be worthy of my lineage."

"I don't think he's afraid of what you can't do. I think he's afraid of what you *can* do. If you want to be with Hunter, he knows you will find a way to do it, and that scares him. Because whether you see it with those violet eyes of yours or not, that man is falling for you."

Her words unnerved me. I didn't want to believe them, so I grabbed a bottle of water and walked off to my room without saying a word. Besides, I had packing to do and a plan to make to get my book back.

***

"Michaela," Signora Tassone called from the front room. "*È ora di andare.*"

It was seven o'clock at night and it was time for us to leave. But I was so tired and had a plane to catch in the morning. I didn't want to attend some village festival tonight.

Someone knocked on my door and I pulled my shoulders back to gather my strength. I would tell Signora Tassone that I wasn't going, that I'd be staying in tonight. But when I opened the door and saw the concern in her eyes, I knew I couldn't disappoint her. "I'll just be a minute, I promise."

She smiled and walked back to the living room.

I threw on a cotton summer dress. It was white with tiny red roses all over it. It had short sleeves and a thin red leather belt. I put on a pair of tennis shoes, since Veronica had warned me there would be a lot of walking and dancing in the streets tonight. *Ugh.* Maybe I should wear heels and use those as an excuse not to dance. But I walked out of my bedroom, tennis shoes on, and out onto the driveway. Veronica sat in the driver's seat with Signora Tassone beside her. I hopped in the back seat. Veronica smiled at me through her rearview mirror and then winked. I smiled but it didn't reach my eyes. It was my last night and I was sad to say goodbye.

The winding road down the mountain into town always left my heart in my throat. It was so narrow that only one vehicle could fit on the road at a time. Drivers had to honk their horns periodically to alert oncoming traffic. When Veronica heard a honk, she slowed down and pulled over to let the other vehicle pass. She did this without any fear or hesitation, and I shook my head each and every time, praying to God that we made it down all right.

The closer we got to town, the more excited I felt. I heard music but it didn't come from a DJ booth or even a band. It came from the villagers themselves. A number of them wore drums strapped to their bodies and pounded a staccato beat with their drumsticks.

Boom, boom, boom. Pause. *Boom, boom, boom.* Repeat.

Voices rang out, but it wasn't singing. The villagers chanted instead. Veronica parked the car, and we weaved our way through the crowd. Bodies surrounded us and Veronica tugged on my arm.

"Girls, I will stay here," said Signora Tassone; then she went to embrace an older lady who stood on the doorstep of one of the apartment buildings.

"*Nonna* likes to watch from Signora Vincenza's balcony," said Veronica. I looked up and saw two seats overlooking the festivities. Assessing the crushing crowd, I wished I could join them.

"What's happening?" I asked Veronica.

"They are celebrating the life of the town's patron saint, Rocco," she told me. People filled the narrow, cobblestone streets. Some pounded on drums, others chanted, and most danced to the rhythm of the beat.

I listened closely to their chant: *"Rocco, Rocco, Rocco, vivo Santo Rocco."* Long live Saint Rocco. But they shouted each word in time with the drumbeat: *Rocco, Rocco, Rocco—Vivo Santo Rocco.* The rhythm hypnotized me. The earth trembled underneath my toes from the pounding of their feet on the pavement.

"*Rocco, Rocco, Rocco—Vivo Santo Rocco*," I repeated the chant.

Veronica smiled at me. Then, she grabbed my hand and pushed us through the crowd. She brought us into the middle of a circle where other men and women danced.

"What do I do?" I asked her, terrified but wanting to dance.

"Two hops on one foot and then two hops on the other. It's kind of like the Russian dance, but try to twist your hips in between hops," she said.

I gave it a shot.

"That's it," she shouted. "Now raise your arms up and hold my hand."

She maneuvered us closer to the others dancing in the center and motioned me to join hands with them. We formed our own circle, and I couldn't believe I was keeping up.

"*Rocco, Rocco, Rocco—Vivo Santo Rocco*," the crowd chanted.

The drumming pulsed in rhythm with my heart. Laughter bubbled up inside of me and it exploded on my lips. There was something primal and beautiful about it all—dancing in the street with strangers, connected by the beat of a drum. I didn't know where we found the energy, but Veronica and I danced and chanted like that for hours.

We'd caught a glimpse of Signora Tassone about an hour ago when she waved goodbye to us. When I'd moved toward Signora Tassone, Veronica shouted in my ear that she would catch a ride with Signora Vincenza's family. I had a feeling Veronica had done this before.

"I need some water," I shouted to Veronica several hours later. She pulled me out of the crowd toward a bar. "I'm surprised they're still open at this hour," I said.

"It's a special night. They are allowed to stay open until morning," she said and ordered us two *limonate*. I sipped my lemonade, watching the waves crash in the ocean, and couldn't help but think of when I was here with Hunter. That felt like a century ago. I still loved him, still wanted to believe that he loved me, but there was so much between us now. And it was not just the ocean that separated us.

I looked up and noticed the dawn breaking and knew the sun would rise soon.

"We should go. I don't want Adam to worry about me if I don't show up for our run. I'll have to apologize for skipping it and then head off to bed."

"You don't have to worry about that," she said.

"Why not?"

"Because Adam is here. He most likely kept an eye on you the whole night." She motioned to the left with her head and I turned in that direction. That's when I saw him. Adam stood by the boardwalk, wearing his usual blue jeans and a white T-shirt.

"How come I didn't notice him earlier?" I asked, more to myself.

"Because he probably didn't want us to see him until now," she said.

Adam held my stare and then brought his hand to his forehead, covering his eyes from the sunrise. I raised my hand, barely touching my forehead, in a strange sort of salute and watched him. He stayed there for only a minute and then left.

"Are you ready to go?" asked Veronica.

I wasn't sure if I wanted to leave, but I was prepared to take the next steps.

"Let's go," I said.

We headed back to Veronica's car just as the sun rose over the ocean.

Five

Hunter

"Laura, what's the status of the reformation campaign ads?" Leo asked.

This was the first formal meeting to discuss manticore business in weeks. Seven of us sat around the large oak boardroom table of Durand Enterprise: Laura, Leo, Thomas, Aunt Elenora, her husband Davis, Aunt Olympia, and James. While I sat at the head of the table, I hadn't said a word and barely listened.

"The ads are performing well and I've started a subcommittee with several kingdom professors to discuss how we can incorporate the ideology of reformation into our education system," Laura explained.

"Good. What about Tommy, Ross? What has he been up to?" Leo asked, turning his attention to Thomas next.

I had asked Thomas to follow Ross when everything went to shit at Jenkins's trial. Ross was a traditionalist and vehemently opposed reformation. So I wanted to make sure he wasn't causing any trouble.

"He hasn't changed his views. He is very much opposed to the lenient ruling. He is saying it would only encourage other manticore rogues to follow in Jenkins's footsteps, since the repercussions are not severe enough to deter them," Thomas informed us.

Leo glanced at me, but I didn't really care what happened to Ross. "Shut him up permanently if you have to, Thomas," I said.

"Hunter, I'm not sure if that's a good idea, especially when we are trying to go about the route of reformation," said Leo.

"You will not change a traditionalist's mind, especially one as old as Ross. He is set in his ways," I warned him.

"Laura, why don't you reach out to Ross," suggested Leo. "Ask him to join your subcommittee as an advisor. This way you can keep an eye on him and perhaps even work on changing his mind."

"That's not going to work," I said stubbornly. Leo gave me a hard stare and then shook his head. I tuned them out as they went about other manticore business.

Only when Davis addressed me directly, did I realize I hadn't been listening for a while. Everyone stared at me with their own version of exasperation on their faces. Davis's face was the worst. His eyes could have skewered me.

"What was that?" I asked.

"I said, Hunter, perhaps you should take some time off," continued Davis. "I know I benefited from my recent time abroad."

The thought appealed to me. I wouldn't mind the extra time to search my father's home. I kept thinking there must be a note, or a journal entry, or something in my mother's room that would offer a clue as to why she'd left for Toronto without telling anyone.

"That's not a bad idea," I began to say. "I—"

"Yes, and I think Leo can take care of manticore business in your absence." Something in Davis's voice awakened my instincts. His words were not harsh, but their meaning weakened my control in manticore business.

"Leo, what do you think of this suggestion?" I asked.

Leo stared at his father for a moment and then said, "I can take care of things for you, if you need some time. I don't mind."

I glanced between Leo and Davis but couldn't decide if this was extremely generous of them or calculating. I tried to ignore my instincts. The last time I'd questioned Leo's loyalty I was wrong, and

I did not want to offend him again. He was a loyal manticore, but even a loyal one would be angry if his honor were called into question a second time.

"All right," I said. "But it won't be for very long."

"No problem. Take your time," he said.

I narrowed my eyes.

"Will you still be attending the charity gala tonight?" Leo asked. "Durand Enterprise is a major donor, and you will have to give a short speech."

"Yes, I'll still go. I already have the speech and it's for a good cause."

"James and I will join you," said Leo, and I nodded once in agreement.

***

A few hours later, James and I were at the gala. We stood at the bar with a glass of scotch in our hands, as we watched Leo make his rounds in the room. He shook hands with all the influential families in New York, and perhaps he even greased a politician's palm or two along the way.

"He's very good at it, you know," said James. "He knows how to work a room. If we were to ever go public with the truth of who we are, Leo would be the perfect spokesperson."

"Yes, he's very good," I admitted. I preferred to be the decision-maker, the one responsible to uphold the rules, while Leo had always been the charmer.

"Um, Hunter, why don't we go outside and get some air before your speech?" James said in a strange voice and put his glass down on the bar.

"Get some air? I'm fine, James. I'm not nervous, just distracted," I told him, but James snatched the drink from my hand and set it on the bar next to his. Then he grabbed my upper arm and pushed me toward the terrace doors at the back of the room.

"James—" I began but stopped mid-sentence. I saw it—I saw why he wanted me away from the bar. Bright chandeliers and shiny decorations hung throughout the room, but a gold shimmer near the ballroom entrance door caught and held my attention. Gold sequins, to be exact. Although I could only see brown curly hair, because her back was turned to me, I knew instantly it was her. The arch of her neck, the silhouette of her body, and her sandalwood scent could never be mistaken for anyone else. My foot involuntarily took a step forward in her direction, but James seized me.

"Hunter," he warned.

"James, you're not going to stop me," I told him.

"This is not the place for you and Michaela to have your big reunion. It's too loud, too crowded, and too human," he whispered the last part. But I didn't care. Nothing would stop me from reaching her.

A man standing next to her turned his head and noticed my approach. His frown and narrowed eyes told me he was not happy about it. He placed his hand on the small of Michaela's back—in the age-old gesture that signaled possession to every man watching—and steered her away from the bar. The gesture stopped me short. *Who is this man?*

Anger rose from my gut straight to my chest, and I could hardly breathe. I needed to keep it in check if I planned to speak with her. I inhaled a deep breath through my nostrils and stared as the man led her to a table closer to the podium.

"Hunter, you're growling," James said next to my ear. It was unnecessary, since I could feel the rumble rise within my throat.

"Why does this scene look familiar?" Leo asked, looking exasperated.

I hadn't seen him approach. My vision was focused on the man who'd just seated himself beside Michaela and poured her a glass of wine. She smiled at him and scanned the room. Her eyes met my intense stare, and they widened marginally. She'd noticed me, of course, yet she didn't react anymore than that.

She still held the wineglass to her mouth, but she hadn't taken a sip yet. I continued to hold her gaze and I hoped she read my desire to speak with her privately. She turned to the man and whispered something in his ear before she stood up. Like a moth to a flame, I followed that short gold dress.

"Hunter," Leo snarled, but I didn't break my stride. "You're on in ten minutes," he called out. I ignored him.

I followed her out through the ballroom doors and into the lobby. She turned her head, saw that I trailed right behind her, and continued to lead me. She took a red-carpeted staircase to the lower levels, and I spotted service staff coming in and out of the kitchen. Her curly hair whipped from side to side as she searched for a place to talk but couldn't seem to find one.

No problem, I'll make one.

I reached forward, grabbed her hand, and gently pulled her into a small alcove at the end of the hallway. With my hands on her shoulders, I turned her back toward the alcove and used my body to shield her from wandering eyes. I moved my hands up against the wall placing them on either side of her head. Though tempted to hold her, I gave her space to move if she needed it.

Her unique violet eyes stared into mine, and tiny sparks raced up my spine. I burned to press my lips to hers but I held myself back. I was still angry with her, angry with our past, angry that we may not have a future.

"Michaela," I whispered harshly. "What are you doing here?"

Besides torturing me and wreaking havoc on my instincts.

"I'm in New York on business. A client asked me to handle one of their launches. They are a sponsor here tonight."

"So that man, the one seated beside you, he's your client?" I asked, feeling relieved I'd overreacted at the touch on her lower back.

"No. He's my...he's my date," she said.

And I felt the pressure in my chest return.

"Your date?"

"Yes," she said, not shying away from my glare.

"Did you know I would be here?" I had to know if she was trying to torture me.

"I did. That's why I brought him," she told me.

"Why?" I worried I was right, and she wanted to play games with my head.

"Because, Hunter. I know how it is when you and I get together," she said with a huff.

"How is it?" I knew, but I wanted to hear her say it.

She turned her head to look at my hands and then at my body, which stood only inches away from hers, then stared back at me pointedly.

"Say it," I whispered.

She closed her eyes but then said what I needed to hear.

"Neither of us thinks clearly when we are together. I needed someone here I could trust to hold me back," she said.

I did not move my hands but instead inched my face down closer to her neck and whispered, "There's no one here to stop us now."

"Yes, there is," she told me and looked over my shoulder.

I turned my head and saw her date standing only twenty feet away. I spun around to walk over and tell him to get lost when Michaela stopped me.

"This is not a competition," she warned me. "I knew I could not control myself if I came here tonight without someone to stop me. Adam knows who and what we are, and he's here to help me say what I need to say and get out unscathed."

"Are you afraid of me now?" I asked, angry she would suggest that I could hurt her.

"Yes. You've already broken my heart once, Hunter. I don't know if I could survive it a second time."

"Michaela, you are the one who left me, remember?" I tried to keep my voice steady. "I never wanted this to end. I still—" She put her hand over my lips to stop me.

"There's much between us that needs to be resolved and that's why I need to speak with you—but not here and not now. Meet me at my hotel room tomorrow afternoon at 4 p.m. Here's where I'm staying."

She handed me a piece of paper with "The Roosevelt Hotel" written on it and the room number 412 scrawled underneath.

"Fine. But we meet alone. You don't need a bodyguard when you're with me, Michaela."

This time the *date* spoke: "That's not happening."

I felt my temperature rise and my fangs lengthen, but I bit down on my lips and held myself in check.

"Think of him more like a chaperone," Michaela said, and her smile soothed my anger.

"Fine. If that's what you want, you can bring your old maid with you."

She smiled at that analogy and moved to leave.

I watched her walk out of my arms and toward another man. She turned back to glance at me, and Adam put his hand on her lower back once again. Before I could react, she swatted it away. The gesture made me irrationally happy and hopeful.

I trailed behind her until we reached the ballroom and Leo grabbed my arm.

"Finally! I've been searching all over for you," he hissed at me. "You're on. Get backstage. You'll be introduced any second."

***

I read the words James had written on the cue cards, but I couldn't tell you what I had said. The audience appreciated it, though, as I received a heartfelt applause at the end. I only thought of those violet eyes that avoided mine every time I looked into the crowd. When I stepped off the stage and returned to my table, my eyes searched for her and her reaction. I was annoyed with how our conversation downstairs had ended. Irritated that she'd walked away, and angry that we were in the same room but she sat next to someone else. Frustration seeped into my gut. While we'd never broken up, it was obvious we were not together either. The limbo was torture. I wanted to hate her for what her mother had done, but the feeling wouldn't stick. I couldn't sit there another minute. My thoughts drove me insane. If we could not talk this over until tomorrow, then I would at least hold her in my arms tonight.

"Where are you going now?" asked James, sounding nervous.

"I'm going to ask Michaela to dance," I said.

"Now?" asked Leo. "We haven't finished dinner yet. It isn't time for dancing."

"There's music playing, so it's perfectly reasonable to dance now," I said and walked across the dance floor toward her.

When I reached her table, all conversation ceased. I stood behind Michaela. She did not notice me until everyone's eyes wandered above her head. She turned around in her seat and I nodded at her.

"Would you do me the honor of dancing with me, Ms. Morrone?" I asked, knowing it would be rude of her to decline my gentlemanly approach. It was a cheap shot, but as I admitted before, I was not a virtuous man. I did not mind stooping low to get what I wanted.

She ground her teeth, arranged a fake smile on her lips, and said, "I don't think the dancing has started yet...Mr. Durand."

I ignored the bulldog seated beside her but I could feel his stare on me.

"Oh, come now, Michaela. Perhaps you can start it off for us," said an older woman at the table. She looked up and gave me a wink. "Perhaps, I can be next."

I smiled and inclined my head to accept her offer. I turned my attention back to Michaela. Her eyes bore into mine. If she could use her powers to stop my heart at this moment, I worried she would. I should have thought this one through.

"Sure. I'll only be a moment," she said to those at her table and put her napkin down.

"Take your time, we will be watching from here," said the older woman.

"That's what I'm afraid of," she said in a low voice when she turned toward me. "Let's go before I stop your beating heart."

I couldn't hold back the laugh that escaped through my throat. "I just had the same thought but didn't think you'd consider it."

"Oh, I'm considering it all right," she said but the smile that followed the statement told me it was only a fantasy—for now.

I reached for her hand and caressed her thumb with mine. I missed the softness of her skin. When we reached the dance floor, I pulled her into my arms and held her closer than I should have. Michaela closed her eyes and I watched her lose herself in the dance while I led our steps. She reacted instinctively to my movements. The symmetry was poetic.

"I missed you," I whispered in her ear. She shivered but said nothing.

My thumb circled the small of her back. "Did you find Nicholas?"

"Yes."

"Did you find the answers you craved?"

"Not all of them," she whispered. "But at least now I know more about who I am."

I bent my head and leaned into her neck. "I discovered some things about the past too."

"You did?" she asked, her eyes closed.

I nodded, and she paled.

"Look, Hunter, not much has changed between us since the last time we saw each other," she said, and her spine straightened beneath the palm of my hand. "I'm still not sure I can trust you or what you are."

Her defensiveness piqued my interest.

"Trust works both ways, Michaela."

She pulled her lips in and turned her head away from me.

I caught a motion a few feet away from us. Leo was escorting one of the politician's wives onto the dance floor. He whispered something in her ear that made her laugh. When his partner turned her head and looked away, Leo caught my eye and gave me a cold stare. He was not happy with me; it seemed a lot of people weren't, but I couldn't bring myself to regret it. Michaela and I would hash this out tomorrow, but tonight I let the world disappear around us.

When the dance ended and I led her back to her table, I promised the older woman I would return for her shortly. "Don't keep me waiting," she warned.

Before I left, Michaela grabbed my hand.

"Hunter?" she said.

I turned back to where she stood next to her chair.

"I forgot to tell you... I need something."

"What is it?" I asked, prepared for anything.

"I need you to bring me back my book."

I wasn't prepared for that.

Six

Michaela

"I can't believe you let him get that close to you," Adam said as he paced the hotel room. He had said this at least nine other times since last night.

When I'd returned to the table after dancing with Hunter, Adam didn't try to hide his disdain for my choice in dance partner. He wore a scowl on his face that scared the other guests at our table. I'd needed to sweeten his sour mood, or at least get him away from the table, so I asked Adam to dance. The dancing worked, at first, or perhaps it was Hunter's narrowed gaze that put a smile on Adam's face. But, when Hunter stood up from the table and walked toward us, I'd worried there would be a scene. Fortunately, Leo intervened and steered Hunter toward the exit. That was the last I saw of him.

"I just don't understand how you can want to be around him, especially knowing the role his kind played in your parents' death," Adam continued.

Despite having trained for years to attack manticores, Adam had never been around one before last night.

His words worked, though. They brought me back to that awful night in my apartment when I'd learned the truth of what Hunter and his family were. It still hurt because I had heard it from someone else.

"Listen, Adam, Hunter will knock on this hotel room door any minute. You need to get it together and focus," I warned him. "We are here to get the book and then get out of New York. I'm not here to explain myself to you."

Adam straightened his back, put his hands on his hips and glared at me. "Fine. It's your life," he said and stalked toward the window.

I waited for any further lectures, but there were none.

"Good," I said and then heard a knock at the door.

I inhaled a deep breath, nodded at Adam, and turned to open the door. Hunter stood there in his usual dark grey suit and white shirt. He took my breath away each and every time I saw him. I hated it.

"Hunter, come in," I said and noticed he held the book I'd asked him to bring. "Thank you for coming."

"Michaela," he said and narrowed his gaze on Adam standing next to the window. He had his back to us. "I see you still felt the need to bring your chaperone."

Then his eyes surveyed the room, taking in the messy bed and suitcases. "Or maybe he was already here," he said without looking up.

Adam had his own room at the hotel, but for some reason I did not disabuse Hunter of the idea that Adam was staying with me.

"That's neither your concern nor your business," I said.

Hunter's eyes narrowed a fraction more, and I knew my words had hit their mark. Good, because I was still angry too.

"Thank you for bringing the book I lent you. I need it back," I said and stuck out my hand to receive it, but he only glanced at my extended arm.

"Why do you want it back?" he asked.

"Because it belongs to me."

"Mmm...well, considering it outlines several ways to hurt me and my kind, I'm hesitant to have this book in the wrong hands."

"You read it?"

"Professor Wallace did and summarized it for me. It is quite remarkable how effortless killing one of us is for you...or someone like you."

I finally dropped my arm and put my hand on my hip instead. "I didn't need the book before and I definitely don't need it now, but it belongs to me and I will have it back," I said.

He assessed me with his eyes as I imagined he would a rival. His narrowed gaze took my measure, but I didn't give him an ounce. I stood tall and showed him that I meant what I said—I would get my book back.

"So, that's it? You are going to take the book back and then leave. Is that right?" he asked.

"Yes, that's right." I didn't deny it.

"No," he said.

"No?" My voice sounded incredulous even to my own ears.

"I'm not going to give you the book and just let you leave. We are going to talk about this, Michaela," he said.

I thought I was ready for this conversation, but I wasn't. I felt terrible admitting it, but I felt stronger when I had the upper hand—when it was Hunter who had wronged me. Now that I knew my mother was responsible for his pain, I was too much of a coward to face him.

"I don't know what you want from me, Hunter," I said.

"The truth."

"Oh, that's rich. You want the truth when you've always kept it from me?"

"I'm sorry, Michaela, but it wasn't only my truth to tell. I needed to protect everyone that depends on our secret," he said, then walked over to sit on the couch. Adam took a step back, distancing himself from Hunter. I appreciated the gesture.

"I need to know, Michaela...do you know all of it?"

"All of it?"

"The whole truth of what happened?"

And then it hit me.

"You know?" I whispered and moved to stand in front of him.

"I know," he said. After sneaking a peek at Adam, he returned his gaze to me. "Did he tell you?"

"No, his father did."

"Did he tell you everything? How they trained her to kill other manticores?"

"Yes," I said weakly. "They still do."

His eyebrows shot up and his lips parted on a soft exhale.

"Are you saying you're now training to be a manticore slayer too?" Hunter asked.

"Those manticores she killed, they were terrible," I responded.

"My mother wasn't."

"Maybe not, but she showed up unannounced, and my mother was only protecting her family."

"And mine couldn't help her instincts when someone held her down. She couldn't refrain herself from fighting back, just as you couldn't stop yourself from taking your next breath."

"Your father didn't have to kill them. He didn't have to seek his revenge," I countered, tears now blurring my vision.

"No, but he did. And if someone killed the woman I love, God help them, Michaela, nothing would stop me from finding them. I regret his actions, but I understand them."

I couldn't stop the tears from falling or the emotions that racketed my body. I gasped for air and could hardly breathe when Hunter stood up and pulled me into his arms.

"Get your dirty hands off of her," shouted Adam, and I saw him take a step toward us. I felt Hunter's body tense as he held himself back, but I didn't trust his instincts right now.

"Adam, stop," I shouted, and Adam stayed where he was.

I extricated myself from Hunter's embrace and wiped the tears from my eyes.

Get it together, Michaela.

Hunter panted, his breathing ragged and his eyes wild. His body wanted to attack, and I had seen what his teeth could do.

"I don't want to fight," I said.

"What do you want, Michaela?" asked Adam, ready to act on my command.

"I want everyone to calm down," I told them and noticed Adam take a step back.

"Don't you *dare* come after me again," Hunter warned Adam in a voice that would instill fear into any living creature. It frightened me. When I glanced up at him, I saw that he sensed my fear.

"I won't hurt you." I believed him but knew it was dangerous to keep him here any longer.

"Tell him. What do you want?" Adam asked me again.

"I want my book back," I said, then extended my hand out to Hunter.

"Is that all?" he asked. I knew he wanted to hear more but I couldn't give it to him. Too much lay between us—secrets, betrayal, and revenge.

But I couldn't get those words out. I didn't think I could get any out without breaking down again, so I just nodded instead.

Hunter stared at me. His eyes held mine until I realized that he wouldn't accept my swift end to this conversation. He opened his mouth to say something—but then his phone rang.

He blinked, looking annoyed by the interruption, but didn't say a word. He pulled his phone out of his jacket pocket and turned his back to take the call.

"What is it, Thomas?" he snarled. "What? How is that possible?"

I glanced back at Adam, who whispered to me, "Are you okay?"

I nodded.

"I have to go," Hunter said when he ended the call.

"What is it?" I asked, concerned now. "Is it Laura?"

"No," he said and then he grabbed my shoulders. "But we're not done here, Michaela."

"Hunter, tell me what happened," I begged him. I needed to know what made him this upset and if there was something I could do to help. "Tell me the truth."

Those particular words affected him because I saw a flash of pain cross his face, and then he closed his eyes and told me, "Thomas just informed me," he opened them again, "that Jenkins has escaped."

Henry Jenkins was a violent manticore who had hurt three humans before Hunter caught him shortly before we met in New York City.

"How?" I asked, confused. "John was his accomplice on the inside, but John is dead. Unless he's enlisted someone new?"

"Or they were always there, waiting for their next move," said Hunter. "I have to go."

"Wait," I said before I could think it through. "I'm coming with you."

"Oh, no you're not," said Hunter at the same time that Adam said, "No way."

"You are not safe at the mansion, and I am not getting you involved with Jenkins. He's a predator."

"And you're not?" sneered Adam.

Hunter didn't respond, but the growl reverberating in his chest told me this was Adam's last and final warning.

"Here is your book, Michaela," he said as he grabbed my hand and placed the book in my palm. "Take it and leave. Go to Toronto and don't come back to New York."

His last words froze me in place and I couldn't move, not even when he pressed his lips to mine. My eyes were still closed when he walked out and slammed the door behind him.

"Bastard," Adam muttered.

I didn't chastise him. I stood speechless with my fingers on my lips. Unsure if Hunter's words or his kiss caused my reaction since both had taken me by surprise.

"Well, at least you've got the book back," Adam said as he took it from me and walked toward my suitcase. "I guess we can go home now."

"We're not going home, especially not now," I told him.

"Why not?"

"Because there's a crazy manticore on the loose," I explained and turned to see a smile spread across his face. "And every ounce of blood in my body wants to track him down and make him pay for what he's done."

"Are you ready to do what it will take?" Adam asked.

"I'm ready," I said and felt my adrenaline soar.

Adam smiled. "Let's do this."

Seven

Michaela

I laid out a large map of Manhattan on the hotel breakfast table. Adam and I stood above it, our heads close together, trying to get our bearings.

"This is where the Durand mansion is located." I pointed to a street I'd circled on the map.

"But you don't think this is where their kingdom is hidden, correct?" Adam asked.

"No, I don't. It's just a home, a nice one with security detail, but when I stayed there it was only family that came in and out. If you're telling me this supposed kingdom includes a courtroom and dungeons, I didn't see any of that."

"What if it is underneath the mansion?"

"That's a possibility," I said, giving merit to the notion. "But I still think I would have encountered other people milling about, or cars parked other than the family's. If there is a kingdom, it's not there. I'm sure of it."

"So we still don't know where Jenkins escaped from, and we don't know where he's going or what his intentions are." Adam was clearly frustrated with our lack of information.

"No, but we can look into where he's been," I said, forming an idea. "We need to research muggings in the area, assaults, anything in the last few months."

"Muggings and assaults in New York? There could be hundreds," said Adam.

"Yes, maybe more. But we need to look for any that have suspicious details in the report. Any unexplained bite marks, scratches, or if the person fell ill afterward, could mean it was a manticore."

"That's a good idea."

"Now we just need to get our hands on those reports."

"I may know someone who can help with that," said Adam.

"You do?"

"My cousin Olivia is a computer genius. She can hack into the police reports, I'm sure."

"Let's call her now," I said, and Adam pulled his cell phone out of his shirt pocket.

While Adam dialed the number on his phone, I walked over to one of my suitcases and unzipped the smaller red one. I had packed three of the tomes I'd found in my home with Hunter last month.

I picked up the smaller one and brought it back to the breakfast table. I skimmed through the tome and opened the chapter I'd bookmarked earlier. I had been studying this page for days now. It was a chant I couldn't master. The language was the same as the others, but the words stuck to the roof of my mouth each time I read them aloud.

Nicholas told me my mother had trouble with this one too; he'd said it was the most important chant for The Sheds. It neutralized a manticore's venom. It was deemed difficult because no one had ever succeeded in neutralizing a manticore's venom before, according to Nicholas. He'd said my mother had tried it once but failed.

If the timing of the chant or the pronunciation of the words weren't perfect, the chant wouldn't work. Instead of neutralizing the venom, the mispronunciation could trigger a manticore's instincts until you had no choice but to stop his heart before he ripped out yours.

The book explained that two glands produced a manticore's venom: one connected to saliva production and the other next to the adrenal gland. Just like humans, the adrenal gland in manticores helped regulate their body's response to stress. If threatened, a manticore's instinct to fight would spark their glands to produce venom. It would then flow through their veins and could be released through the teeth or fingernails. Once it started, Nicholas said there was no way for a manticore to stop his attack. But I didn't agree with this. Hunter had told me he could control his instincts, and I wanted to believe him. He said he'd learned to rein in his anger over the years. I had to believe that was possible.

"All right, Olivia's on it, but it's going to take some time to hack into the system and look for the details you mentioned," Adam said as he walked back to join me at the table. "What are you working on?"

"I'm practicing the venom-neutralizing chant," I replied.

"Nicholas said you don't have to worry about that one. He mentioned it's really difficult to master and that your mother was never able to learn it either."

"I'm not my mother," I mumbled under my breath, and I focused on the words again.

Ecce venenum! Audi vocem meam. Tu non opus, non volebant, non opus. Ego dici tibi aquam et ignem te deorsum. Fac me sicut torrens qui te timidum. Hoc autem novam mortem et vitam.

I repeated the words over and over again but still heard my hesitation and stutter while reciting them. My finger hovered over a translation I'd written in the margin: *Poison behold! Listen to my voice. You are no longer needed, no longer wanted, no longer necessary. I claim thine fire and water thee down. Make thee as timid as a brook. I take this death and bring you a new life.*

I had no difficulty repeating the translation; the words rushed through my lips like a waterfall. I chanted them over and over again. I said them ten times, twenty, and then once more.

I lost track of the time and the next thing I heard was Adam's voice pulling me back. "Michaela, did you hear what I said?" he asked.

"No. What is it, Adam?"

"Olivia thinks she's found something. She's emailing the reports over to me now."

I closed my book and sat next to Adam on the bed, waiting for Olivia's email. I couldn't help but notice his cologne. It smelled like the ocean, not offensive or strong, just inviting. I held my breath as I peeked over his arm to see his phone.

"Here we go," he said and opened the email. There were three files attached.

"It's difficult to read over your shoulder," I said. "Why don't you send them to me so I can take a look at the same time."

Adam turned his head toward me and must have noticed my discomfort. He gave me one of his rare smiles.

"Sure thing," he said.

He airdropped the files to my phone, and I sat back down at the breakfast table to review the reports.

The first one had taken place more than six months ago. The report described a twenty-six-year-old woman with bite marks on her wrist and shoulder. The second incident had happened three months ago, and the photographs depicted scratches made by some sort of large cat. The scratches were visible on the man's torso and went right through his shirt. The last report was filed about a month ago. Actually, it was the same night as the Hugo Boss party. The woman hadn't reported any injuries, but Olivia still flagged this case.

I continued to read the report. At one point, the woman stated her attacker had disappeared into thin air. He was there one minute and then gone the next, was how the woman described it. The police officer had said he suspected she suffered from hallucinations.

"This last incident, the one in September," I said. "Why do you think Olivia sent us this one?"

I gave Adam a minute to catch up and read the report.

"Let me call her and ask," he said while dialing the number. "Liv, hey, it's me. That last report you sent, the one near Main and First street...yeah, why did you flag it?"

He waited, nodding his head while Olivia explained. "Okay, thanks. Hold on."

He turned to me, "She says that while there were no injuries, she trusts the woman's statement and does not believe she was hallucinating."

I nodded in agreement. "Only a manticore could move that fast," I whispered, but Adam heard me.

"Thanks, Liv. Good work," Adam said and ended the call.

When Adam had nearly killed Hunter and I at the airport, I'd seen how quickly a manticore could move. Hunter was one step ahead of the bullet itself. When I'd watched Hunter fight John, the moves were a blur to me. I thought fear made my vision fuzzy, but I knew now it was more than that.

"We need to speak to each of the wounded," I said. "See the injuries for ourselves and decide if what they experienced could have been caused by a manticore."

"I don't think they're going to open up to a couple of strangers knocking on their door. Maybe we say we are police and want to follow up on their case," he suggested.

The thought of lying to someone who had already been hurt didn't sit well with me. "No, we tell them the truth."

"The truth?" he said while his eyes searched mine for any hint of humor. I wasn't kidding.

"The truth," I repeated. "Those people, they've been through enough and I'm not going to lie to them." And then, because I couldn't hold it in any longer, I said, "I'm tired of secrets. I told you, I'm not my mother, Adam."

Adam's face changed to an expression I'd never seen on him before. He looked contrite.

"I'm sorry," he said in a low voice.

"For what?" I asked, thinking of the number of times Adam had frustrated me.

"For what happened at the airport, for scaring you. For making you think someone was trying to kill *you.* I know I've said you weren't my target, but I've never apologized for how my actions made you feel. I'm sorry you were there and that I scared you," he said, then reached across the table to hold my hand.

His thumb rubbed back and forth along mine. Despite his gentle touch I knew he could hurt me, but not for the reason he apologized for now. I was afraid of Adam, scared of how my blood raced whenever his broad shoulders were close to me.

He laced his fingers with mine and gently tugged me forward to stand in front of him. I had to look up to face him. So, I kept my head down.

He ran his free hand along my hair; his fingers caught on my curls, but he didn't let go. The pull on my scalp was gentle and sent a tingle down my spine. He caressed my curls until his fingers reached the ends of the strands, and then he tugged on those too. The tug raised my head up and forced me to meet his stare.

He brought his face closer to mine and I knew where this would lead. A part of me wanted to stop him, while another part of me longed to know if kissing him would make everything I felt for Hunter go away.

I closed my eyes, relaxed my lips, and invited him in. He didn't miss his cue and pressed his mouth softly against mine. I parted my lips, and he didn't hesitate. His tongue explored my mouth, and I fought my way through to explore his. The hand on my back moved lower and then lower still. I gasped at the touch, but Adam sealed my mouth with his again. He held my body tightly against his, and I could feel his arousal. I didn't want this to go any further.

"Wait," I said and placed my hand on his chest. I reached behind me for his hand and brought it up between us.

His eyes searched mine for clues as to his next move. I shook my head and took a step back.

"I can't do this," I said.

"Were you thinking of him while you kissed me?" His voice was hoarse.

"No," I said, because it was the truth. "But it was the first time I didn't think of him."

"I don't understand," he said, running his fingers through his hair. "He is a monster. He could hurt you, kill you, in the most brutal way. You could never have a life with him. I could give you more. You just have to let me."

"Everything I am should repel me from him. My genes, my past, my future. But I can't move past the idea that there's a way for us to be together, a way to..." An idea popped into my head, but I shook it off before any hope could take root in the notion.

Adam didn't notice; he walked away irritated halfway through my speech.

"I know being with you would be so easy, and a big part of me wants that right now. I want a normal life, a family," I said. "But I love him."

"Stop. I can't stand to hear you talk like that about him. It makes me angry, frustrated...and I don't know what else but I can't handle it." He grabbed his jacket and reached to open the door.

"Where are you going?"

"I need some air to clear my thoughts." He shut the door behind him. I stood alone in the room with only my guilt.

I could be with Adam. It would be easy, and Nicholas would be thrilled. It would work with little effort at all. But I loved Hunter and had promised him that we'd find a way to make it work. I intended to keep that promise. I just didn't know how. The idea popped back into my head but I quickly uprooted it, not wanting the thought to germinate in my mind. It was too risky, and I had already lost too much.

***

It was early evening when someone knocked on my hotel room door. I checked the peephole and saw Adam standing on the other side. He wore the same clothes but his hair was wet.

I opened the door but didn't invite him in. He didn't step forward to join me either.

"Ready?" he asked.

"For what?"

"To find the woman with the bite marks."

"Adam, about what happened earlier..."

"I don't want to talk about it."

His clipped toned cut off any explanation I had prepared, so I just nodded once. He was right—there wasn't much else to talk about. At least not with Adam. I closed the door but only for a second to grab my coat and phone, and then I joined him in the hallway.

"Did you call a cab?" I asked.

"No. I paid cash and rented a motorcycle. I don't want any trail leading to her home."

"Good thinking," I said. "But a motorcycle?"

"Have you ever ridden on one before?"

"No, I haven't. I've never had a death wish."

"Funny, I thought that's exactly what we were arguing about earlier."

"Adam—"

"Forget I brought it up," he said, holding his hand up. "Let's do what we're trained to do and hunt this manticore."

I smiled in agreement.

When we reached the front of the building, a large black and chrome bike waited for us. Adam hopped on and passed me a helmet. He strapped his under his chin while I straddled the bike and wrapped my arms around him as tightly as I could.

"Do you trust me?" he asked.

"Not entirely," I said truthfully.

Adam laughed and then kick-started the engine. It roared to life and we took off like a bullet. I closed my eyes, afraid I would fall off if I opened them.

"Michaela, if you hold on any tighter you're going to leave a mark."

"Can you slow down?" I asked with my eyes still closed.

"I'm going the speed limit."

"Yes, but the limit feels different when I don't have two tons of metal separating my face from the pavement."

He slowed the bike down, just a few clicks less, but it was enough for me to open my eyes. "How far is this place?" I asked.

"Not far. Maybe twenty minutes from here."

I mustered the will to turn my head to the side. I pressed my cheek to Adam's back and anchored myself to him.

As he drove, I couldn't help but smile. New York was even more beautiful at night. The city lit up like a Broadway show—from the storefronts to the rooftop billboards—and right now I felt like one of its stars. Regardless of the time, there were always people walking along the streets and several cars on the road. No one noticed you because you were just another cast member in this play, and anonymity was part of the ticket. To get lost in a city so big wasn't unusual, but you could find yourself here too.

A few minutes later, Adam drove through the Brooklyn Bridge.

Being suspended over water was both terrifying and exhilarating. Shortly after we passed the bridge, he turned onto a residential street and parked in front of a brownstone home.

"This is it," he said.

The house was tall and narrow but looked cozy, like something I would love to live in. I unwound my arms from Adam's waist and raised one leg at a time to climb down from the bike.

"Her name is Stacey Barns," he said. I nodded. I remembered it, as well. I remembered all the details from her report.

I walked up to her door and, before I changed my mind, I rang the doorbell and waited.

A few seconds later, a voice over the doorbell speaker said, "Can I help you?"

"Yes. Hi, my name is Michaela, and this is Adam. We were hoping to speak with you."

"Speak to me about what?"

"About an incident you experienced about six months ago. You filed a police report."

"Are you the police?"

"No."

"Then I don't have to speak with you. Goodbye."

"You don't have to, but I am hoping you'd want to."

"And why would I want that?"

"Because we want to find the man that attacked you and bring him to justice."

She paused. I had prepared a response if she asked me how I knew this information, but she didn't.

"If the police couldn't find him, what makes you think you can?"

"I have a special set of skills that helps me catch predators like him, but I'll need your help."

Stacey didn't respond to this directly, but a few minutes later a woman with short-cropped hair and a diamond piercing in her nose answered the door. She was striking.

"What do you want to know?"

"Can we come in?" Adam asked, looking around. I knew he was checking to make sure no one had followed us. Stacey peeked around, too, and then stepped outside.

"It's better if we talk outside."

I didn't blame her for not trusting us. Bad experiences often made good people distrustful.

We took a seat on her porch, and I decided to start. "Were you able to see the face of the man who attacked you?"

"I did. But it was dark and his features were nondescript. He had blond hair and a medium build. I couldn't see anything that would distinguish him from a million other guys walking around."

"The incident happened at 8 p.m. on a Monday night. Do you usually take that route at that time?" asked Adam.

"Yes. That's when my shift ends at the bar and I walk over to the subway. I take the same route every night. In hindsight, I see how obvious that is."

"This isn't something you're responsible for. This is on him, not you," I assured her.

She nodded, but I could tell bringing up the incident again had made her nervous, especially when she pulled out a pack of cigarettes from her back pocket.

"Smoke?" she offered.

I shook my head but Adam took one. "Thanks," he said.

She pulled out her lighter and he pulled in a drag. I caught Stacey staring at Adam. I understood why. He was easy on the eyes, especially when one's eyes were focused on his mouth. But while Adam distracted her, I took the opportunity to examine her wrists. Her black sweater covered her shoulders but not her wrists. There were faint markings on the right one.

"Is it okay if I take a look at those?" I asked her, pointing to her wrist. "The markings."

She shrugged and extended her wrist to me.

"Did you get these that night?" I asked.

She nodded again. "Yeah. When I tried to fight back, the bastard bit me." The markings were thin lines. "I know they don't look like much, but they hurt like hell."

"Hurt how?" asked Adam.

She looked away and blew out a puff of smoke while holding her cigarette. When she looked back at us she said, "I know this sounds crazy, but it felt like a snake bite or something. It was painful, sore, and then it started to swell. I was worried it would get infected, so I went to the emergency room."

"I don't think you're crazy. I think you're smart for taking it seriously," said Adam.

She nodded, and I agreed with him. "He's right. It could have been much worse if you didn't go to the hospital."

"Yeah, they said they had to treat it like a snake bite because I was showing all the symptoms, but I don't remember him holding a damn snake. That's the craziest part."

"Do you remember anything else about the incident?" I asked.

"I remember being scared and confused. I didn't know if he was trying to rob me or kill me," she said and took a deep breath after she said this last part.

"I'm sorry you have to rehash this, but any clue as to what he wanted with you would really help us." I hated having to push her for the details.

"That's the thing, I don't know what he wanted. He didn't steal my purse or anything else...he just bit me, said 'my kind are worthless,' and ran. I'm thinking it's probably some fucked-up hate crime."

She was looking out into the street, holding her cigarette, when I asked, "Do you recall if you'd ever seen him before?"

"At the time, I told the police I didn't." She flicked her cigarette over the railing, scattering the ashes onto the ground. "But months later, I thought I remembered him coming to the bar where I worked. I thought I saw him there a few times. I don't know if he was stalking me, or if it was just a 'wrong place at the wrong time' sort of thing."

Then she looked me in the eye and asked, "How are you going to bring this guy to justice if you don't know where he is?"

"Because I won't stop until I do," I told her.

"Is this personal for you too?" she asked.

"Yes," I said. "But not in the same way as it is for you. He hurt you and I don't want him to hurt anyone else."

"Do you want us to keep you posted, or do you want to just forget the whole thing?" Adam asked.

"Honey, I'll never forget it. So yeah, let me know, maybe this way I'll sleep again at night." Stacey finished her cigarette and put it out on the step when she stood up. "Unless you have anything else, I'm going to go."

"Yes, of course," I said. "Thank you for talking to us."

She nodded and then went inside.

"Well, that was painful and I fear not very productive," I said to Adam.

"Maybe," he said. "Doesn't it seem odd to you that he didn't do more than bite her? Like, what was the point of the assault?"

"I don't know. Maybe it was just to get the attention of the king. But if it's not too late, let's see if we can talk to the guy from the second report," I replied.

Adam pulled up the report on his phone and punched in the address on his GPS app.

"It's not too far from here, actually. Maybe this predator keeps it local."

"Maybe," I said and walked over to the bike. As I straddled the bike behind him, Adam dropped his cigarette and drove off a little faster this time. I didn't complain.

Eight

Hunter

"You know, the least you could do is provide interesting conversation for this stakeout," Leo said from the passenger seat of the car.

"My idea of interesting doesn't include clothing advice," Thomas muttered from the back seat.

"Well, I've never held your bad taste in tailors against you, Thomas," Leo countered.

"Will you two stop bickering like a bunch of grumpy old men?" I shouted.

That shut them up. I knew we were all frustrated. We had been tracking Jenkins for days and had come up empty. We'd followed his scent from Central Park to Brooklyn but lost it shortly after we crossed the bridge. There were a couple of streets that had a lingering scent, but it was mixed up with others that threw us off. So, we'd been parked at the intersection of these two streets for hours, looking for any kind of Jenkins sighting. The wait was torture.

"You know, James does provide great family discounts if..." Leo started up again, but I raised my hand and he shut his mouth. I thought I saw movement at the house down the street. I had watched it for some time. I thought it suspicious that no one had come or gone from the home in nearly twenty-four hours, until now.

"A red car just pulled into the driveway." I pointed to the grey house with aluminum siding.

"Can you see who's inside?" asked Thomas, sticking his head between Leo and me to get a better view from the back seat.

"No, I haven't seen anyone leave yet," I said. "Wait, the garage door is opening." I leaned forward, but I couldn't see if anyone was in the garage because the tall hedges beside the house blocked my view. "I'm going to drive closer."

I started the engine and shifted the car into Drive. At the same time, the red car pulled out of the driveway. "There's someone in the back seat," I said. "Whoever was in the house must have called a car service."

"Well, gentlemen, let's put our hunting skills to work then." Leo leaned back in his seat, but his fingers curled into a fist. I couldn't agree more. Adrenaline pumped in my veins as I followed the car. I tried to keep my distance, but I didn't want to lose him. This was the first real lead we'd had so far.

The red car sped along the road for another five minutes until it pulled up next to a yellow-painted house. It appeared to be a triplex. This time tall trees—not hedges—blocked our view. I moved the car closer and watched as a figure stepped out of the back seat and walked toward the side of the home. I parked the car and got out to follow on foot.

"Is it him?" asked Leo in a deep baritone. His voice had changed. He'd lost his cavalier attitude and become a predator. Our prey was getting away.

"I don't know, but we can't lose him." I walked toward the side of the house where I spied a side door. Thomas and Leo were right behind me. The figure ahead had moved too quickly; I didn't see if he had forced his way in or if he had used a key. Regardless, we had to follow him inside because that kind of speed only meant one thing. He was a manticore.

"It's him," I said.

"Are you sure?" Leo asked.

"Yes."

It was nearly 9:00 p.m. and the sun had already set. I silently thanked the darkness for providing us cover until we reached the side door. I wasn't surprised to find the door unlocked and didn't hesitate to make my way inside. The house was eerily quiet for a triplex. No sound or movement indicated which direction Jenkins had gone, but I picked up his scent to my left and raced up the stairs. When I reached the second level, the door to my left was wide open and I spotted the bastard. Only, he was not alone. He held a woman in front of him with a knife to her throat.

"Your tracking skills are weak. When you couldn't find the apartment I was staying at, I took matters into my own hands and marked my scent on that home you were staking out."

"If you were so eager to meet with us, Jenkins, why not just show yourself?"

"Because that was not part of my plan. You see, I have some unfinished business here with this one." He sneered down at the woman. Her hands trembled but she did not make a sound while he held her against his sweaty body. When I looked closely at her face and long red hair, I recognized her. She was the woman Jenkins had attacked in the alley last month, when we had first captured him.

"Let her go, Jenkins. It's over."

"That's where you're wrong, Hunter. It has only just begun. I told you before, I will not follow some rules that were forced upon me. I am a free manticore. I have no master and no lion pride. I am a lone hunter."

"You are not alone now. You are surrounded. There are three of us and only one of you."

"Well, maybe I have more friends here than you think I do," Jenkins said and glanced at Leo. I turned to look at him, too, but Leo's face was blank.

"What does he mean by that?" I asked.

Leo shook his head. "I have no idea."

"I think this is it. I think this is Scarlet Reynold's apartment up ahead." A woman's voice called from the hallway right before I smelled her scent. It hit me like a typhoon, and I felt momentarily unsteady. *Michaela.*

"Hunter?" she said when she entered the room.

"What are you doing here?" I growled at her but did not turn my attention away from Jenkins. I knew he could move faster than us. I hadn't forgotten all those times he had gotten away.

"I told you to go home." The need to protect her rose up and consumed me. I couldn't think when she was in danger. All I could do was react, and I didn't want her around when my control hung on a razor's edge.

"Yes, you did tell me to go. But I had other plans," she said without hesitation.

"Leave now, then. This doesn't concern you," I told her and prayed that she listened this time.

"Oh no, you should stay Michaela." A grin spread across Jenkins's face. "Watch as I finish my final act."

"What are you talking about, Jenkins?" My head spun as I tried to keep my eye on the predator before me and forget the woman behind me.

"I don't like loose ends, and Scarlet, here, is a loose end. I didn't get a chance to savor this one and I keep thinking, does she taste like strawberries or wine?" Jenkins sniffed Scarlet's red hair. "I knew Hunter would come after me and now he has to decide—save the girl or kill me? He won't have time to do both, and I already know which one he will choose. Tell me I'm wrong, Hunter. Which one will it be?"

He was right. I would save the girl, and I would lose precious time while he got away. Leo and Thomas were not as fast as me.

"Maybe I'll just get a lick while I wait for you to decide." Jenkins stuck out his tongue next to Scarlet's ear.

Scarlet, who was still held at knife-point, flinched but responded with a threat of her own.

"Touch me and I will kill you myself," she said.

I raised my eyebrows at this. I was impressed by her confident words. But Jenkins only laughed. "Oh, I do regret not sinking my teeth into you. But I'll fix that soon enough."

"No, you won't," said Michaela, and I backed up toward her instinctively before she made a move closer to Jenkins.

"She's got this," whispered Adam when he saw my movements. I didn't doubt Michaela could take care of herself, but Jenkins was a predator like I had never seen before. He was fast, ruthless, and lethal.

"You're out of moves, Jenkins," I shouted, hoping he believed me. My eye caught a movement. Scarlet raised her arm and inched her hand closer to the table. A pair of black scissors laid next to a scrapbook. I read her intent and appreciated her will to fight but I shook my head when she caught my eyes. She wouldn't be fast enough and then he'd kill her.

"Am I out of moves, Leo?" Jenkins asked, looking directly at my cousin. Again, I stared at Leo, wondering if he could have betrayed us.

"Yes, you are," Leo responded.

"Well then, there's only one more thing to do," he said and opened his mouth.

His fangs were already out, and I knew he would sink them into Scarlet's neck. Everyone moved at once. Scarlet reached for the scissors, distracting Jenkins, and then my hands wrapped around Jenkins's neck two seconds later. I turned slightly to the right and saw Leo holding Scarlet in his arms. I did not dare look behind me to see where Michaela was, but I heard her voice.

"Don't do it, Hunter," she said. "That's not what your father ordered."

"She's right, Hunter," said Leo. "We need to bring him back to the kingdom."

Leo's suggestion grated on my nerves. I wondered if he was the one who'd released Jenkins from his cell in the first place. Jenkins had certainly implied that he was a "friend" a few moments ago.

"No," I said. "His chance for rehabilitation is gone. We are going to handle this my way now." Then I put my face right in front of Jenkins's and said, "Just like I warned him I would."

"Hunter," Leo called, but I didn't hear the rest. I only heard blood rushing in my ears and the loud instinct to kill my prey. I had hunted for days and had finally captured him. I would not release him. I squeezed his neck and felt Jenkins try to take a breath, but my fingers nearly closed up his passageway. He kicked his feet relentlessly, but while he was faster, I was stronger.

"Wait," said Scarlet and her voice made me pause. "Not until I've said my piece."

Leo still held her, but when she looked pointedly down at his arms he released her. Jenkins turned his eyes toward her, but I didn't loosen my hold on his neck.

"I hate you," she said from behind me. "I hate what you did to me. I hate that I've been afraid every day since that night."

The anger in her voice fueled mine.

Jenkins did not say a word. He couldn't; he could barely breathe with the pressure I was forcing around his throat. He didn't deserve to speak to her.

"What do you want me to do with him, Scarlet?" I asked, knowing that as much as I wanted to end his life now, I would let him go if she asked it of me.

The silence in the room felt heavy. Everyone held their breath, waiting for Scarlet's command.

"Kill him," she whispered, and I inhaled a deep breath through my nostrils and reveled in the satisfaction those words permitted.

A growl reverberated in my chest and venom rushed to my mouth. Jenkins didn't plan to go down without a fight, as he bared his teeth now too.

"Stop! Don't do it, Hunter," Michaela shouted, but I didn't listen.

"What if there's another way?" said Adam.

"Who the hell is he?" asked Leo beside me.

"Michaela, try the neutralizing chant," said Adam.

"Adam, no, I haven't mastered it yet." I had no idea what they were talking about and didn't care now that my instincts roared to life. It took all my concentration not to sink my teeth into Jenkins's throat that second.

"This feels like the right place to try," whispered Adam.

The venom tasted sweet on my tongue. I was losing control and didn't want Michaela here to see it. "Everyone out!" I shouted. "I'm taking care of Jenkins myself. This ends tonight."

Michaela's voice rang in my ears, but I didn't understand what she said. She repeated the words again and then when I thought she had finished she said them once more.

Her words confused me, and they affected Jenkins, as well. His body convulsed and his eyes grew larger, but I did not ease my grip in case this was his plan for escape. His eyes bulged out and then focused behind me to where Michaela stood. Whatever Jenkins was before, he became a pure killer now, and his target was Michaela.

He fought against my grip. His body grew stronger, as though he'd been infused with a burst of energy and strength. I was losing my stranglehold on him. Then Jenkins put his arms between mine as if he were about to pray and in one swift movement broke through my grip.

He raced straight for Michaela, so I didn't hesitate. But before I could grab Jenkins again, Scarlet shot out, arm raised above her head and stabbed Jenkins in the leg with the scissors. Jenkins roared, his head up in the air, and then redirected his fury to a new fight—to Scarlet. This was one fight Scarlet could not win. Without losing another second, I wrapped my biceps between Jenkins' head and twisted in one rapid motion, snapping his neck. He crumpled to the ground, lifeless.

The room fell silent. There was nothing but my own heavy breathing. I tried taking large gulps of air to calm the killer instincts raging inside me, but my blood raced. It had been a long time since I had killed someone. I was losing control. I wanted to order everyone out, but I was afraid speaking would compromise my focus. Thankfully, Thomas noticed my struggle and moved everyone into action. "Leo, help me get Jenkins up and in the car," he said. "We need to bring him back with us."

"I just need another minute." Leo held Scarlet in his arms where she had fallen to the ground. She stared at Jenkins's lifeless body, but I couldn't tell if she was shocked or relieved.

Thomas grabbed the scissors in Jenkins's thigh and pulled them out. He wiped them clean on Jenkins' shirt and then handed them to Scarlet. With a shaky hand she took the scissors and tried to place them back on the table. But her hand shook so badly she could not grasp them and they fell to the floor. Leo left the scissors on the ground and picked up Scarlet instead. He put his hands on her arms and pulled her into his chest. Scarlet closed her eyes and sank into his embrace.

"Hunter," Michaela called to me, but I wasn't ready to speak yet. She stepped toward me, but Adam stopped her with his hand. While I appreciated his intervention, a growl still grew in my chest and I couldn't stop the snarl that escaped my mouth. Michaela paused and I felt unworthy of her.

"Michaela, let's go," Adam said. "It's over."

Feelings of loss and regret washed over me and encompassed

the anger, dragging it down deep into the pit of my stomach. The thought that I would never see Michaela again—and this was the last thing she would remember of me—was unbearable.

I closed my eyes and focused on my breathing. I counted to ten and prayed that when I opened my eyes, she would still be there. Eight, seven, six...another deep breath...four, three, two, one.

When I opened my eyes, she stood in front of me and waited. Her eyes pleaded with me, but I didn't know what she wanted from me.

"Don't go," I said to her.

"I won't."

"Meet me tomorrow. Before you leave, meet with me." I took another breath, finally the anger was starting to subside. "Please," I begged her.

"All right. Where?"

"My apartment."

"Michaela, I don't think this is a good idea," said Adam, but Michaela ignored his warning.

"What time?"

"Six o'clock. I'll pick you up at your hotel."

"No, I'll meet you there."

"Fine. Come to the sixteenth floor," I said, feeling in control again.

"I'll see you tomorrow," she said and continued to stare at me.

"Tomorrow," I agreed and took one more breath before finally exhaling.

When Michaela and Adam left, I turned to Thomas. "Let's get this piece of shit out of here." I bent to pick up Jenkins's shoulders while Thomas picked up his legs. Leo squeezed Scarlet's hand and then cleared the way for us as we raced to the car and dumped Jenkins's body in the trunk. It all happened in less than a minute, and then we were gone.

Nine

Michaela

Adam insisted on dropping me off in front of Hunter's building the next evening. We stood, arguing, outside the building's front doors.

"Promise me you will leave if he doesn't seem in control of himself," Adam repeated. "Or if you feel uncomfortable and want to leave for any reason, you call me. I'll stay close by and I can be here in less than five minutes."

"I promise, Adam," I said to appease him, and hoped he wouldn't make me agree to anything else. He gripped my shoulder. I placed my hand on top of his and asked him with my eyes to let me go. He loosened his fingers and stepped away. I took one last look at Adam and made my way to Hunter.

The white walls and grand staircase in the building's foyer were as imposing as ever. As I walked toward the elevator, I realized I had never been inside Hunter's apartment. The last time I came, he had laid out a picnic on the rooftop and shown me the world—well, just Manhattan, but it felt like it was everything I needed at the time.

I stepped into the elevator, pressed the button for the sixteenth floor, and steadied my heart while I watched the doors close. When they opened, Hunter was there with a smile. He was leaning against the casing of his apartment door, hands in his pockets. He wore grey pants and a black sweater that matched his dark hair.

"I knew you would be punctual," he said.

"You think you know me so well, do you?" I stepped off the elevator.

"I do." His smile turned into a wider grin.

I smiled back and didn't argue his point. I didn't want to argue tonight. Regardless of what happened in his apartment, I didn't want to leave this city with animosity, uncertainty, or regrets.

Hunter pushed off the casing and turned to open his door. "Come in," he said and motioned for me to enter first. I stepped inside and was surprised by what I saw. Just like the foyer, his apartment was modern and bright. Large windows lined the penthouse, uncovered by any drapery, and all the walls and furniture were white. No clutter; everything in its place. No books, but lots of technology—even the refrigerator had a screen on it.

"This is nothing like how I pictured your place," I told him.

"What do you mean?"

"Well, I thought it would look similar to your family's home, you know, old-money cozy."

He laughed at this. "I've never heard that term before," he said.

"I think I just made it up." I laughed.

"Well, I'm sorry to disappoint you."

"I'm not disappointed, just surprised. But I admit I don't have a good track record of figuring you out. You haven't really made it easy for me."

He looked at me but then turned and walked over to the kitchen.

"Can I get you something to drink?

"Do you have diet soda?"

"Would sparkling water work?"

"Sure," I said.

As he prepared the drinks, I peeked at his photographs. I recognized Thomas, Laura, and Leo. There were some others I didn't recognize. I wondered if I would ever meet them.

"Hunter, what are we doing here?"

"What do you mean? I'm pouring you a drink."

"I mean, what am I doing here?"

He didn't answer me; instead he picked up a knife and sliced a lemon. I walked over to him and put my hand on his. When he didn't drop the knife, I tugged on the blade. It didn't budge since he was holding on tightly.

"Let go, or you'll hurt me," I said.

He stared at me with those amber eyes that I had looked into a million times before. I wondered if I really knew the man behind them.

"I'm sorry, Michaela," he said, holding me in place with his eyes.

"I seem to be getting a lot of apologies lately," I said. "What for, Hunter?"

"For everything. For not telling you the truth. For not putting you first. For not loving you hard enough so that no one could ever make you doubt my feelings and motives. I wanted you to heal my father, yes, but I loved you."

"Loved?" The finality of the word made my blood run cold.

At this, Hunter finally looked away. I knew I had put him on the spot, but I needed to know. "I was shocked when I found out what happened to my mother. My father told me she was killed by an enemy soldier. I was furious when I learned the truth."

"I guess in a way she was killed by an enemy. I understand your anger," I said. This time I avoided his eyes and stared at the knife instead.

"But the more I thought about it, the more I realized I wasn't angry with your mother. I was angry with my father. Yes, your mother killed mine, but I understand she acted in self-defense. She had no choice when a manticore was coming after her and her child. But my father had a choice, and he chose revenge. He chose to murder her and two other innocent people. I know he was grieving, and I understand the sentiment. Trust me, I do. I would kill anyone that hurt you. But I don't know how we get past this. Every time I see you, I'm reminded of my father's actions."

The pain in Hunter's eyes gutted me because it added to the heavy burden of my own. I was so angry with him for lying to me and with his father for the role he played in my parents' death. But hearing Hunter's apology, I felt my anger dissipate. And then my heart stopped when I heard him speak of his love for me in the past tense. I still loved him. I loved his empathy and his passion. I didn't want to lose him. I knew it was hypocritical since I was the one who asked him for time, but now that he was threatening to walk away, I couldn't bare it. I wanted to work it out, find a way, but I needed him to want it too.

"Then, you can't get past this? There is no future for us?" I asked.

"Tell me, can you get past it, Michaela?"

"Yes," I whispered. "Because I am not my mother and you are not your father, Hunter. It is terrible what happened to our mothers, but we don't have to let that stop us. We don't have to let the past dictate our future."

He walked away. I was not getting through to him. There was something else he hid from me.

"What are you not telling me?" When he walked past me, I followed him to the living room. "What are you afraid of?" I grabbed his arm and turned him until he faced me.

"You," he said and let out a breath. He ran his fingers through his hair and sat on the couch.

"You're afraid of me?" I asked in a low voice. Then a memory of John, dead on the ground, flashed in my mind. "I understand. What I did to John, it was an accident. I—"

He shook his head in disbelief. "I'm not afraid *of* you. I'm afraid *for* you! Open your eyes. You now know what I am. I am a predator. You saw what I am capable of with my bare hands. I would love to say that I didn't want to kill the bastard, but I can't. I wanted to kill him the first time I tracked him down. I wanted to kill him when I spoke to him in his prison cell. And I definitely wanted to kill him when I saw him go after you." Hunter clenched and unclenched his fist. "It felt good to finally do it and be rid of him." His voice shook when he stared up at me. "Look closely. Don't you see what I am? I am a killer."

I kept my mouth shut and processed everything Hunter had said. Finally, some insight into how he saw himself.

Finally, I understood.

"It isn't your father you can't forgive—it's yourself. Every time you see me, it isn't your father's actions you see, it's your own. Because you know that if it were you in his place, you would have done the same. You would do it still. It's not him you hate, it's you."

"What do you want from me, Michaela?" he asked, sounding tortured.

"The truth." I grabbed his hand when he tried to turn away.

"Fine, you're right," he said and he grabbed both my shoulders and stared into my eyes. "I hate what I am and what my instincts are. How can I trust a killer to be around the person I love the most? Especially when that killer is me. I can't do it. I can't risk it."

"You can't or you won't?" I glared at him. "What if I told you that you don't get to decide for me? What if I told you I could protect myself?"

"What are you talking about?" he said and let go of my arms.

"Try me," I said.

"Don't be ridiculous, I—"

"Try me," I whispered this time and got into my fighting stance.

He raised his eyebrow at me and then weakly reached for me. I easily pulled his arm back behind him and held him there.

"Cute move, I'll give you that. But you don't have the strength to hold me here." I couldn't see his face, but I heard the warning in his voice.

"Try me," I whispered again and then began my chant.

Hunter pulled his arm away, but I held on. His tense muscles softened in my grip. I let go and his arm fell limply by his side. He turned to me, his mouth wide open. When he tried to raise his arm, it only came up a few inches. He shook his head and tried again. He grunted. His forehead glistened from his efforts. His large eyes caught mine, but I couldn't tell if he was shocked or scared.

I reversed the chant and saw the moment it worked because Hunter raised his arm straight up in the air. He inhaled a gulp of air and let it out. He didn't smile.

"What the hell did you do?"

"I convinced your mind to believe the muscle in your arm did not work. It's similar to hypnosis."

He raised his arm up and down again, seeming to reassure himself. "I see you learned a few things from those books. Could you do that with any manticore, or just the ones whose minds and hearts you already own?" he asked, and finally a smile tugged on his lips.

"I've only tried it on you, but theoretically it works on any manticore."

"That will be a cool parlor trick one day."

"It's more than a parlor trick. Do you believe me now? Do you believe I can take care of myself? I don't need you to use what you are as an excuse to keep us from being together. I want to be with you, Hunter."

His smile faded and he stared right into my eyes. He stalked toward me, and his amber eyes burned. I felt like his prey. For a second, I thought he would try to scare me again, but then his hand shot out and held my head. I closed my eyes, preparing for the onslaught. I wasn't disappointed.

He kissed me wildly and ruthlessly. He did not hold back. He walked me backward toward the couch. Then, he lifted me up, guiding my legs around his waist, and brought us crashing down into the cushions. He didn't apologize for landing hard on top of me, nor did I want him to. I only wanted more of him—more of whatever this was.

I pulled on the hem of his black sweater and raised it up over his chest. His muscled stomach clenched. He paused our kiss only to pull the sweater off his head. He then did the same with my sweater. His rough skin on mine made me shiver everywhere. The heat from his body warmed my blood, and I smiled through his relentless kissing.

He pulled his mouth away from my lips and used his tongue to explore my neck, slowly moving down to my collarbone, and landing at the space between my breasts. I held his head there. I wanted to feel him close to my heart. I wanted him to hear it race in my chest.

He wrestled his way out of my grip, and I laughed because his kisses tickled my stomach. He moved lower still.

"I love you," I whispered.

He raised his head and then his arms to plant another kiss on my lips. He pulled back to look at me and whispered back, "I love you too." His amber eyes glowed.

He brought his lips to my ear, distracting me while his fingers worked on my zipper. He pulled down my jeans and stripped them off me. The world around us faded away. Our past, our hurdles, everything. I thought of nothing other than being with Hunter. I closed my eyes and inhaled. He smelled like the trees after the rain. I explored his body with my fingertips, every inch, every muscle, every sinew. His back arched at my touch.

"Michaela," Hunter whispered, and he sounded like he was in agony.

I felt a rumble on my chest. For a moment, I thought it was me. The rumble started as a purr, a soft sound next to my heart, but then as we continued it got louder. A growl echoed in the room, and Hunter became more frantic. His kisses were unmerciful, and he used every inch of his mouth to explore my neck: his lips, his tongue, his teeth—

"Ow!" I gasped at the pain.

Hunter snapped his head up and put his hand on my neck. When he pulled it away, bright red blood dripped from his fingers.

"*Fuck!*" he shouted.

Then he dropped his mouth to my neck again and pulled and sucked at the wound.

"Hunter, what are you doing?" I tried to pull him off of me.

He stood up and spit the blood into a glass nearby. He left the room and returned a few minutes later with a white cloth. He placed the cloth on my neck and it stung like hell.

"Ow! Ow! Stop that!" I shouted and pulled down on his arm.

"Hold still. It's hydrogen peroxide. I need to clean the wound," he bit out.

I relented and sucked in a breath to relieve the pain. It started to subside. He tossed the cloth in the trash and then sat next to me on the couch. He fastened a bandage to my neck and then held my face in both of his hands.

"How do you feel, Michaela?" he asked.

"I don't know," I answered truthfully. "I don't know what the hell just happened."

"Are you dizzy? Nauseated? Numb?"

"You're the one making me dizzy. I'm fine," I told him.

He stared at me, probably deciding if he should believe me. Then he raised himself up and walked away from me. "Dammit! This is exactly what I was afraid of," he said.

"It's just a cut, Hunter. I'm fine."

He turned his face toward me. His eyes were stricken and the vein on his neck throbbed.

"How can you say that it's just a cut? It's not. It's a bite from me. You know what that means, don't you? You know the poison it wields."

For a second, I panicked. I hadn't thought about how he'd cut me, that it was with his teeth. But I remained calm and kept my voice even. "You sucked out the poison and cleaned the wound, right? So I'll be fine."

"Yes," he said and took a calming breath. "The wound isn't deep. I think I got it all out. It should be all right."

"See. You were prepared. We can do this," I said and grabbed his hand to pull him back on the couch. But he resisted. The bite had killed the mood. I wondered if I could bring it back to life.

I kissed his cheek and then placed my mouth to his jaw. He stiffened but otherwise didn't seem affected by my endeavor. He remained seated on the couch, his hands curled into fists at his sides.

"Hunter, forget it." Kiss. "It was an accident." Kiss. "I'm fine."

He pulled his head back and put both his hands on my shoulders.

"How can we be together, if we can never really be together?" he asked me.

I didn't know how to answer him.

"Even if we can work through our parents' past, and I can get the entire manticore kingdom to accept you as my future queen, what will that mean for us if we can't truly be together?"

"Sex isn't everything," I hedged.

"No, but it shouldn't be a death sentence either."

"What do you want me to say? This is who we are. This is our cross to bear. Can you handle that?"

"I could if it didn't risk your life, Michaela."

I threw my hands up in the air in frustration. "I looked!" I shouted. "I looked for any kind of mention of someone like me being with someone like you and I didn't find anything."

He nodded, accepting this conclusion.

"But I also didn't find any mention of a manticore's venom

killing a Shed. Yes, it describes how deadly the venom is to humans, but it says nothing of its effects on The Sheds. We don't know for sure that your venom would hurt me. Maybe...maybe, we try it in small doses. Like what just happened now. Maybe we wait and see what sort of effect it has on me."

"Absolutely not. I'm not taking that risk. You are not an experiment."

I knew he wouldn't agree to that; the scene earlier was testament enough.

"I wish there was some way you could protect yourself from my venom. The same way you controlled my mind, you could control my venom too."

His words shocked me, and it must have shown on my face. He stared at me, narrowed his eyes, and then stood in front of me. I remained seated on the couch. He bent down on one knee to look me in the eye.

"What is it?" he asked.

I didn't answer him. I put my jeans back on instead. He tried again. "I can see it on your face. There's something you're not telling me."

I had always been a terrible liar. Once, when I was fifteen, I'd lied to my parents about attending a college party. I gave myself away when I asked if they would be upset if I visited a friend in her dorm room. This time, my face—not my words—gave me away.

"There is a chant in one of the books," I began but wanted to play it down, especially since I had not mastered it yet.

"Yes..."

"The chant is supposed to neutralize a manticore's venom."

"For how long?" he asked.

"Indefinitely," I responded.

He stared at me and then a smile spread across his face. A laugh escaped his lips. He jumped up from the floor and lifted me up with him.

"Michaela! This is wonderful! This is amazing," he said. "I asked Professor Wallace to find something like this for us, but he said there wasn't anything in that first book."

I shook my head. So much for playing it down.

There was only one chapter on this chant. I wasn't surprised Professor Wallace hadn't come across it in the first book.

"What's wrong? Why aren't you excited?" he asked. "Why didn't you tell me about this sooner?"

"Because, Hunter, I can't do it!" I shouted at him.

"What do you mean you can't?" he asked, his eyebrows arching.

"When Adam suggested I try something on Jenkins, he meant the neutralizing chant. He knew I was having trouble with it and figured it was worth trying on Jenkins."

"Is that why Jenkins went mad when you recited those words?"

"I think so."

"Adam was willing to risk you standing in front of a manticore whose instincts would be triggered like that?" he asked, clearly getting angry now.

"In his defense, Adam's never met a manticore before. I don't think he understood what could have happened."

"I'll be happy to make him understand," he said. I ignored the chill that ran down my spine when he said it.

"It obviously didn't work, as I knew it wouldn't," I said.

"Why did you know it wouldn't work?"

"Because when I say a chant, I feel it roll off my tongue. The words fall from my mouth and echo in my mind. But with this one, they get stuck. It's as if they don't want to work with me—like the words are holding on to my lips, not wanting to get out."

"Mmm," he said.

"My mother wasn't able to get the chant to work either. In fact,

Nicholas can't recall a single instance where the chant did work for any Shed. I think it's a dud. I think they messed up the wording with this one and it will never work. Not for anyone, and definitely not for me. So we have to think of another way."

"What if I'm willing to risk it? What if you tie me up so that I can't hurt you, and you try it on me?" he asked, grabbing my hands. His hands shook, and I wasn't sure if it was from excitement or fear.

"No," I said.

"It may be our only way, Michaela."

"I don't know what the other risks of the chant are. What if it's more than just triggering the instincts? What if it changes you in other ways? What if it eventually kills you? I'm not taking that chance."

Hunter sighed. "I won't change your mind on this, will I?" he asked.

I shook my head emphatically.

"All right. We will have to think of another way," he said and pulled me into his embrace.

I took another deep breath and sank deeper into his arms. I was just about to tell him everything would be okay, when my cell phone rang. "I should get this." I scurried off the couch and grabbed my phone from the kitchen table. I wasn't surprised to see Adam's name. I knew he would check up on me.

"Adam? Hey, I'm fine, you don't—"

"Michaela, you've got to get out of there," he said. "It's a trap."

"What? What are you talking about?"

"Get out of there now!" he shouted. "Ten guys in suits rushed into the building a minute ago and one of them said your name."

I glanced at Hunter, and he looked just as confused as I was. I thought Adam had to be mistaken.

"There's no trap, Adam," I said but then the door to Hunter's apartment flew open, and several large burly men in black suits raced in with their guns drawn.

"Uh, Adam. I'll have to call you back," I said and ended the call.

Ten

Michaela

"What the hell is going on here?" Hunter shouted and stood in front of me.

I peeked from behind and counted ten men, just as Adam had said.

"Mr. Durand, we have orders to arrest Michaela Morrone. We were told she would be here," said one of the men. "Ma'am, is that you?"

Before I could answer him, Hunter interjected.

"Orders? Given by whom?" he asked, his hands on his hips.

"By our commander," the bigger one replied.

"I am your commander while my father rests," Hunter snarled.

"No, sir. We were told that Leo Durand is the one giving orders right now, and he just ordered Michaela's arrest."

He handed Hunter a piece of paper, and I saw my name in the middle of it. Up top, it read: *The Office of the Manticore Kingdom*, and an insignia with a lion and a scorpion was stamped beside it.

"There has been a mistake," Hunter said, but the big one didn't stop to listen. He stepped forward and I panicked. I hadn't studied how to defend myself against ten manticores—two maybe, but ten was ambitious.

"Don't you dare touch her," Hunter growled, and I could tell by the sound of his voice that he was losing the grip on his control.

Hunter could defend himself, but I thought ten manticores were beyond his capabilities, as well.

"Hunter, it's okay. Let me go with them peacefully, and you can clear this up with Leo in the meantime. I'm sure it's all a big misunderstanding," I said and prayed to God that I was right. Otherwise, I had walked into my own nightmare. I shifted to get around Hunter, but he shot out his arm and held me back. I placed a hand on his arm and walked around him.

"I'll be right behind you in my car, Michaela. I'm going to take care of this immediately," he said.

"I know you will," I reassured him and myself.

The bigger one directed me to the elevator, and we made our way down and exited into the lobby.

"Michaela!" Adam shouted when he saw us coming.

"Adam, get back," I warned him. "I'm fine. It's all just a big misunderstanding. Hunter is going to clear it up."

His eyebrows pressed together, and I saw him take measure of all the manticores around me. I shook my head. It would be suicide for him to attempt my escape from here. *Not here*, I mouthed to him. Fortunately, he didn't overestimate himself. He took a step back and allowed us to leave the building without any incident.

A black car with tinted windows waited outside of Hunter's building. The big one opened the back door for me. He got into the car and sat himself next to me in the back seat.

"Drive," he said, and the car took off.

I tried to remain calm. I inhaled a deep breath, counted to five and let it out. I did that several times until my heartbeat slowed down. I focused on something other than where they were taking me and what would happen once I got there.

I needed to confirm if they were all manticores. I remembered a passage in one of the books that identified a manticore's features: amber eyes for the most dominant ones and then brown with a gold rim for the rest. I turned to examine the big one's eyes; he looked straight ahead, but I saw only brown with a gold rim. The book must have meant dominance in accordance to rank and not necessarily size. All ten men were quite large and tall. I suspected most manticores looked like them. I closed my eyes and listened for the most distinguishing feature—their heartbeats. I hadn't had the chance to test this yet, but according to the book a manticore's heartbeat had a specific rhythm. If a human's heartbeat went something like *ba-boom, ba-boom, ba-boom*, a manticore's was slightly faster and lengthier, so more like *ba-ba-boom, ba-ba-boom, ba-ba-boom.*

I narrowed my focus and listened. At first, a faint flutter persisted in my head. Then I heard it: *ba-ba-boom, ba-ba-boom.* The sound came from the big one beside me. I focused on the driver next and heard it again. *Ba-ba-boom, ba-ba-boom.* My own heart fluttered in my chest. I'd done it. I figured out they were all manticores.

Based on my readings and my suspicions with John, I knew I could control a manticore's heart. So I decided to try something. I didn't want to stop their hearts, of course, I only wanted to test my abilities.

I took a deep breath and held it. I recited a chant that helped me focus. I envisioned holding their hearts in my hand. I squeezed and listened. I listened for any change in the staccato of their heartbeats: *ba-ba-boom, ba-ba-boom.* Another deep breath. *Ba-ba...boom, ba-ba...boom.* There it was! A falter in their heartbeats. All of them. I'd made that happen. I felt elated. I'd controlled all three manticores in this car. I wondered how many more could I control at once.

Hunter

I grabbed my keys and raced out the door after them. When I reached the lobby, a hand grabbed onto my arm. I nearly snatched it off in my anger, until I recognized the face. It was Adam.

"What do you want?" I shouted.

"To come with you," he said. "You're going after Michaela, right?"

"Yes, I am, but you're not coming with me." I glared at his hand still holding my arm. "Now, get out of my way. You've already cost me time."

Surprisingly, he let go and didn't argue.

When I reached my car, I dialed Leo's number. After three rings, he answered.

"Hunter?"

I bit my tongue so as not to shout and roar at him. I needed answers. *Why did you have her arrested? Why did you betray me?* I settled for the former.

"Why did you do it?" I asked, my voice trembling.

"Do what? What's wrong?" he asked. His confusion seemed genuine.

"Ten manticores just stormed my apartment and took Michaela with them," I said carefully.

"They what? Why?" he asked.

"Because you told them to," I said.

"I did what? No, I didn't."

"They said they had orders to arrest her and the orders were given by you."

"I did not give those orders, Hunter. Why would I?"

"That's what I'm trying to figure out."

"Someone else wants her, and I—" I didn't hear the rest of what he said because another call beeped through. "It's your mother," I said.

A long pause, then Leo said, "You should take the call."

I did. "Hello?"

"Hunter? Hunter, are you alone?" asked Aunt Elenora. I had never seen or heard her frantic before. It made me nervous.

"Yes, what is it?" I asked.

"It's Michaela. You need to find her," she said.

"What do you know about what's happened?" I asked, worried my suspicions of Aunt Elenora were coming to fruition.

"I overheard your uncle Theodore tell the guards to arrest her. He said they were Leo's orders, but I know Leo did not give that command," she explained.

"Yes, he just confirmed the same with me," I said. "Did Theodore say anything else?"

"Yes, he told them to bring her to the dungeons. That he is arresting her for the murder of his son."

"What!"

"Yes, he means to put her on trial for John's death and for interfering with the arrest of Jenkins."

Fuck!

"All right, I'm heading there now. Thank you, Elenora," I said and ended the call. I dialed Leo's number again. This time he answered after the first ring. "Meet me at the dungeons," I said. "That's where they're taking her. I need you there. It's time I take my place in command again."

I ended the call and headed straight for Central Park, where our kingdom and its dungeons were hidden away.

Eleven

Michaela

The smell of rot and mold and God knows what else stung my nose. I held my breath and then inhaled through my mouth. There were no lights, only whatever illumination seeped through the cells from the hallway lamps. A cold cement floor and steel bars surrounded me. There was nothing else inside the cell. I sat on the dirty floor and shuddered to think where I was supposed to relieve myself.

The burly men hadn't bothered to blindfold me when they'd brought me here. That worried me. They thought I wouldn't live to tell another soul where their dungeons were hidden. I shook my head. All this time, they'd hidden their kingdom underneath our noses. My mother, Nicholas, and others before them had searched for the Manticore Kingdom. I had found it but would die here if Hunter couldn't get me out. The irony was not lost on me. I wished I'd never had desired to see it.

"It is immensely satisfying seeing you inside there," said a voice, and I turned to see who it was.

I couldn't stop the gasp that escaped from my lips. I placed a hand over my mouth to keep me steady. If I was only worried before, I was terrified now. *Theodore.* He could only want one thing from me: my life for his son's.

"It wasn't Leo who ordered my arrest. It was you," I said, the realization dawning on me.

"Yes."

"What do you want from me?" I asked, hoping it wasn't as fatal as I imagined.

"I want you to face the consequences of murdering my son," he said, and it gave me hope.

"I'm so sorry, Theodore. I really am. I didn't intend to kill him. I just wanted to stop him. But I accidently stopped his heart. I didn't have control over my powers then, but I do now." I feared the explanation would be futile, but it felt good expressing it because it was the truth.

"Sometimes the intent is not a bad one, but the action that follows it is. Your world punishes actions as well as intentions, do they not? Manslaughter, for example, is the act of murder without malice aforethought, and it is punishable, is it not?"

His question was rhetorical, and I wasn't fooled by his soft voice. He wasn't here to dispute the law; he'd come for satisfaction, just like he said. If I kept him talking, maybe I could buy myself some time until Hunter arrived.

"What is the punishment for manslaughter in your world?" I asked, admittedly ignorant of their laws.

He smiled and walked closer to me. He pointed his finger and sliced it across his neck. "Death," he whispered.

A cold shiver ran through my body, and I found it difficult to breathe. I tried to calm my heart and took in a deep breath.

Think, Michaela!

There was no point in attacking him. I would still be stuck in this cell. My best move was to wait for Hunter; he had to be close.

"Theodore, are you down here?" someone called from the stairs.

Theodore pursed his lips, annoyed to have been disturbed, but called out, "Yes, I'm here."

A man I'd never seen before stepped down the stairs and walked toward us.

"I've spoken to Olympia. She is going to get the king settled and ready to hear her plea."

"There will be no plea, Davis," said Theodore. "She is guilty. Five witnesses saw her kill my son. Even if Hunter denies it, the others cannot. They saw it with their own eyes."

"Then, it should be a swift trial," he said and glanced at me. He took his time inspecting me from head to toe, and I did the same. Grey strands salted his hair. He had a wide mouth and a Roman nose. He was handsome and reminded me of someone.

"I can see the attraction," said Davis. "Those eyes are alluring, and if their power holds true—dangerous."

"All the more reason to take care of the girl before she becomes a problem," said Theodore.

"Mmm, the idea has merit," he said and then looked at me. "What do you say?"

Before I could respond, a commotion ensued. Hunter shouted, and his voice boomed off the walls. I heard him before I saw him come down the stairs.

"Get her out of there," he shouted.

Theodore walked over to stand in front of Hunter.

"She is under arrest and waiting to see the king," he said. "She's been lawfully charged with murder."

Hunter growled and tried again. "Lawfully? You lied and used Leo's name to charge her. I said, get her out of there."

"No," Theodore said, staring Hunter down. Theodore's eyes bulged and a vein in his forehead throbbed. He sneered, and I caught a glimpse of his fangs. I worried that Hunter would pay for my mistakes. I was about to accept the trial but was interrupted again. Someone came down the stairs.

"Let her go, Theodore," said a female voice. It was Elenora.

"No," said Theodore again. This time a few of the security guards stood with him in front of my cell, blocking the door.

"Are you going to fight your family on this?" she asked.

"Yes. Because I am fighting *for* my family—for my son," he said. The pain in his voice pierced my heart. A renewed sense of guilt hit me in the chest.

"Unfortunately, there's no need for this little showdown," said Elenora. "I came down to tell you, the king is prepared to see her now. I'm here to bring her up."

"No, I want a public trial," said Theodore. "I want everyone to know what she is and the truth of what happened to my son."

"Do you really want everyone to know the whole truth about your son and the traitor he was?" said Elenora. "It is best for the entire family if that matter is kept from the rest of the kingdom. We cannot risk anyone doubting our family's strength or ability to rule. We do not need Tommy Ross, or any other upstart, to think our family is weak and attempt a move for the throne himself. Now, I will take Michaela upstairs to the king and you will step aside."

"I'll do it," said Hunter.

"Forgive me, Hunter, but I don't trust that you will. You will only try to get her away just like you did the last time. No. She is finally going to face the consequences of her actions. Let's go, my dear," she said and pulled a key from her coat pocket.

"Step aside," she ordered the guards, and they did.

She unlocked my cell.

I nodded my agreement to Hunter. In a way, I was relieved to finally put the incident behind me. I just hoped it wouldn't cost me my life.

Elenora led me up the cement stairwell. I nearly tripped on the first step, since it was quite dark, but it didn't bother any of the manticores. She held my arm and helped me the rest of the way up.

"We've never had a human in here, you know," she said cheerfully, as though I should be honored by that distinction. "Never thought we'd need to. That is until you came along."

I murmured an "oh" under my breath. I didn't know how I felt about Elenora. Hunter didn't trust her and that was enough to make me wary.

"I never got the chance to meet your mother, but I'm sure you know that. I would have found it a pleasure to hold her arm, just as I am holding yours."

When I didn't respond, she glanced at me and smiled. "You don't trust me? Well, it's prudent of you to be careful. You never know whom you can trust in a houseful of manticores," she said and then laughed.

We reached a hallway with several doors and an elevator all the way at the end. Two security guards flanked the elevator. The doors opened, and Leo stepped out of the lift. He frowned and walked toward us.

"Mother, what are you doing?" he asked, staring pointedly at her hand on my arm.

"Oh, darling, always thinking the worst of me. I am taking her to the king," Elenora said.

"Where's Hunter?"

"I'm here," he responded from behind.

Leo joined us as Elenora opened one of the doors that led into another hallway. This one was wider, and several ceremonial photographs of men and women in military uniform hung on the walls. We stood in front of two large wood-panelled doors that looked to be at least fifteen feet tall. Two security guards pulled on the brass handles to open those doors, and we all walked inside.

This was no ordinary courtroom. There were several rows of wooden pews but no benches for attorneys.

"Where does the jury sit?" I asked.

"The king is the jury and executioner, and he sits over there," said Elenora. She pointed to the back of the room where a brass throne sat empty.

Elenora led me to a glass box on wheels with a single pew inside.

"You don't need to put her in there," said Hunter. He looked ready to break the glass.

"We must follow procedure, Hunter. After all, this is not a family meeting," said Davis.

Hunter frowned, not pacified by the arguments, but sat next to Leo in the pew closest to me. Theodore, Davis, Elenora, and about ten armed guards sat in pews behind them.

Once we were all seated, the back door opened and a man wearing a military uniform walked through and faced us. "Ladies and gentlemen, King Marsel Durand."

Everyone stood and I followed their lead. I recognized the king, even though he looked nothing like the frail person I had last seen. His stride was sure, and he did not falter in his step. He held his back straight and his head high.

"Please, sit down," he said, looking around the room and then to me. His eyes reflected pain, like it hurt him to see me. I worried this did not bode well for me.

"I'm told, Leo, you've charged this woman with the death of John Durand. Is that correct?" asked the king.

Leo stood up. "No, sire, I did not. My uncle lied about that to get her here. I believe this entire trial needs to be dismissed."

Hunter exhaled a breath of relief following this statement.

"Sire," began Theodore, but the king raised his hand to cut him off.

"While the method to arrest Ms. Morrone may have been deceitful, I still believe this trial has merit and will continue."

"What?" said Hunter, disbelief clear in his voice. Leo grabbed his arm and pulled him to sit, but Hunter didn't relent easily. Leo had to hold him down. He obviously had not expected this from his father. Now I was really nervous.

"Let us hear your arguments, Theodore," said the king.

Theodore stood up, straightened his jacket, and walked to stand in front of the throne to address his king. "This woman is guilty of murder. She is responsible for the death of my son, John. She killed him, and there are at least five witnesses who can attest to it," said Theodore.

"No need," the king said as he waved this off. "I've heard the story recounted several times and I believe what you say is true. Michaela is responsible for John's death."

Hunter raised his hand to interject again, but Leo had a tight grip on his other arm. Leo whispered in his ear, and Hunter mumbled back but remained seated.

Theodore took a step back, clearly stunned by this admission of guilt from the king, and then pushed forward. "You see, it is an undisputed claim," he said and pointed his finger at me. "She killed him and must be punished accordingly. She must die for what she did."

Fear gripped my body and I couldn't move, could barely breathe. My blood ran cold, and I shivered. But I remained silent.

The king turned to glare at me. "Michaela, was it your intention to kill John?" he asked.

Relieved I could proclaim it formally and apologize to everyone, I took a deep breath before firmly denying the allegation. "I had no intention of killing John," I said. "I only wanted to stop him. I am so sorry."

I turned my head to look at Theodore when I said this, but the contempt in his eyes had not softened.

"You see, sire," Theodore said to the king. "She admits it, she has no control over her power. If she had no intention to kill John but did so anyway, how can any manticore be safe around her? How can you protect us if you let her go? For the safety of all manticores, she must die."

His words defeated me. I lost control of my fears and a sob escaped from my mouth.

"This is ridiculous," shouted Hunter and stood up to address his father. "John was a traitor. He admitted it himself in front of all those witnesses," he sneered. "John deserved what he got, and I only regret I didn't do it myself."

Theodore stared at Hunter, but Hunter did not relent. "Your son betrayed his king. Seeking to blame another for his ultimate demise is pathetic."

"You bastard," growled Theodore. "John deserved a trial—more than she does," he said and pointed at me again. "She had no right to kill him!"

"No, it was my right!" Hunter roared back.

"That's enough," said the king. "Theodore is right."

The words slapped me and I turned to see Hunter flinch, as well.

"What?" he whispered.

"It was not Michaela's place to kill John. She is not a manticore, and it was not her right to kill one of our own. She must be punished for this," said the king.

"Father, please," pleaded Hunter, but the king raised his hand again.

"She will not be put to death," King Marsel said. "However, she is sentenced to sixty years in our dungeons."

A gasp echoed in the room, but it didn't come from me. Olympia held her hand to her mouth. I hadn't noticed her or Laura join us. My focus had been entirely on the king. And he'd just sentenced me to life in that cold, dirty, empty cell. I couldn't do it.

"Please," I begged him. "Don't do this. I didn't mean to harm him. I may not have been in control of my powers then, but I am now."

"Marsel, I think the girl can serve us better outside of the dungeons," said Elenora. "Perhaps she can be sentenced to work as our healer. She would be a force for us rather than forgotten."

"No," said Hunter, wrenching his arm out of Leo's grasp. "Michaela is not a tool for us to use, nor is she going to be a prisoner."

He approached the throne and dropped to his knees.

"Father, I beg you," he said. "Let her go. She did not ask for any of this. I sought her out in her own home. I brought her here. You should be thanking Michaela for saving your life, not condemning hers."

The king dropped his head and looked away from his son. Then he placed both hands down on the armrests and rose from the throne. He stood in front of Hunter.

"You are right. I do owe her my life. If I believe she can take John's life without touching him, then I must also believe she is responsible for saving mine," said the king.

"Thank you, Father," said Hunter, starting to rise. "Then you will let her go?"

"I will let her go," he said, and I let out another sob—this one from relief. "On one condition," he added.

The room fell silent, as we all waited to hear what the king had to say. "I will forgive her crime in exchange for saving my life. But she is still a danger to our kind, and I will not have her around my son and heir. Michaela is free to go...but, Hunter, you must set her free, as well. You must let her go and never see her again."

That's when I realized, I was never on trial. This was all about Hunter, and the king wanting him to be with a manticore instead of me.

"Why are you doing this?" The pain in Hunter's voice broke my heart. He had not realized his father's motivation yet.

"She and her family are a danger to us all," said the king.

"I don't have any family left. You made sure of that," I told him, angry that he dared to speak of my family.

The king flinched but otherwise did not respond.

"She has an aunt," said Theodore. "We must lock them both up."

"My aunt doesn't have any powers—leave her alone!" I shouted at him.

Theodore ground his jaw, and I heard his growl from twenty feet away.

"Marsel, you must lock her in the dungeons. Hunter is not going to give her up," Theodore shouted back.

Hunter gazed at me. His eyes pleaded with me and his shoulders dropped in defeat. Agony flashed across his face, but he managed to say clearly, "I will give her up." Then he glared at his father and growled with his fists clenched at his sides. "Now let her go."

"Hunter, no!" I shouted. "You promised me. You promised me we'd find a way!"

But he ignored me. He stared at his father, waiting for a response. The king nodded and then turned to the guard, "Let her go."

The guard did not stand to do the king's bidding; in fact, he didn't move at all. He just gazed straight ahead.

"Guard," the king said again, this time more sternly.

"I was afraid this might happen," said Theodore, now walking toward the king. "I was afraid you'd prove to be the same reformer, or relent to your son's affections, or worse—what I hadn't even planned—offer her freedom despite finding her guilty. Pathetic," Theodore spat in his face.

"What do you think you're doing, Uncle?" warned Hunter.

"I am taking her," he said, his eyes blazing at the king. "She's coming with me, and no one will stop me."

"You're going to need more than ten manticores to stop me," said Hunter. He rose to his feet to defend himself against the approaching guards. But at that moment, one of the guards opened the door and ten more armed manticores walked in, their guns raised and pointed at Hunter and his father.

Leo rose from his seat and stood next to Hunter.

"Leo," shouted Elenora. "Don't get yourself involved in this."

"This is treason," Leo said. "And I won't sit and watch as my uncle betrays his king and his people."

"This does not concern you, Leo," said Theodore. "I just want the girl."

"Well, that's not going to happen," Leo replied.

"So be it," said Theodore, and then to the guard closest to Hunter, he said, "Take care of him."

Coward! He wouldn't even fight his own battles. Theodore watched as a guard raised his arms and swung at Hunter. Hunter blocked the punch but the next one hit him in the gut. Leo tried to pull the guard off of Hunter, but another one lifted Leo up from behind.

I shouldn't have been surprised to see Laura jump into the fray. She landed an impressive kick into the guard's stomach that sent him windmilling across the room. Hunter spun around and pulled the guard's arm around his back until it broke. The manticore's scream pierced my ears. I covered them as I watched the guard fall to the ground, clutching his arm in pain. Leo and Laura wrestled with their assailants. Another manticore reached for Hunter. There would be ten more after him. I was surprised they didn't all pounce on the three of them at once and finish this quickly.

I hadn't seen Theodore's approach until he was only ten feet away. But Hunter saw him. "Father, stop him!" he shouted, but the king hesitated. He looked between me and his son. I was on my own. That was fine with me. I waited for an opening. I stepped out of the glass box, my fingers curled into a fist, prepared to face Theodore.

"Don't come any closer," I warned him. "I don't want to hurt you."

This gave him pause, and frustration mounted on his face.

"You are outmatched, Uncle," Hunter shouted as he fought off the next guard. "She is more powerful than you."

"That may be so," said Theodore, "But is she faster than a bullet?"

At his words, the remaining guards turned and pointed their guns at me. I realized why they hadn't bothered to fight Hunter at once. Their target was me. It always had been.

"Theodore, stop this," said the king, finally.

"No, this ends today," Theodore responded.

I closed my eyes and tried something I never had before. I had no idea if this would work, but I didn't have time to consider it. I was out of options. I repeated the words I'd practiced. The ones that helped me control their thoughts. I envisioned each guard, one by one. I envisioned whispering the words softly into their ears, just like a lullaby.

"Surrender yourself to me now," said Theodore.

I didn't respond, instead focusing on my words. He shouted this time. "Surrender yourself, or I'll have them shoot you."

I shook my head and opened my eyes. I smiled at the scene before me. Theodore was fixated on me and hadn't noticed. When he saw my smile, he turned around. All twenty guards lay on the floor.

"My God!" he said. "She's killed them! She's killed them all!" He turned to the king. "Do you see how powerful she is? Do you see why we must take care of her before she kills us too?"

The king stared at me, horrified, as did Hunter and the rest of his family. I was a little hurt that they thought so poorly of me. But I didn't have a great track record.

"They are not dead," I assured them. "I merely suggested in their minds that they needed to sleep for the next twelve hours. They'll probably feel better than ever when they wake up tomorrow."

Shocked and then desperate, Theodore tried again. "It doesn't matter that they are still alive. Look at the power she wields. Look at what she can do so effortlessly." He waved his hand over the courtroom and the sleeping manticores.

"I cannot blame her for her powers," said the king. "Do we not ask the same for ourselves? She did not harm anyone here today, but you, Theodore...you disobeyed your king."

Theodore's face turned red, and his chest heaved and fell. He panted while his shoulders rose with each breath. His deranged face terrified me. I worried he would lose control at any moment.

"You!" he said. "You did this and you won't stop. But I will stop you, even if I must use my own bare hands." He shook his hands in front of him and curled them as though he imagined my neck between them.

Having lost his army, Theodore was desperate, but he wasn't weak. He knew it was over for him and he wanted it to be over for me, as well. I saw that desperation in his eyes right before he threw his body on top of mine. I thought I was prepared for his attack, but he was faster and stronger than I'd anticipated. When he raised his head to roar his anger, his fangs grew and venom dripped from their tips. My heart raced, and I scrambled to get away from him. I needed time to chant, think, or say goodbye. I turned my head violently from side to side, but I couldn't see Hunter. All I saw was a vengeful father's face in front of me before he sank his teeth into my neck. Then I saw nothing at all.

Twelve

Hunter

I didn't know how I would save her. It didn't matter. I knew I wouldn't get there in time. It was too late. His fangs bit into the soft flesh at her neck.

"No!" I roared and raced toward my uncle.

I hesitated, afraid to throw him off of her. If his teeth were lodged in her neck, pulling him away would only tear the skin at her throat. Instead, I stopped resisting my anger. I let it flow freely through me. My own fangs lengthened, and I tasted the sweet venom on my tongue. Then I attacked.

My nails tore through his shirt and clawed my uncle's back. He roared his head up and released Michaela. With her free, I readied to finish him. I aimed for his throat, but he was prepared and strong. He grabbed my jacket and threw me effortlessly to the side. I fell to the ground but jumped back up and continued to fight him. I dropped my right shoulder and rushed straight into his abdomen, pushing him to the ground. He landed a few punches to my kidneys, but they were nothing compared to the pain I felt imagining Michaela dead on the ground.

"You bastard," I shouted, and my eyes stung from the unshed tears. We wrestled on the floor as I attempted to gain the upper hand and straddle him. He was sharper than I had assumed, and he got away. He used a pew to lift himself up.

"You killed her!" I yelled.

"It was retribution for my son," he sneered. "I enjoyed every second of it. I can still taste her skin on my tongue."

A red haze clouded my eyes, and adrenaline rushed through my blood. My rage blinded me, but I still raced toward him. I grabbed his collar with one hand and his leg with the other, then swung his body up into the air and roared. Gathering all my strength, I threw him onto the pews. He landed awkwardly on the wooden edge and fell to the ground. His body went limp. He didn't move, and I prayed that he was dead. If he wasn't, I was ready to take him on all over again.

I stood there a few minutes, sucking in air, watching for movement from the heap of bones on the floor. Nothing. Satisfied that it was over, I walked over to Michaela.

No longer able to hold them back, tears streamed down my face. When I reached her, I rubbed the tears off with my shirt sleeve. I gently lifted her head. Her face looked peaceful; remnants of a smile lingered on her lips. I reached for her hand and felt a faint pulse. She wasn't dead yet. If the poison had not taken hold, I thought maybe we could rid her of it.

"Get the physician," I yelled. "Meet me at the mansion, it's closer."

Laura raced out of the room.

I slowly slid one arm under Michaela's neck and the other under her knees, then lifted her body off the ground. Her head lolled to the side, away from me. I carried her like a ragdoll and avoided looking at my father when I passed him.

"Hunter, wait," he said.

I couldn't talk right now, especially not to him. So, I kept my mouth shut and walked out of the courtroom and into the hallway. Footsteps raced after me. Leo ran past me to get to the elevator first; he held the door while I carried Michaela in. The doors shut and I closed my eyes, praying like I never had before. Praying that it was not too late.

Leo drove us to the mansion in my car and ran every red light on the way.

When we arrived, Laura was waiting for us outside.

"The physician is in your old room," she said. "I figured that's where you'd want to bring her."

I nodded because my throat still felt too tight to speak. I climbed the stairs and walked down the hallway toward my room. I laid Michaela gently on top of the bed. The last time we were in this bed, she had been full of life, mischief, and hope. I worried she had none of those left.

"Move aside, Hunter, so I can examine her," said the physician, surprising me. I hadn't noticed him when I'd come in. I stepped back and allowed him to get close to her.

He placed his ear to her heart. "The heartbeat is slow but steady. That's a good sign," he said.

I took a deep breath, hope rising in my heart. I watched as he examined the violent wound on her neck. The teeth marks were jagged, as if my uncle had shaken his head back and forth while biting her to cause more pain. I wished I could kill him again just for that.

"The wound is large and deep," explained the physician. "Did you manage to suck any of the poison out?"

"I tried in the car on the way over, but I didn't know how much of it was venom. There was so much blood coming from the wound, I was afraid she would bleed out. I tried to staunch the blood at the same time." I ran a hand through my hair. "Is it too late to try it now?" I asked.

"I'm afraid so. The venom would have already traveled through her body."

"Wouldn't we see signs of the poisoning by now? Wouldn't she be dying or in some sort of pain?" I recalled witnessing other manticore attacks. "Every time I've seen our poison injected, death was imminent. That's why I thought we had time. She was so calm."

"Not necessarily. Every human reacts differently to our venom. To some, it is a quick poisoning, while to others, it is a slow and torturous death. I am surprised, with the size of this wound, that it was not quick for her."

"No, but torturous instead?"

"I don't know for sure," he hedged. "The venom could cause paralysis, which might be why she does not look like she's suffering. However, it could still be killing her slowly inside. We're just not seeing it. Perhaps it's better this way," he said.

"Better? For whom, Doctor?" I said and grabbed him by his shirt collar. "For us monsters that don't have to witness what our poison does?"

Laura's hand covered mine and she unfurled my fist. "Let him go, Hunter. Do not take your anger out on him. It's not his fault."

I didn't let go. I couldn't. I was angry and I didn't care who I hurt. If Michaela died, why did anyone else deserve to live? Dark, murderous thoughts raced through my mind. I imagined myself a dark avenging angel, killing other manticores for the monsters they truly were.

"Hunter, look at me," said Laura. My sister was one of the good ones. She always kept her anger in check. I should have envied her, but I didn't.

"If Michaela is indeed dying, then killing the doctor or any other manticore is not going to change that," she said.

"No, but at least another predator will be off the streets," I said. The doctor gulped and his eyes widened.

"You don't mean that," she said.

"I do, Laura," I said but let go of the physician. He scampered to the other side of the bed. "Father is wrong. We are not capable of rehabilitation. We are killers. It's in our nature and perhaps we do not deserve to assimilate with humans. We are far too dangerous to be around them."

"Manticores are not killing humans. Humans kill other humans too. There is good and bad in all of us. Some of us just let the good stay closer to the top while keeping a tight lid on the bad."

I considered her words and turned to look at Michaela. Her good was always visible, it was always on top. If she died, she would not die alone.

I lay down next to her on the bed and wrapped my arms around her. It killed me to imagine her in pain right now but unable to show it. I tucked her head under my chin and ran my hand up and down her arm. I wanted her to feel only my touch, nothing else.

Movement on the other side of the room rustled in my ear, but I didn't open my eyes. I imagined it was Laura, shuffling the doctor and anyone else out. The soft click of the door signaled I was alone with Michaela. I closed my eyes and held on tighter. Whatever time I had left, I planned to spend it with her in my arms.

Thirteen

Michaela

Sweat trickled down my neck, and my body flushed from the heat. I could hardly breathe. A heavy blanket covered my face and limbs. I squeezed my eyes and then opened them a sliver. I didn't recognize, at first, where I was.

Then, I spotted the tall mahogany antique dresser, the red upholstered Louis XIV chair, and the Persian rug in the center. It was Hunter's old bedroom. Memories flooded my mind of the last time I was in this room. I smiled.

The heavy blanket turned out to be a heavy male. I grinned as I squirmed around to face him. I placed my hand on his cheek and felt stubble underneath my fingertips. His eyes fluttered open, but his mouth remained shut. His amber eyes widened and then he lifted himself up on his elbow, hovering his body over mine.

"Michaela," he whispered. "Am I dreaming?"

His question surprised me. *Could this be a dream? Am I dead and this is heaven?*

As much as I loved waking up in this bed with Hunter, I wanted to be alive in it. The thought of me dying brought back a terrible vision: Theodore roaring, and his fangs inching closer to me. The memory urged my hand to my neck. My fingers felt a bandage there. *Ouch! Not a dream, not in heaven, and definitely not dead.*

"No, I'm pretty sure this is real life. My neck hurts worse than the time Mr. Whiskers bit me."

"Mr. Whiskers?" he said and then shook his head. "Michaela, I don't believe it..." he said and frowned. He squeezed his eyes shut and didn't open them.

"Are you all right, Hunter?" I asked him.

He laughed and continued to laugh until he fell back onto the bed.

I was more than a little worried about him.

"*Am I all right*? Am *I* all right? Yes, Michaela! I'm more than all right. You're alive and talking. I didn't want to hope that this was possible."

"What were you expecting?"

He stopped laughing and reached for me. He cupped my cheek.

"Do you remember what happened to you in the courtroom?"

I recalled my latest memory and shuddered.

"Yes, your uncle attacked me."

He nodded and pulled me into his arms. "Yes. He bit you, Michaela. The wound is quite large. We are certain his venom entered your body. We thought you were dying," he said.

"How long have I been unconscious?"

He glanced down at his watch, "About three hours."

Oh, well, that wasn't so bad. I'd taken naps longer than that.

"Have you been in here with me the whole time," I asked, but I read the answer in his tired eyes. He nodded, and I reached for him this time. I lay on top of him, placed my hand on his cheek, and brought my lips to rest on his mouth. I kissed him gently, and he barely moved his mouth. I knew he was holding back, afraid of hurting me. But I was fine—better than fine, in fact. I felt alive and ready to take control of my life again.

I pushed myself up onto Hunter and straddled his hips. He chuckled and raised his arms behind his head. I leaned down for another kiss but then laughed when he tickled behind my knees. He knew my weakness.

"Hunter!" I chastised.

"Checking that everything is the way it should be," he said.

I snatched his hands and tugged them up above his head. "Everything is exactly the way it should be," I told him and leaned down to kiss him again.

"Well now, Laura, it seems our Michaela is in fact not dying," Leo teased from the doorway. "She's very much in good health and spirits."

I smirked because I couldn't argue with that. I twisted to see him over my shoulder but I didn't get up. Laura averted her gaze, and I cringed for making her uncomfortable. No one would want to catch their sibling in bed. I relented, swung my leg off of Hunter, and stood next to the bed.

"Don't you know to knock first," Hunter grumbled at them.

"I thought this was a sick room, not a college dorm room," said Leo. "You should have at least put a tie on the door handle."

Having turned back around, Laura walked over to me and extended her arms. I opened mine, too, and embraced her.

"I'm so glad you're okay," she said. "I was worried we'd lost you, even before we really got to know you better."

I peeked up at Hunter, remembering the trial and his father's ruling. "Are we going to get the chance? Am I a free woman?" I asked.

Hunter didn't respond immediately, so Laura interjected. "Yes, my father declared it so."

"He also asked Hunter to forsake me," I reminded them. "Does this mean I must leave?"

"Absolutely not," said Hunter, but Laura and Leo gave each other a wary look.

"I'd like an audience with the king," I told them.

"You'd what?" asked Leo.

"I want to speak with the king," I repeated.

"I'll have to see when he's available," Leo said too casually. "But first, he asked to speak with you, Hunter."

"I'm looking forward to it," Hunter said, and straightened his shirt before giving me a soft kiss. He turned and walked out of the room with Leo.

"Come, I'll help set up a bath for you," said Laura. "I'm sure you'll want to wash the day off."

"That does sound nice," I said, hoping they had a soap strong enough to wash my worries away too.

I wasn't concerned about the king hurting Hunter; I was worried about Hunter offending his father. The last thing I wanted was Hunter losing his family because of me. I wouldn't wish that on anyone.

"Is your father a reasonable man, Laura?" I asked. My experience with the king was quite limited so far.

"He is. But with you, it seems to be personal, Michaela. I don't know what he's going to do," she replied. She wrung her hands, and her worried eyes glanced at mine.

"I appreciate your honesty. And it's personal for me too."

"Yes, I imagine it is," she said softly. "I'd love to hear your side of the story, if you're willing to share it."

I thought about her offer and decided I could really use an ally right now. I nodded, and she squeezed me with another hug before leading me to the bathroom. She passed me a towel when we got there.

"First, you bathe, then we talk," she said.

"Deal."

Hunter

"I'll be just outside the door," Leo assured me when we reached my father's study.

"Leo, you don't have to worry. I'll be able to control myself," I told him.

"It's not you I'm worried about, Hunter," he said. "I've never seen him like this."

Leo was right. My father had always been logical and methodical. His mannerisms put everyone at ease. But his conduct at Michaela's trial concerned me. His decision to keep Michaela away from us—away from me—was not logical but personal. And that was unlike him.

I knocked on the door once and then let myself in. My father sat at his desk, staring at my mother's portrait as he usually did when he was deep in thought.

I strode into the room and sat on the brown leather couch across from his desk.

"What do you think she would have done about Michaela?" he asked.

"I don't know, Father." I huffed, frustrated that he'd spoken of Michaela like she was some business predicament, instead of the woman I loved. "Mother would probably tell you to follow your heart."

He always smiled when I mentioned my mother. He frowned now.

"But it's not her decision I came here for," I said. "It's yours."

"I already gave you my decision, Hunter. Michaela cannot stay here. She is too dangerous to manticores. She is too powerful and barely in control of this power."

"She was quite in control when she handled twenty manticore guards without hurting a single one of them," I argued.

"Yes, and it only showed me that she could have just as easily stopped their hearts at the same time," he shot back. "How do you think other manticores will respond to that threat? There will be someone who will want to make sure a power like hers cannot be used against them. They will kill her, Hunter. I also know they will kill you to get to her because you will stand in their way. I won't allow that to happen, especially if I can prevent it first. You are my son and heir. I must protect the kingdom and the future of this family. Michaela must go. You will find someone else. I know you will."

"So, that's it? You label her a threat and tell me to just forget about her. Tell me to toss her back into the sea like a fish I caught on a hook. I can't do that. I love her. I trust her. She would not hurt anyone intentionally."

"How can you know that? How much time have you really spent with her?"

"Enough to know what's in her heart, to know that her soul is good and kind. To know that she is a better being than me. But I am weak. I cannot stay away from her. I tried father, but I know that I can't do it. Don't ask it of me."

"I am not asking, Hunter. I demand it," he threatened. His tone made me lean back. He had never spoken to me like this before.

"Is this really about her powers or is it about her mother, Lucia?" I asked, needing to know the truth.

"Don't speak of that woman in my presence," he sneered.

"Why not? Did you even give Lucia the chance to explain herself?" I asked.

"Explain herself? There was nothing she could have said that would have made me forgive her. She killed my wife! She killed the only woman I've ever loved and will ever love. She took her from me."

"You are doing the same to me now."

"What are you talking about? I am not going to kill Michaela. She is not her mother. I won't hold her responsible for her sins, but I'll be damned before I allow Lucia's daughter to ruin our kingdom and our future."

"If you send her away and command me to forget her, you might as well kill me," I said.

"Don't be dramatic, Hunter," he warned me.

But I shook my head. "Dramatic? I am being honest with you, Father. A piece of you died along with my mother. If you knew she still roamed this earth and you could not be with her, would your life not be hell? Is that what you condemn me to?"

He looked uncomfortable but then cleared his throat. "I've made my decision and it is final," he said.

I stood to leave. It was pointless. Nothing I said, dramatic or otherwise, would make a difference.

"Fine. Then I've made a decision, as well," I said. "I renounce the throne. I renounce the kingdom. I'll leave today with Michaela and will never step foot in your house again."

"You wouldn't," he said, a threat lingering in his voice.

"Why not? I would be a terrible ruler with resentment in my heart. Our people do not deserve that, and I do not deserve to be bitter."

I walked out of the room and didn't look back. I knew when I'd entered his study that this was a possibility, and I'd recognized the look of determination in his eyes. I didn't know the words I would say but I knew the risk I was willing to take. I wasn't afraid to lose it all. Not when I stood to gain so much more with her.

When I returned to my old bedroom, Michaela was not there. I searched for her downstairs and found her in the breakfast room, seated next to Laura. They held their heads close together. Judging by the frown on Laura's face, the conversation was a serious one.

Michaela's hair was wet and she had pulled it into a braid. She wore a pair of grey lounge pants and a white T-shirt. Laura must have lent those to her.

"Hunter," Laura said when she spotted me in the doorway. "How did your talk with Father go?"

"As expected," I told her.

"Can I see him now?" Michaela asked.

"Not right now," I said. "It's not a good time. A lot has happened today."

She nodded but didn't respond.

"Are you ready to go?" I asked her, itching to leave this place.

She glanced down at her clothes, "Is it all right if I borrow these for the day, Laura?"

"Of course," said Laura. "Where are you going, Hunter?"

"Back to my place. Michaela and I will be more comfortable there."

Laura and I stared at each other for a few minutes. I knew Laura had guessed that the conversation with our sire had not gone well.

"When will you be back?" she asked.

"I'm not sure," I said. *Let it go!*

She twisted her lips, preparing to argue, but must have decided she would leave it for now. "I'll come check on you tomorrow, Michaela."

"Thanks, Laura. I appreciate your kindness," said Michaela. "I'll go grab my clothes and things from your room, Hunter. Then I'll be ready to leave."

"I'll be here," I said and watched her leave the room.

"I take it Father didn't change his mind?" Laura asked, rising from her chair.

"No," I told her.

"What are you going to do?" She crossed her arms and leaned her hip against the table.

"What I need to do. Get Michaela away from here and start our lives together. On our own."

"Hunter, don't do this. I'm sure Father will come around. Be patient."

"He will not change his mind. You should have seen his face. He hates her." I stared at my sister. "He may say it's for the good of the kingdom, but I know it's because he can't stand to be in the same room as her. I will not put her through that. She doesn't deserve it and neither do I."

"It will be impossible for you to be with her and still be the heir. As your partner, she will be involved."

"That's why I have renounced my claim to the throne."

"You did what?" She uncrossed her arms and held up her palms.

I didn't respond because I knew she'd heard me. I raised my eyebrow instead.

"Hunter, you can't do that. Who will take over?"

"You. You are a ferocious leader. You are brilliant, strategic, and you know how to take charge."

"Thank you. But I don't want it. I did not have decades to prepare for this as you have, and it's not what I want. Don't put me in this position."

"I don't have a choice, Laura. Father will not have her here and I won't be here without her."

"There must be some way to work this out," she said and sat down at the table again.

"Everything doesn't always work out the way we want it to."

"Maybe, but I don't think we've tried hard enough yet."

I walked over to where she sat holding her forehead in the palm of her hand. I didn't want to hurt Laura. I pulled her up and wrapped my arms around her.

"This isn't goodbye," I assured her. "I will see you soon." Laura leaned her cheek against my shoulder, but otherwise didn't respond.

I did say goodbye, however, to the kingdom.

Fourteen

Michaela

"What's that on your arm?" Hunter asked me while driving back to his apartment. I'd brought my hand to the stick shift to hold his while he drove, and he must have noticed the band-aid on the inside of my elbow.

"Oh, the physician came in while you were speaking to your father. He wanted to take a sample of my blood to check if the venom had caused any permanent damage to my cells."

"How do you feel?" he asked me for the fourth time that day.

"I feel great, Hunter," I answered truthfully. "Just a little guilty. I should go to the hotel room and let Adam know I'm all right. He must be worried."

"That reminds me," he said and reached into the inside pocket of his jacket. "Leo found this on the courtroom floor when he went back in to clean up."

He handed me my cell, and I was so relieved. My entire life was in that phone.

"Fantastic. I was worried I had lost it." I swiped up to unlock the screen, happy I still had some battery life left. I'd missed thirteen calls—eleven were from Adam. I dialed his number first.

"Michaela?" he answered after half a ring. "Is that you?"

"Yes, it's me. I'm all right," I assured him.

"Oh, thank God!" he whispered, and sucked in a deep breath. "Are you hurt? Do you need me to come get you?"

"No, I'm fine. I'm staying with Hunter today, but I'll be back tomorrow to pack and board our flight."

"Are you with him right now?" he asked.

"Yes, why?"

Adam didn't respond. I thought the line had dropped, but then I heard him say, "Okay, I'll see you tomorrow," right before he ended the call.

I peeked up at Hunter, but he stared ahead and didn't say a word for a few minutes.

"Your flight leaves tomorrow?" he finally asked.

"Yes. 10 a.m."

"Then, I guess we will have to make tonight count." He turned to face me and pinned me with his gaze. "You up for it, Ms. Morrone?"

"I think I can handle anything you dish out, Mr. Durand."

"Oh, I believe you. I think you can handle ten of me," he said.

"Or twenty," I joked, but then he frowned.

"Too soon?" I asked, wrinkling my brow.

"Yeah, too soon," he said, but a smile tugged on his lips and he shook his head.

I looked down at the sweats I wore. "I'm going to need something to wear. Can you drop me off at my hotel to pick up some things?"

"If you promise to wear the gold dress tonight."

I smirked at this. "Deal."

He pulled his car up to the front door of my hotel and I turned to him, "I'll just be a few minutes," I said, then raced out of the car so I could keep my word.

Damn! I'd left my purse at Hunter's apartment when I'd been arrested, so I didn't have the room key with me. I walked over to the concierge to plead my case. Unfortunately, the concierge wasn't inclined to help. He frowned at my lack of ID and denied me entry into my own room. *Ugh.*

Then I remembered I'd given Adam the second key to my room. I pulled my cell phone out of my back pocket and dialed his number. He answered immediately.

"Hello?"

"Adam, hey. Can you meet me in front of my hotel room? I don't have my key on me, and I need to get inside to collect a few things."

"Sure, I'll meet you there."

"Thanks," I said and took the elevator to the fourth floor.

Since his room was down the hall from mine, Adam arrived at my door first.

"Thank you—you're a lifesaver," I told him.

He examined my face, and then his eyes roamed down to my neck. He raised his arm to reach for my bandage, but I held his hand up in the air.

"I'm fine," I said.

"What happened?"

"I got bitten, but I'm fine."

"What? You were bitten by a manticore?" I wasn't sure if he was referring to Hunter's bite or Theodore's. I thought it safer to blame the latter.

"Yes, Hunter's uncle—"

"Mother f—"

"It wasn't Hunter's fault,"

"The hell it wasn't. What are you doing, Michaela? You could have been killed, and now you're going back to his apartment for more? Do you have a death wish?"

"No, I don't. I very much want to live, actually."

"Then stop tempting fate by spending time with him."

"I'm not having this conversation with you, Adam. I don't owe you any explanation."

He raked his fingers through his hair and grunted his frustration.

"I will bring you and your father up to speed with everything that happened, I promise. But not today."

"Is that all we get? A briefing?"

"I got the book back, didn't I? Mission accomplished. What else do you want from me?"

"Are you really that blind? I want to be with you, Michaela!"

My head snapped back and I stood there. I wasn't prepared for his declaration.

"I'm sorry, Adam, but I can't be with you when I still love him."

Adam stared at me, his eyes searching mine. He rubbed the back of his neck and then dropped his head. He stayed like that a few minutes until he reached forward and opened my door. "I'll see you in the lobby tomorrow morning," he said and turned to leave. His back muscles tensed as he strode away.

I considered calling out to him; I didn't want him to leave angry with me. But I didn't know what to say. So, I said nothing at all and watched him step inside his room without looking back.

I packed my things and headed back to Hunter's car. "Sorry, I got held up."

"No problem," he said and drove off.

***

I found my purse on Hunter's couch where I had left it. I put my cell phone inside. I didn't want any distractions during my last night here.

"I've already bathed, so I won't be long before we can leave," I called out before heading to the guest bedroom to change.

"Take your time," he told me, and then walked over. He reached me in three strides and kissed me gently on the mouth. His fingers caressed my hair, moved to my temple, and then down my cheek. He smoothed out a strand of hair that had escaped my braid and tucked it behind my ear.

"I don't know what I would have done if I'd lost you," he said.

"You don't need to worry about that," I assured him, and he nodded. "I just need thirty minutes to get ready."

"Michaela?" He stopped me before I could enter the room.

"Yes, Hunter?" I asked, turning my head to look at him over my shoulder.

"Lock your door," he said with a devilish smile.

I laughed recalling when he had first said that in my apartment. "Are you sure?" I teased, holding the door open.

"Yes...for now."

Once inside the locked room, I unravelled my braid and shook out my curls. I laid the gold dress on the bed and then sat near the window to apply my makeup.

Thirty minutes later, I opened the guest room door. Hunter stood with his back against the kitchen counter, talking on his cell phone.

He faltered on his last word and then held up his index finger. I raised my eyebrows at the command but decided I would have some fun with him instead. I slowly walked—*the* walk—up to him. I put one foot directly in front of the other and swayed my hips from side to side. It worked. I had his attention. His eyes followed my every step. His gaze glued to my body. He said something about amalgamations to the person on the other end of the call, but I ignored it. My interest was focused on *this* merger.

I placed the palm of my hand on his chest and pushed him toward the chair. He sat down and looked up. Then, growled an order into the phone. I ran my hand along the back of his suit jacket, brushing his collar and the back of his neck at the same time. Goosebumps rose on his skin wherever I touched him. I walked around until I stood in front of him, but I turned my body and faced away from him.

With his free right hand, he clutched my hip and squeezed hard, then massaged the spot. I stepped back and sat myself on his right leg, next to his free hand. He still held his phone with his left hand but moved his right one from my hip to the top of my thigh. His hand inched toward the hem of my dress, which had ridden to mid-thigh. He pushed his way underneath my dress but didn't stop there. His hand persisted around my panties until he cupped my sensitive flesh. My head fell back onto his shoulder from the pleasure of it.

"I've got to go, Leo," he growled. "I'll talk to you tomorrow."

He ended the call and threw his phone onto the table. He reached out and held my face while he ravaged my mouth. He explored my mouth with his tongue, and the feelings that arose made my head spin. I gripped his hair with both of my hands to steady myself and answered his kiss.

"Let's go to your room," I panted.

He brought his head down to my neck, hovering his lips over my bandage, "We can't, Michaela. But I can take care of you," he said.

He slipped his fingers inside me, and I gasped. I held on to his neck as his hand moved slowly and steadily across my flesh. I felt myself hovering on the brink. "Hunter," I whispered.

"Let go, Michaela," he said. "I've got you."

When the intensity climaxed, I let myself fall, knowing he was there to catch me. I fell until I could hardly take a breath. When I finally raised my head up from his shoulder, I held his face in my hands and searched his eyes.

"I want you to fall with me," I said.

He didn't respond; he just kissed my nose and gently raised me from his lap.

"Hunter," I began to argue.

"Let's not talk about it now. I have a whole night planned and it's already better than I imagined," he smiled. "Give me a minute and I'll join you out front."

I nodded and watched him go. I thought back to all the Shed stories Nicholas had told me, and all the chapters I'd read in the books. Even though a relationship between a Shed and a manticore had not been told before, if I could believe in these supernatural beings, then I had to believe anything was possible.

Fifteen

Michaela

We dined at Savor. The food was just as good as the first time I ate there, but it was much more romantic this time with Hunter next to me. He reached for my hand as we exited the restaurant.

"Are you up for a walk?" he asked me, but then glanced down at my shoes.

"Don't worry, these are my comfortable heels," I reassured him. "I can walk a red carpet and tear down banners in these heels. I've done it many times."

"Great, it's only a few blocks," he said.

"What is? Where are we going?"

"Central Park for a carriage ride. You mentioned the last time you were here that you wanted one."

I couldn't believe he'd remembered.

"That sounds wonderful," I said and snuggled into his arm. He tugged me against his body and we walked side by side the short distance to the park.

At the park entrance, there was a queue of carriages out front. We walked up to the first one, and Hunter held my hand as I climbed up the steps. The horse closest to us stamped his foot and let out a snort. The driver patted down his mane and hushed him soothingly. The horse calmed down. "He's never done that before," said the driver, turning back toward us. Hunter just smiled in return.

"I'm glad you brought a coat. It's gotten cold tonight," Hunter said when he sat down beside me.

"I don't leave home without a jacket or sweater. I hate being cold."

I wrapped my arms around his chest, and he brought his arm over my shoulder. The carriage rocked back and then we were off.

The sound of the horses' hooves clopping on the pavement, and the old brick bridge in the distance, had me believing we were in a different place and perhaps a different time.

"What are you thinking?" he asked me.

I laughed. "You don't want to know."

"Try me."

"Well, I was thinking how this feels like we've been transported back about two hundred years. It feels terribly romantic to be in an open carriage, in your arms, with the beauty of nature all around us."

"It is lovely," he said. "I travel to the park at least once a week. But I've never taken a carriage before. I don't think I ever would have if you hadn't mentioned it."

"That's the best part about loving someone. You open your mind to new perspectives."

"Yes, that's true."

"I, for example, will never lock a door again without thinking of you."

He chuckled.

"I never appreciated how tiny those locks were until I was in your apartment and contemplated breaking one to get to you."

"You're right. The lock wouldn't have stood a chance."

"No, it wouldn't have. But I'm very good at controlling myself when I'm around you, Michaela. I love you more than anything. That's why I think we can make this work. It may not be like most relationships, but we can be together. We can have a life together."

The onslaught of happiness that his words filled me with rocked me back farther into my seat. A tear escaped before I could control myself.

"You're crying," he said, bringing his hand to my cheek.

"It's been a long time since I've let someone in. I love you too, Hunter."

He pulled me closer into his embrace and squeezed until it felt as though he was hugging my heart from the inside. I squeezed back and hoped he felt it too.

We didn't speak for the rest of the ride. A smile sealed my lips and I didn't want to say or do anything but enjoy the moment.

When the carriage ride was over, Hunter walked us over to a bench.

"Are you warm enough to sit for a while?"

"Yes." I flipped up the collar of my jacket. I pulled out a blue silk scarf from my pocket and wrapped it around my neck.

We sat on a bench just outside the park. He held my hand, and we stared at the cars and people passing by.

Hunter interrupted the moment with his next words. "Michaela, there's something I want to say to you."

This sounded ominous, and I couldn't help the knot that formed at the bottom of my stomach.

"There's a lot about me you don't know," he continued.

I raised my head to interrupt him, to tell him I knew enough, when he said, "But there will be plenty of time to catch you up."

I smiled at that.

"I have not lived the life of a saint. As you know, I've done terrible things. I've killed manticores. I've hunted them and punished them. I've had dark thoughts, and I don't know if I could express them to you without darkening your light. But, in spite of all of this, or maybe because of it, I want to be better...for you, and for myself."

He sucked in a breath. "You have given me hope. I want to give you support and unconditional love beyond this night."

"I've been thinking about a long-distance relationship, too, and I want to make it work. I always have."

"That's not what I'm saying," he explained, and I frowned.

"Oh. Okay. Then I don't understand," I said.

"While you were getting ready tonight, I went into my safe and retrieved an item from my family's collection. I wasn't sure how I would give this to you because I hadn't really planned it." He pulled a box out of his pocket. "So much has happened today, but I know one thing—I don't want a long-distance relationship with you... I want a lifetime."

He dropped down onto one knee. "Will you marry me, Michaela? I don't want to spend a single day without you."

Tears rushed to my eyes, and my vision blurred. I blinked and they spilled over onto my cheeks. I swiped at them, but it was useless because more tears took their place.

"I don't know what to say." One hand covered my mouth, while the other pushed against my racing heart.

"Say yes." He chuckled.

"Yes! A hundred times, yes," I shouted and threw my arms around his neck.

I hadn't noticed the crowd until they applauded. I peeked around Hunter and saw a handful of people cheering us on. I laughed and bent forward into an awkward seated bow.

Hunter rose from the ground, picked me up, and swung me into his arms. I laughed again and held on tightly until he pulled me down slowly against his body. I caught his lips on the way down.

"Let's go home," I said, and he nodded in agreement.

We walked back to Savor to pick up Hunter's car. I wanted to call my friend Dev and my aunt Julie to tell them the good news.

When I checked my phone in the car, I noticed I had a missed call from Laura.

"Laura just called me," I said. "Did she know you would propose tonight? Is she calling to congratulate us?"

"I didn't tell anyone," he said.

"Mmm, let me just make sure it's nothing important." I dialed her number to call her back.

"Michaela?" she answered immediately.

"Hi, Laura. Is everything all right?"

"Are you with Hunter? I'd like to tell him at the same time."

"I am. Do you want me to put the call on speaker?"

"Yes, that would be great." I pressed the speaker button.

"Go ahead."

"The physician just came by here," she began.

"Did he find anything wrong with Michaela's blood?" Hunter asked. His voice had a serious edge now.

"He didn't find any damage to her cells," she said, and I sighed a breath of relief. Hunter did the same.

"But the thing is, he didn't find any trace of the venom either. In less than four hours, the venom had completely left your system. He said that would be impossible. There could be traces of venom for days in a human's body."

"Did you say anything to him, Laura, about Michaela?" Hunter's voice sounded panicked.

"Of course not, Hunter," she said. "As a physician he will not reveal anything about his patient. However, we both know that the kingdom is small and gossip abounds."

"They won't figure out what she is," Hunter said, his words a promise rather than a reassurance.

"No, but they'll know she's not completely human. They'll know there's something special about her."

"Well, she's not going to be here when they do."

"What do you mean?" asked Laura.

Hunter turned his head and muted my phone. "Do you want to tell her?"

"Go ahead," I said and smiled. He unmuted the phone.

"I just proposed to Michaela and she accepted. We're getting married and we will both be leaving New York."

"Married? Wow, congratulations. I'm happy for you both."

"Thank you," I said and grinned. I was a little surprised about Hunter leaving New York, we hadn't had a chance to talk about the logistics yet. But there was time for that.

"Well, I'll let you two go. I just wanted to give you the heads-up."

"Thanks, Laura. I'll talk to you tomorrow." I ended the call.

Hunter didn't say anything immediately after the call and neither did I. I didn't know about him, but I was contemplating the implications of what my blood results meant.

"Do you think it's possible that your uncle didn't inject venom into my body?" I asked him since that was my first thought.

He shook his head. "Even when I didn't want to bite your neck, venom was released through my teeth. It's instinct. He can't control it. I don't think he would have wanted to stop it anyway."

I shuddered at the memory. Then another thought entered my mind.

"What if I am immune to the venom? What if my blood counteracts it as soon as it enters my body?"

"But you fell unconscious after my uncle attacked you," he said.

"Yes. But I could have fainted from fear. God knows I was scared to death. It's not inconceivable to think that my consciousness and body would retreat and try to heal from such an attack."

Hunter stared ahead at the road but furrowed his brow.

"I don't think your venom can hurt me," I reiterated.

He turned his head and I saw the conflict in his amber eyes. A part of me also feared to hope, but I wanted to believe it could be true.

By the time we arrived at his apartment, Hunter still hadn't indicted if he thought my theory possible. I didn't pressure him. I'd give him time to process the information. My mind, however, was made up. I chose hope.

When we entered his apartment, he dropped his keys on the console table and took off his jacket. He grabbed mine and hung them both on the coat rack next to the door. He walked back to me. I searched those amber eyes and this time saw determination. He had made a decision.

He reached for my hand and led me to his room. He uttered no words, no explanation, no plea. He did not smile, but his brow wasn't furrowed either. After he closed his door, he walked toward me and unbuttoned his shirt. His chiseled muscles flexed when he slipped it off his shoulders.

"Are you ready, Michaela?" he asked me in a husky voice.

I could only nod in response.

With his hands on my shoulders, he turned me around and swept my long hair to the side. He tugged on the zipper of my gold-sequined dress, and the cool air on my skin made me shiver.

"I've wanted to do this from the moment you walked out of that changeroom," he said. "I've imagined it a million times in my mind since then."

His lips found my neck and he kissed the sensitive spot at my shoulder. He pushed the straps off my shoulders until the dress pooled at my feet. He raised my hand and helped me step out of the dress. Wearing only my black lace bra and panties, I turned to face him.

"You are gorgeous," he said as he stared at me.

His voice did not falter; he did not look away. I knew he spoke the truth.

"I loved you from the moment you kissed me at James's apartment," I told him. "Maybe I even loved you a little at Starbucks," I said with a laugh.

He smiled, too, perhaps recalling the awkwardness of our first meeting.

He gently grasped my face, his fingers burrowing in the back of my hair. He tilted my head up until I stood staring into his eyes. I saw the moment his emotions changed. When he turned from loving to lover.

He grabbed my hips and pulled me up onto his body. I wrapped my legs around his waist. He laid me down on his bed, and I tugged his chest down on top of me. I basked in the feel of his weight on me. I held on tighter, hugging him closer. He raised his head and lifted himself onto his elbows, then kissed me like I was the air he needed to breathe. Inhaling his familiar woodsy scent intoxicated me. The room spun.

I surrendered to him and forgot everything else. My thoughts centered on Hunter's lips trailing down my stomach, his hands pulling off my clothes, his breath tickling my thighs. Then I couldn't think at all.

He moved his body up and hovered on top of me, waiting. His brow furrowed.

I smiled and nodded.

He shut his eyes, briefly. When he opened them, I could feel him nudge inside me. I raised my hips to urge him farther, and he needed no more invitation. He pushed forward and the feeling of completeness made me gasp. He caught it with his lips and slowly rocked inside me in a timeless rhythm. I clawed at his back.

"Let go, Michaela," he whispered.

"I want you to fall with me," I pleaded with him.

He said nothing to my plea; instead he raised himself above me and quickened his pace. I held on tightly, until I couldn't hold on any longer. When he saw me let go, he let his body break free too. I grasped his shoulders as we fell together and landed in each other's arms.

Sixteen

Michaela

Hunter held my hand the entire car ride to the airport. I hadn't got much sleep last night, but I wasn't upset about it. I smiled and turned to read his expression. He kept his attention on the road, but I couldn't help but sense his thoughts were elsewhere.

"You're going to call me as soon as you land?" he asked me again.

"Yes," I said. "When are you planning to fly out?"

"I'm going to need a few days to organize myself and hand work off. Then I'll need time to pack up my apartment. I should be there by Friday," he said.

"Will you have my ring back by then?" I asked, rubbing the empty space on my ring finger.

"Yes, I should have it resized by then," he said, then grabbed my left hand and squeezed it.

He pulled over at the departures drop-off and came around to open my door. He held out his hand to help me out, and I took it. He gently tugged me into his embrace and kissed me softly. He kissed my top lip first and then sucked on my bottom. I forgot everything around me and focused on memorizing each movement of his lips. The memory would help get me through the next few days.

When he stepped back, and I caught my breath, he said, "Call me. Don't forget."

I huffed but secretly enjoyed his concern. He handed me my suitcase, and I gave him one last hug before I left.

"I'll call you, Hunter," I said. "I love you."

"I love you too," he said and leaned up against his car as he watched me go. I smiled over my shoulder and walked through the automated glass doors.

When I found the airline counter, Adam was already there waiting for me. I'd dreaded this conversation all morning. I had texted him earlier to let him know I wouldn't be meeting him in the hotel lobby but at the airport instead. He didn't respond, but my phone indicated he had read the message.

I walked up to him and prepared myself for the inevitable argument.

"Hi, Adam," I said and waited for him to berate me.

He looked up and stared at me. His eyes roamed over my face and body. I raised my eyebrow, anticipating his questions.

"Are you okay?" he asked.

"Yes," I said.

"Good," he responded, and then he walked away and got into line.

Huh, is that his only question?

I should have been happy, not disappointed. I wanted him to start an argument so I could tell him that Hunter was not a monster, that he was my fiancé. But since Adam said nothing else—hadn't brought up Hunter—it felt strange to blurt it out. So, I decided to wait for the right time.

We were seated next to each other on the plane. We had booked the seats before we'd left. I expected him to change them after last night, but maybe he hadn't been able to switch them at the last minute.

The plane wasn't full, so it was just Adam and me in our row. He knew I preferred the aisle seat, so he sat himself next to the window. But when he pulled down the window shade and then his baseball cap over his eyes—the universal sign for "I don't want to talk,"—then pretended to go to sleep, I suspected he'd sat himself there to get away from me. I sighed an annoyed breath and pulled out my laptop. I had a lot of work to catch up on anyway.

I planned out media strategies and caught up on product knowledge for an upcoming launch. I spent most of the time building a media plan for a skincare client and sneaking peeks at Adam. At one point, he put on his headphones, and that was the only response I got from him.

After we landed, we walked over to our arrival gate. I was about to tell Adam goodbye, when I heard someone call my name. I turned and saw Nicholas waving us down. He had a huge grin on his face. I groaned; I didn't need to disappoint another Giannis right now. Adam rolled his eyes. If possible, he looked less pleased to see his father than I did.

"It's so great to see you both," said Nicholas, patting his son's shoulder. Adam kept his vow of silence, even in his father's presence. "I heard you got it?"

"Yes, Nicholas, I got the book back," I assured him.

"Good, good. Let me drive you back to your home, where you can return it to its rightful place. I want to hear about how you were able to get it back from him. Did he try to win you back? Did you find out where their kingdom is? Did—"

"There's a lot I have to catch you up on," I said as we got into Nicholas's car. Adam sat in the back seat, so I took the front. After Nicholas got in, I took a deep breath and started at the beginning. I told him about seeing Hunter at the gala and getting my book back the next day.

"Well, that's fantastic. If you got it back so quickly, what took you so long to come home?" he asked. I told him about Jenkins and the process of taking him down.

"I tried the venom-neutralizing chant, but it didn't work. It only seemed to incite his anger and instincts more," I explained.

"That's okay, Michaela. It appears to be a very difficult chant. No one has had any success with it yet. But I know you will master it. I can feel you are special," Nicholas said.

I heard a snort from the back seat.

Nicholas pulled the car up to my building, but I didn't want to have this conversation again. I needed to get it off my chest now.

"There's more I need to tell you both," I said. "Would you like to come in?"

"Sure, of course. Adam, go get her suitcase," said Nicholas, pointing to his son and then hitching his thumb up toward the trunk.

Adam went without a word. He was still in his brooding-villain mood.

When we got inside, I prepared coffee as I knew we would need it. Once I had a steaming cup in front of each of us, I explained everything. "So, after I was attacked, the physician took a sample of my blood," I told them. "He said there was no trace of venom in there."

"Really?" asked Nicholas. "This is incredible. Everything I've read says there have been traces of venom in the blood for days. But of course, these cases were all human—none were from a Shed."

"I believe my blood counteracts the venom. I'm sure I am immune to its poison," I said.

Nicholas nodded and pinched his chin between his thumb and index finger. Adam looked at me for the first time in hours. His eyes had grown larger.

"So, their venom can't hurt you?" he asked.

"No, it can't," I assured him.

"And you're sure of this because of the blood sample?" he asked, emphasizing the last three words. I understood what he was asking me.

"No, not just the blood sample," I admitted. "I slept with Hunter." I looked up, avoiding their eyes for the next part. "We didn't use protection because I'm on the pill and I'm only telling you so you know that a Shed's blood is immune to bites and um, other things." I hastened to say.

Nicholas's eyebrows nearly touched his hairline. It would have been comical if Adam's flaring nostrils didn't make me cringe. I usually only mentioned my private encounters to Dev, but I knew the circumstances here were different.

"Oh, I see," said Nicholas, and he wrung his hands awkwardly. "And was it for research? Were you testing your theory?" he asked, his eyes hopeful.

"No, Nicholas, it was not for research. It was for all the other reasons two people make love. Normal reasons."

"Michaela, this seems risky," said Nicholas. "He can lose control and you could get hurt. I advise you to end this before something terrible happens."

Adam gripped the edge of my kitchen table, and I feared he would break it. Instead, he pushed his chair back, scraping the legs across the tiles, and stood up. He strode over to the window but didn't say anything. I turned back to Nicholas.

"I appreciate your concern. I really do. But you have no reason to be worried. Hunter won't hurt me... He loves me."

"What if he's only using you?" he asked me.

"To what end?"

"To wield you as a weapon?" said Nicholas. "To guarantee no manticore will ever try to take the throne."

"He is not like that," I said.

"And you know this because you've spent, what, six weeks with the guy?" Adam snarled. "You say he's good, but all I've seen is a monster. A monster that can break another monster's neck in less time than I can take a breath. Open your eyes, Michaela, and see what's right in front of you."

"You cannot judge someone's character solely on their actions," I said.

"That's exactly how I judge someone's character. I judge them not by what they tell me I want to hear but by what they do when things go bad. When the shit hits the fan, what are his instincts?" He glared at me, but I didn't respond. So he continued to push. "I can tell you what his instincts are—to kill. He is a killer, Michaela."

"He isn't the only one who has killed," I shot back. "I judge someone by his intentions, and Hunter's are good."

"But, Michaela," said Nicholas, trying to calm us both down with his placating tone. "Sheds and manticores are not meant to be together. They are natural enemies. It is nature's intention for it to be that way."

"Well, those are not my intentions. Some people believe that animals are intended to be on this earth to feed humans, but I don't see them that way."

"What are you talking about?" said Adam, annoyed with my argument. "We are not talking about having a pet. We are talking about letting a monster into your life—into your bed."

"That's it, isn't it? You're upset that I let him into my bed and not you."

At this, Nicholas's eyebrows shot up again.

Adam didn't notice because he only stared at me.

"That's not what this is about," he said. "I care about you, Michaela. I don't want to see you hurt by something that only cares about himself. He has no intention of being with you. He is the heir to the Manticore Kingdom for Chrissake. He has to marry another manticore and will toss you aside when he is done with you."

"That's not true," I said with conviction.

Adam shook his head and walked away.

"That's not true," I repeated. "Because he just asked me to marry him, and I said yes."

Adam stopped walking and stood frozen in place. He didn't move. "What did you say?" he asked quietly.

"I said he proposed," I told him. "We are getting married."

"Married?" he asked again. "You are going to marry Hunter?"

"Yes," I said, and I finally drew in a breath now that I'd got it all off my chest.

Adam turned around and reached me in two strides. I had to tilt my head back to look him in the eye.

"Is this what you want? Is this really what you want, Michaela?" he asked me, and I felt the emotions pulsating inside of him. His eyes burned like a fire had been lit behind them, and he clearly fought to hold back his next words. His lips pursed, but he waited for my response.

"Yes," I said with a smile, to show him it was exactly what I wanted, what I had always wanted.

"Fine," he spat, curling his hands into fists. He turned on his heels and marched toward the front of my apartment.

"Thank you, Adam. You're going to like him once you get to know him," I said, hoping beyond hope.

"I won't ever like him, but I will accept it. Don't ask anything more of me," he said and then walked out my front door.

I stared at my closed door but didn't chase him.

"I have to admit, I am surprised by this announcement," said Nicholas. "I know your mother said something about manticores not being all that we thought they were. But then, when she was killed by them, I thought they had only deceived her into believing that. I thought they had manipulated her into trusting them only to kill her."

"You're wrong. They are not all monsters. Hunter and Laura, they are good. So are many others too. You'll see," I said.

"What about your heritage? What about being a Shed?" he asked.

"That's all I've ever known, and my purpose in life revolves around training you."

"I will always be a Shed. Marrying Hunter will not change who I am. Simply because I have the ability to kill manticores doesn't mean I should. That makes me no better than the beasts you claim them to be."

Nicholas stood still, and his eyes grew somber.

"Our focus will change now. We will find a new path together," I assured him, rising to stand next to him. "I promise I won't abandon you, Nicholas."

Nicholas smiled and opened his arms to me. I stepped into his embrace. He held on tightly, and for the first time since I lost my father, I felt like a little girl again.

"Thank you for revealing who I am and helping me unravel what I can do. I never would have been able to read those books and know my history without you. I will forever be grateful for that."

"I am happy to know The Sheds will continue, albeit with a new focus," he said. "I won't lie, it will be nice to rest for a little while. I've been waiting for you my whole life. Now that I've found you and understand who you are, I feel like I've been set free."

I smiled and held both of his hands.

"I'll see you soon, Michaela," he said and walked toward the front door.

"Goodbye, Nicholas," I said and closed the door behind him. I shut my eyes and thought back to the very first time I heard Nicholas's voice over the phone in this very apartment. I was confused, lost, and uncertain. Now, I'm none of those things. As Nicholas said, in knowing the truth, I was free. Free from doubt, certain of my journey ahead.

Hunter

I was uncertain of my path ahead. I knew nothing else but how to be the heir to the Manticore Kingdom. My future was planned out for me the day I was born. I knew what lay ahead with each passing year. Today, that future was gone. In its place, a blank page, a future I could finally plan out for myself.

I went to my office after dropping Michaela off at the airport. Other than my private daytimer and a few files, there wasn't much for me to pack up. I'd asked Laura, Leo, and Thomas to meet me in the boardroom. They were already seated when I arrived.

Laura jumped up and gave me a hug when I entered.

"Congratulations, big brother!" she said with a squeal. "I knew you would follow your heart."

"You did?" I asked skeptically. "I recall you telling me to stay away from her at the TIFF afterparty because she's human."

"I didn't tell you to stay away from her," she said as she smacked my shoulder. "I simply wanted to make sure you knew what you were getting into."

"Yes, well I didn't," I said. "But I do now."

Laura's beaming smile told me she knew what I was about to say.

"I asked Michaela to marry me, and she accepted my proposal."

Leo and Thomas sat staring at me dumbfounded. I'd expected their reaction.

"Also, I will be leaving New York City by the end of the week," I added. "I have called a company meeting this afternoon to let everyone know. I will be working remotely from Toronto, and plan to attend at least bi-monthly meetings here in New York until all accounts are successfully transferred to a new manager." I paused and waited for any questions. They had none. So, I continued.

"Thomas, you will take care of the day-to-day business meetings I cannot be present for. You and I will have weekly briefings to discuss what will be said at these meetings. Does that work for you?"

Thomas's brow furrowed but he nodded, "Yes, Hunter, that's fine with me."

"As for the Manticore Kingdom, I have renounced my duties and claim to the throne."

"You've what?" shouted Leo. Apparently, walking away from Durand Enterprise was understandable but the kingdom was not.

"I asked Laura to take my place, but she has turned down the offer. We both decided, Leo, that you would make an excellent leader. Laura will suggest the king claim you as his heir."

At this, Leo fell back into his chair with a big huff. "I don't know what to say. I am honored you both think so highly of me," he said. "I admit, I was concerned you were having doubts about me again, Hunter."

"I was concerned when Jenkins insinuated that you and he were friends, but I understand that was just a ploy he used to turn our attention away from him."

Leo nodded noncommittally. "Have you spoken to your father about this?" he asked.

"I have not. My father and I... Well, we are no longer speaking. He was not happy when I chose Michaela over the kingdom."

"I can't imagine he would be happy about that," Leo responded.

"I will tell him," Laura said. "He needs to know that he has the support of both of his children in this decision."

"I'm not too sure he's going to be happy to hear it," said Leo. "Regardless of the messenger."

Seventeen

Michaela

"I think I've died and gone to heaven," Dev said when we walked into the bridal store. I couldn't tell Dev what had truly happened in New York City, but I did tell him that Hunter had proposed, and I'd said yes. After we both stopped crying, I asked Dev if he would be my man of honor; he agreed, and then we both started crying again. After he wiped his tears away, his exact words to me were, "You're going to need my help. You don't know the first thing about color coordination."

He was right, of course, but now that we were in the dress shop, I had my doubts.

"How hard can it be to color-coordinate white?" I asked him as we perused the aisles.

"White is not a color. It is a shade," he said. "And that's not the color we are coordinating. I think the wedding colors should be gold and purple. The color of your eyes and Hunter's."

"Don't you think that's a bit mushy?" I asked him.

"It's a wedding, Michaela! It's the only time when mushy is expected."

I shrugged my agreement and continued to sort through dresses.

"This one is beautiful," said Aunt Julie, pulling out a long gown with a princess cut.

I had asked her to join Dev and me for our outing. I wanted her to be a part of my special day. I was also trying to build a closer relationship with her. I realized that I needed to own my role in feeling alone for most of my life. My aunt Julie had always been there for me; I'd just never allowed myself to reach out to her. I thought it would be a betrayal to my mother, as though I was seeking someone else out to replace her. I understood now how wrong that was.

"That is beautiful, Aunt Julie," I said, and I touched the gauzy fabric. "I think I'll try it on."

Aunt Julie handed me the dress, and I walked it to the change room where Dev had already placed four other dresses.

As I tried on the first one Dev had selected, I heard him call out to me.

"Have you booked the church yet?"

"They are completely booked for the rest of the year," I called back. "Besides, Hunter isn't Catholic so we wouldn't be able to be married there unless he converts."

"Mmm, I guess I'll have to do it then."

"Do what?" I asked while the bridal store employee, who was in the changeroom with me, zipped me up.

"Be the officiant at your wedding," he said.

I walked out of the changeroom and didn't look in the mirror, I looked at Aunt Julie and Dev's reactions instead. They were both smiling.

"It's lovely, dear," said Aunt Julie.

"I like how it accentuates your curves," said Dev.

I walked toward the mirror and saw the sleek white dress cling to every inch of my body. It was pretty but it wasn't me. I shook my head and walked back into the changeroom.

Next, I tried on the princess-cut dress with the big tulle skirt, which Aunt Julie had picked out.

"Do you mean to tell me you have a license to marry us, Dev?" I asked him.

"Yes, I got it a couple of years ago when I was planning Dave and

Marc's wedding. I belong to a spiritual church, and I've kept my license active. It's good money as a side hustle."

"I didn't know this about you," I said as I walked out of the changeroom for a second time.

"Well, we all keep secrets, Michaela," he said with a wink. "It's what makes life interesting."

I smiled at his remark, and we both gave each other a smug grin. He knew I was keeping something from him, but he was fine with it. That's why I loved Dev. We knew each other so well.

"Oh, that's very pretty, Michaela," Aunt Julie said.

"Very princess-like," Dev replied, but I wasn't sure from his tone if that was a compliment.

When I walked over to the mirror, I did not recognize my reflection. The dress was stunning, but it overpowered me. I shook my head and the woman with the pin cushions frowned and sat back down again. I walked back to the changeroom.

I didn't even bother coming out of the changeroom with the third one.

"What about that one?" I said, reaching for a dress that hung on the rack near the changerooms. The lace caught my attention, along with the shimmery fabric underneath.

"We just got this one in. Would you like to try it?" asked the woman with the pin cushions. I could see the hope in her eyes.

"Yes, I would."

She handed the dress to her colleague in the changeroom, who helped me slip it on and smoothly zipped me up. When I turned around to face her, she beamed at me. I couldn't help but smile back.

When I stepped outside and assessed the looks on Dev's and Aunt Julie's faces, I was disappointed to see they were not smiling.

"You don't like it?" I asked, feeling disappointed. "Aunt Julie, you don't think it looks lovely?"

She shook her head and looked like she was about to cry.

"Dev?"

"This is the one," he said as he rose to his feet. He escorted me to the mirror. "Take a look for yourself."

In the mirror's reflection, I saw my best friend smiling back at me. Then, I saw myself for the first time in the dress. The sweetheart bodice fit snugly down to my waist but then the lace fell freely to the ground. When I twisted and turned my waist, light reflected off the shimmering fabric underneath, and I felt like a constellation of stars in the sky. I felt like a goddess. I smiled at my reflection.

I nodded and agreed with Dev. "You're right. This is the one," I told him.

Aunt Julie joined us at the mirror, her hands clasped together in front of her lips. Her mascara had run, and she wiped at another tear falling down her cheek.

"You look beautiful, Michaela," she said. "I wish..."

"I know," I said, because I couldn't bear it if she finished that sentence. "I wish that too."

"I brought something—in case you did find the dress today." She reached into her purse and pulled out a purple velvet pouch. She untied the drawstring and drew out a necklace.

"This belonged to your grandmother and then your mother," she said as she reached around my neck to secure the necklace on me. "I was saving it to give it to you on a special day. I think your wedding day is a good one."

I touched the stone in the middle of the necklace. "Is this an amethyst?" I asked.

"It is," she said with a smile.

"An amethyst stone is said to have special powers," Dev added.

His comment took me by surprise, but I was curious to know more. "How so?"

"It helps to purify negative energy and rein in one's focus. Among other things, of course. It will be perfect for a wedding day."

"Thank you, Aunt Julie," I said and continued to grasp the stone. I glanced back at my reflection in the mirror.

"That necklace definitely brings out your eyes," said Dev. "I'm sticking with my gold and violet theme."

"Is this the one?" the woman with the pin cushions asked, she kept her face blank, but she clutched her pin cushion.

"It is," I said.

She lifted onto her tiptoes and offered me an excited clap, smacking the pin cushion. She hurried to measure the hem before I could change my mind.

***

On the car ride back, I drove Dev home first.

"So, we are in agreement. Since Julie will be hosting the wedding in her backyard and I will be the officiant," said Dev, "we don't need to wait. I can have this all planned out in three weeks."

"Three weeks," I repeated, getting cold feet.

"Is something wrong?" asked Dev.

"No, I just have to make sure that works for the groom. He is, after all, getting married too," I said, relieved I'd bought myself some time.

"Okay, speak to Hunter and then let me know," Dev said as he shuffled out of the back seat, but then he turned to say, "You know, it's crazy that I haven't even met him yet."

"Crazy," I repeated.

"We'll remedy that this weekend," he told me. "I'll have you both over to my place for dinner."

He waved goodbye to us, and I pulled out onto the street and drove back to Aunt Julie's house—my family home.

"It's going to be strange introducing Hunter to my friends," I told Aunt Julie.

"Why's that?"

"Because it seems so normal, and there's been nothing normal about our relationship since we've met." I had told my aunt Julie the truth about Hunter and his family before I'd left for Italy. I was a mess and needed her comfort. Besides, since he hadn't been the one to tell her, he hadn't broken any rules.

"Well, you are both extraordinary beings. I don't expect your relationship to be anything less."

"That's the thing... I'm not sure I can do *normal* anymore," I said sincerely.

"You will figure this out, the both of you together."

I nodded and pictured spending my usual Friday nights with Dev watching old episodes of *Buffy the Vampire Slayer*, this time with Hunter there, and I couldn't help but cringe.

***

"You don't need to be nervous," I told Hunter. "He's going to love you."

"I'm not nervous," said Hunter, pulling a black sweater over his head. I caught a glimpse of his tight abs and wanted to run my hands over them again.

"He's really kind but he can be sarcastic," I continued, gawking at him as he moved his suitcase into my closet. "So, don't worry if you don't get his sense of humor at first."

"I'm not worried," said Hunter.

Hunter had arrived at my apartment while I was still at work. I'd told him to make himself at home. He'd taken a shower and brewed me a cup of coffee by the time I got in. But I couldn't drink it; I was too nervous about tonight.

"If he says..." I began, but Hunter reached me in two strides and stopped my next words by placing two fingers on my lips.

"Michaela, stop fretting," he said. "It's going to be fine."

"I'm not fretting," I said, annoyed by the remark. "I'm just trying to prepare you for tonight."

"I'm not a client who needs to be prepped for an interview," he reminded me.

I scrunched up my nose because it had sort of sounded like media training—slash 'Dev training'—a moment ago.

"You're right," I said. "It'll be fine."

But I worried the entire way over that they were going to hate each other.

Dev's place was just up the street from mine, so Hunter and I walked there. He held my hand, and I relaxed a little. The night air was getting colder. I already had my coat on, but Hunter had said he was fine with a light jacket.

I knocked on Dev's door, inhaled a big gulp of air, and fixed a smile on my face. Dev opened the door immediately, but he forgot to fix his smile. He had the same look on his face that he got when we are bargain-shopping together—determined, focused, and prepared to ask for an extra discount.

"Hunter, I presume?" he extended his hand and Hunter shook it.

"It's a pleasure to meet you, Dev."

"Charming. Won't you both come in. Can I get you a glass of wine?" he asked as Hunter and I walked into Dev's kitchen.

"We drink wine now on Friday nights?" I asked Dev, confused.

"We do," he snapped. "White or red, Hunter?"

"Red, if you have," said Hunter, unzipping his jacket. "Or a beer is fine, too, if you don't have a bottle opened."

Dev smiled but it didn't reach his eyes.

"Michaela, would you like some wine?"

"Um, sure."

Dev reached for a bottle opener as I took Hunter's jacket and hung it next to my coat. Hunter walked toward Dev and made himself comfortable on a stool at the counter.

Dev expertly removed the cork from the bottle in a matter of minutes, and I was genuinely impressed. "Didn't know you could do that," I said for the second time this week.

He smiled but continued to stare at Hunter with his "don't mess with me" shopping look.

"So, Hunter, Michaela tells me you work in property development. Are you successful?" Dev asked.

"Yes."

"How successful?"

"Enough that she wouldn't need to work if she no longer wishes to." Both Dev and I raised our eyebrows at this.

"When it comes to sex, do you ensure her pleasure as well as your own?"

"Dev!" I shouted, embarrassed he would bring money and sex up in the first three minutes of meeting Hunter.

"'Ladies first' has always been my motto," said Hunter, unfazed by the question.

"Are you threatened by a successful woman?"

"No."

"Are you threatened by an independent one?"

"No," he said without hesitation, not shying away from Dev's stare.

"Mmm..." continued Dev, and I thought he was satisfied with the answers and prayed that he was done.

"Are you finished?" I asked, annoyed.

"Almost," he said.

"Cat-person or dog-person?" Dev asked Hunter while pointing his finger at him.

"Cat."

"Team Edward or Jacob?"

"Jacob."

"Italian or Mexican?"

"Both."

"Swanson or Geller?"

"Definitely Gellar"

"Okay, I approve," said Dev and poured the wine.

I exhaled a deep breath and took a big gulp of wine from my glass. Dev and Hunter walked over to the couch and sat next to each other. I smiled, relieved that my best friend and my fiancé seemed to get along. This could work. We'd find a way to make this work.

"Are you coming, Michaela?" Hunter stretched out his arm behind the couch to grab my hand. I snuggled up next to him and couldn't think of a better way to spend the rest of my life.

Eighteen

Michaela

Hunter agreed to marry in three weeks. He'd said he would be fine marrying in three days, but I told him Dev needed time to mail out the invitations. We invited all of Hunter's family, but only Laura, Leo, and Thomas would be attending. I invited everyone at work, and they all accepted. I imagined they were curious to see if it was a shotgun wedding. I'd caught my coworker Emily staring at my midsection a few times.

The lead-up to the wedding had been considerably smooth. I kept telling Hunter I worried this meant the wedding day would be a disaster. But he told me it just meant we had a terrific wedding planner. I couldn't help but agree. Dev was a dream. He'd picked and mailed the invitations. After I'd chosen the flowers, he'd ordered them and the décor to be delivered to Aunt Julie's place. He'd even planned the rehearsal dinner for us, which was tonight. Hunter told me his family had just arrived in Toronto.

"Which hotel are they staying at?" I asked, while getting ready for dinner. I was in the bedroom, trying to decide which earrings I should wear.

"The Four Seasons," he said. "They checked in about an hour ago. Laura texted me that they're looking forward to tonight."

"Me too," I shouted back. But it was unnecessary as Hunter had just entered the bedroom. I had seen him dressed earlier, but I still caught my breath when I saw him walk in. He wore a dark blue suit with an amber tie.

"You look stunning," he said and walked over to stand behind me. I examined our reflection in the mirror. He put his hands on my bare shoulders and smoothed them down my arms. "That dress really makes your eyes stand out."

I'd decided to wear a short, white, fitted dress with a gold belt. He brushed my hair to the side and placed a kiss to my neck, right on my scar.

"I am eager to marry you, Michaela. I want to finally intertwine our lives, knowing we belong together and that no one and nothing can stop us."

I turned to face him and put my arms around his neck. "We did it, Hunter," I said. "We found our way. It wasn't some chant or prophecy in an old book, it was us. We decided it would be so and made it happen."

"To think of all the time we wasted, when I should have just believed that something that felt so right could not be wrong."

He pulled me closer and put his lips on mine. The kiss was soft and slow. I sighed into his lips and took my time enjoying the feel of his mouth pressed against mine.

"We should go," he whispered as he loosened his hold on me. "Everyone will be waiting."

I grabbed my purse and we headed to the restaurant.

***

Hunter was right, most people were already at the restaurant by the time we arrived.

"Where's Leo?" Hunter asked Laura soon after we greeted everyone.

"He will be joining us shortly—he must have gotten held up," Laura said with a grin. She was obviously holding something back.

"Held up? Doing what?" asked Hunter. Thomas mumbled something under his breath and Laura nudged him, but then they both started laughing. She was definitely hiding something. I would interrogate Hunter later, in case he figured it out.

"Were you able to get ahold of Nicholas or Adam?" I asked Dev after I managed to get him alone.

"They're both back in Italy. I don't think they'll make it to the wedding," he said gently, trying to break the news to me.

"I understand. Thanks for trying," I told him. "I love this restaurant you chose, by the way."

The restaurant was a mansion converted into a bistro. The owners had kept the walls as they were originally built, lending a cozy feel to the place. The restaurant was not open concept, but instead there were dining tables set up in various rooms of the house. Dev had chosen the parlor to host our dinner. The room was smaller but ensured privacy. The walls were papered in a white damask print, and the curtains were royal blue velour. A cream-colored carpet lined the floor, and the credenza was filled with plates and saucers that looked like they could belong to a dukedom, if not a kingdom.

As the waiters passed around hors d'oeuvres, Hunter grabbed my hand and whispered in my ear, "Come with me. We need to finish what we started in your apartment, otherwise I can't think when I see you in that dress."

"Are you serious?" I giggled.

"Yes," he deadpanned. I laughed again and pulled his hand to my waist. He steered me out into the hallway and walked us toward the alcove near the back.

"Hunter, we can't. This is a public place," I scolded him.

"I just want to kiss you, maybe touch you," he whispered. When we rounded the corner, he pulled me toward him, and our bodies collided with hard muscle instead of a wall. Shocked to find another couple there, I averted my eyes, mortified. I grabbed Hunter's hand to get the heck out of there as fast as we could, when he pulled his arm away.

"Leo?" Hunter asked. The man's back was still toward us. He now turned his head slightly, shielding the other person, and I saw that it was in fact Leo.

I caught a glimpse of red hair at the same time Hunter asked in disbelief, "Scarlet?" Then in anger, "What the hell is going on?"

Leo dropped his arms, and Scarlet straightened her blouse. She cleared her throat and said, "Hello, Michaela. Hi, Hunter," then extended her hand forward. "It's great to see you again."

Hunter stared at her hand, still in shock, but I moved forward and shook it.

"We weren't expecting you, Scarlet, but I am very happy to see you. How are you?" I asked.

"Fine, fine. Just a little humiliated," she said and grimaced.

I smiled at her. "Well, you shouldn't be. You were only caught because you were here first," I said.

Our banter hadn't softened Hunter's face. He did not smile, and his eyebrows were still drawn together, as though he couldn't believe what was right in front of him.

"Come with me," I said to Scarlet. "I will introduce you to the rest of the party." I led her to our private room. She looked back at Leo, but he nodded to her and then returned to his stare-down with Hunter.

"Are you sure we should leave them alone?" asked Scarlet.

"They'll be fine," I reassured her. "Hunter's in a good mood."

"If that's how he looks when he's in a good mood, I'd hate to see him when he's in a bad one."

"You already have," I reminded her, and felt her hand tremble in mine.

When I returned to the parlor with Scarlet, Thomas and Laura didn't look surprised. They must have been waiting for this little bomb to explode, and their smiles confirmed it. Hunter and Leo returned only a few minutes later, thankfully neither showing any bruises.

"Is everything all right?" I asked Hunter when he sat himself next to me at the dinner table.

"I don't know," he said.

"Well, what did you two talk about?" I asked, impatient that he was giving me so little.

"It wasn't really much of a discussion. I berated him for taking advantage of a woman who was hurt. He denied that, of course, and said it wasn't what it looked like. He said he knew what he was doing and would keep his distance."

"Well, that doesn't sound so bad," I said.

"Yes, except that's exactly what I said about you, and look where we are now."

"Oh," I said and snuck a peek at Leo and Scarlet. He gazed at her with the fierceness of a knight prepared to battle any dragon that came for his princess. She looked oblivious to the path before her. Yes, Hunter was right; it did look familiar.

"Can I have everyone's attention?" said Laura, standing up from the table with her champagne glass.

"When Hunter asked me to be his Best Woman, I naturally agreed," she said, giving Hunter a cheeky smile. He chuckled. "I have never seen my brother happier, nor have I ever met a woman worthier of his love. You have fought battles and overcome enormous obstacles to be here today. I can't tell you that the road ahead will be an easy one, but I do know that whatever comes your way, you will always have each other, and this family, to support and love you forever."

"Here, here," said Dev.

"Cheers," said Aunt Julie with a smile so bright she reminded me of my mother.

"To a lifetime together," I said to Hunter, and he kissed my mouth.

"And a thousand more," he whispered.

Nineteen

Michaela

I brushed the curtain away from my old bedroom window and watched Dev orchestrate the wedding preparations outside. Hunter had spent the night at my apartment, and I'd slept at Aunt Julie's instead. It felt like a dream to wake up in my childhood bedroom on my wedding day.

There was a large white tent covering half of the backyard with several wooden tables and chairs inside. The florist arranged the centerpieces on the black linen tablecloths: a white orchid in a square glass vase surrounded by tiny candles on a bed of green moss.

White roses and green vines covered the wooden gazebo my father had built when I was a little girl. Soon, Hunter and I would say our vows inside the gazebo. Dev and Aunt Julie were arranging white garden chairs in front of it for our guests. Everything was perfect.

"Michaela," Aunt Julie called from the doorway. "Are you ready to get dressed, dear?"

My aunt was already dressed, and she wore something new. A royal blue off the shoulder dress. She'd curled her hair and piled it up high; she reminded me of a Grecian goddess.

"You look wonderful," I told her.

"Thank you. So do you."

I'd done my own hair and makeup. I was pleased with the way they'd both turned out. So far, my wayward curls were behaving.

"I'm ready," I said. She reached for my dress, which hung from the armoire. She helped me slip into the gown without stepping on the hem and then pulled the dress up. She zipped up the back and then turned to pick up my veil. It matched the French lace of my dress but was much longer and trailed behind my gown. She secured the veil to the top of my head with a few pins, but I stopped her from covering my face. "I don't want anything between Hunter and me today, not even a piece of lace."

"I understand," she replied. "Your mother did the same."

"She did? I didn't know that."

"She broke a lot of traditions, much like her daughter."

I smiled. "I don't like being told what not to do."

"No, you don't let anyone limit what you can do," she said. "There's a difference."

Her fingers lingered on the lace trim framing my face.

"I'm proud of you, Michaela," she said. "I know your parents would be as well, if they were here."

My eyes watered, and I quickly fanned them with my hand.

"Don't cry. Dev will kill me if I ruin your makeup or this moment," said Aunt Julie.

"You're not ruining it," I assured her. "Thank you. For everything you've done for me, even though I haven't always appreciated it."

She hugged me tightly, and I held her closer than I'd ever allowed myself before. She released me, murmuring she didn't want to crush my lace.

"Let me get your shoes." She helped me slip on the three-inch heels.

"Are you sure about these?" she asked, looking terrified at the curve of my foot.

"Absolutely," I told her and smirked.

A knock at the door startled us both.

"I asked him to wait until I came downstairs," Aunt Julie muttered.

"Asked who?" I blurted out then panicked. "It's not Hunter, is it? He can't see me before the wedding." I suddenly became superstitious.

"It's not Hunter," said a male voice.

"Nicholas!" I shouted and ran to embrace him. "You came."

"Yes, we wouldn't miss your wedding," he said.

"We?" I asked.

"I wasn't going to let the old guy travel by himself," Adam said from the hallway. I grinned at him, and a smile tugged at his lips.

"I'm happy you came, both of you," I said.

Adam took a moment to respond, his eyes roaming over my dress. "I'm glad I came too. I will never forget how you look right now," he said.

"Thank you." I reached over and hugged him. "Are Veronica and Signora Tassone here too?" I raised myself onto my toes, looking over their shoulders.

"No, they really couldn't make it," said Adam. "Signora Tassone is afraid to fly, and Veronica did not want to leave her alone. She sent you a video message. Check your phone later."

"I will. I miss them."

"Hunter has just arrived," said Aunt Julie, gazing out the window. "The ceremony will begin soon."

"Nicholas," I said, coming to a spontaneous decision. "I had planned to walk down the aisle by myself, but I would love it if you walked with me. It would mean a lot to me to have your blessing for this next step in my life."

"It would be my honor," he answered, his hand to his heart.

We walked down the stairs and caught Dev in the hallway.

"There's my gorgeous bride," he said.

"Dev, I don't know how to thank you for everything you've done. It all looks perfect," I said.

"I know, it looks fantastic," he said without hesitation. "Everyone is here, and we are ready to begin whenever you are. Are you ready?"

"I am."

"Great, see you at the altar," he replied and leaned across Nicholas to give me a kiss on the cheek.

I spotted Hunter inside the gazebo. He tapped his fingers against his thigh. I thought he looked nervous. I smiled, because one look at him and my nerves were gone. I was ready to get married. I wrapped my fingers around Nicholas's arm and he led me toward the backyard. Dev signaled the violinist, and she began to play Canon in D. I waited for the first few notes and then stepped forward. The guests turned and watched Nicholas escort me down the aisle. My eyes didn't stray to look at their faces. I stared ahead at Hunter. His hands were now still by his sides and his face serene. He smiled at me, and I smiled back. My heart soared along with the sound of the violin. I held back my tears and focused on my smile because at this moment I was happy. I had never been happier in all my life. When we reached Hunter, Nicholas gave him a nod and then turned to me and squeezed both my hands. He kissed each of my cheeks before he released me and sat next to Adam. Hunter reached for my hand and we turned to face Dev.

"Dear friends," said Dev. "We are gathered here today to celebrate the love between Hunter Durand and Michaela Morrone in blessed matrimony. We are here to bear witness to their union and to support them as they begin their journey together. The bride and groom have prepared their vows."

Dev nodded to me to go first.

I forced myself to breathe steadily and recite the words I'd written down a week ago.

"Hunter, from the moment I met you, you've been my guiding

light whenever I was lost. You've helped me find myself and realize dreams I never allowed myself to dream before. With you, I feel I can conquer anything—nothing is insurmountable. I promise to love, cherish, and honor you through sickness and in health all the days of my life."

Dev beamed at me and then turned his attention to Hunter. Hunter did not take in a breath but squeezed both of my hands before he spoke.

"Michaela, my life began the day I met you. My world had no light until you shined upon it. If I helped you find yourself, then you helped me save myself. No matter what falls before us, no matter how dark the night or how heavy the burden, I will be there and help you carry it. I promise to love, cherish, and honor you all the days of my life."

A tear fell down my cheek and my heart nearly burst. Hunter rubbed his thumb across my face to wipe it away.

Dev cleared his throat before he continued, "With the power vested in me, I now pronounce you husband and wife. You may kiss the bride."

Hunter dropped his hand to my waist and in a sweeping motion brought me into his arms. He kissed me like I was the most cherished person in the world, and in that moment I believed that I was.

The guests applauded, and I felt Hunter's smile break on my lips. "We'll finish this later," he whispered, and I couldn't wait for him to keep that promise.

***

We greeted our guests after the ceremony, and I thanked my boss, Suzanne, for coming. Before she left, she whispered in my ear, "Looks like that vacation you took did you well, Michaela. I may have to take some time off, as well."

We both laughed just as my coworker Tricia came up to us.

"What's so funny?" she asked.

"Nothing," I said, because old habits die hard.

"It was a beautiful ceremony," she continued, making me feel a little guilty about my last comment.

"Thank you, Tricia," I said sincerely.

Adam and Nicholas gathered around to congratulate us, and I noticed Tricia eyeing Adam like he was the next big account acquisition.

"I'm Tricia Sullivan," she said to Adam and stuck out her hand.

Adam stared at it for a second and then said, "I'm not interested."

I was shocked. Tricia may be terribly competitive, but she didn't deserve rudeness from him.

"Adam," I admonished him, but Tricia stopped me. "It's all right, Michaela. I'm not interested either. I was just being polite."

"I can't believe Adam would say something like that," I told Hunter afterward.

"I can't blame the guy. I'd be miserable, too, if the roles were reversed. Cut him some slack, just for today. Then you can be mad at him. In fact, I believe that's a great idea."

"Oh stop," I laughed and swatted his shoulder.

By the time we sat down to dinner, I was starving. I'd chosen my favorite Italian restaurant to cater the food. I would always order the penne alla vodka when I was a kid, so naturally that was on the menu tonight, along with eggplant parmigiana and osso bucco.

I ate too much. I was relieved when Hunter stood up and asked me to dance. We opened the floor with Ben E. King's "Stand by Me." I was lost in the song and didn't catch my bearings until Shania Twain's "From this Moment On" came on, and several couples joined us on the dance floor. Thomas and Laura stood up along with Leo and Scarlet. Even Nicholas asked my aunt Julie to dance. Adam sat at the table, looking preoccupied with his drink.

"He's here," Dev whispered in my ear. I followed his gaze to see who he was referring to and spotted a tall, muscular man with glasses. I had never seen him before.

"Is that Mr. English Breakfast Tea?" I asked with a grin.

"It sure is," Dev said with a grin.

"Well, what are you waiting for?" I pushed his arm. "Go get him."

Dev squeezed my hand and walked across the dance floor to meet the man whose face beamed when he saw Dev's approach.

"How are you enjoying your wedding day, Mrs. Durand?" Hunter asked while we swayed to the music.

"It's perfect," I said. "I love how weddings bring people together. I don't want it to end."

"Well, it's not over yet. I've got a little surprise for you." He checked his watch and then said, "It's almost time."

He pointed up to the sky, and seconds later there was a loud hissing sound quickly followed by an explosion of violet.

"Fireworks," I said, and pressed my hands together.

"I didn't want to wait for a child of ours to be born. I wanted to light the sky up in violet tonight, in your honor."

"Thank you," I whispered. I put my head on his shoulder and he wrapped his arms around me as we watched the display of violet lights in the sky. Hunter held me tightly until he whisked me away to fulfill his earlier promise.

Twenty

Hunter

I would never tire of waking up next to Michaela. Her peacefulness calmed the restlessness in me. I dressed quickly and closed the door carefully when I left the apartment. Every day this week, I'd set my alarm to wake up before her. I picked up coffees and cream cheese bagels for us to share before we went our separate ways to work.

"I'll take a caramel macchiato decaf with almond milk, extra hot and extra caramel, and a double espresso to go," I said to the barista.

I wanted to book a European tour for our honeymoon, but Michaela preferred to wait until summer when she could take three weeks off work. She said she felt guilty about the time off she'd taken already. I was fine to wait. I'd seen Europe hundreds of times, but I looked forward to exploring it with Michaela now.

"Hunter," the barista called out.

"Thanks," I said and grabbed our order. On my way back to the apartment, I studied the homes in the neighborhood again. We'd started looking at houses in the area, but nothing had piqued our interest yet.

I knew Michaela was in the shower from the screeching of the old pipes. I was tempted to undress and join her. I unraveled my tie but hesitated when the water turned off. I wasn't going to let that stop me, however. I unbuttoned my shirt and walked into the bathroom.

She stepped out of the shower, soaking wet and naked. The scene had me considering all sorts of positions.

"Oh, no you don't," she said when she saw me unzipping my pants. "I cannot be late to work again this week. It's embarrassing coming up with lame excuses no one buys anyway."

"Then stop making excuses," I said and took off my shirt.

"Hunter, I mean it. I am determined to make it to work on time today."

"I am determined, as well." I grinned at her.

She laughed but still held her towel close to her body, "You are incorrigible, insatiable, and completely..."

"Yours," I said to complete her sentence.

When I saw her smile, I knew I had won. She relented and I took my time.

***

I was buttoning my shirt, after showering for the second time that morning, when I heard Michaela shout from the kitchen.

"Hunter, your phone's ringing! It rang the entire time you were in the shower. I think it's important."

I'd scheduled my first weekly call with Thomas for this morning. We'd been in touch by email and shared a few conference calls with investors, but we hadn't caught up privately yet. It wasn't easy working remotely—I felt disconnected. But I'd promised myself I would make this work for Michaela. I refused to have a long-distance marriage.

After I had dressed, I checked my phone. There were two missed calls from Thomas and three from Laura. A knot grew in the pit of my stomach.

"I've got to run," said Michaela. She snatched her purse and planted a kiss on my lips before heading out. "I'll call you later."

"Talk to you later," I said and smiled, hiding my concern from her. She left and I called Laura.

Michaela

An uneasiness stirred in my stomach as I drove to work. While Hunter had smiled when I left, he hadn't kissed me goodbye. He hadn't complained about work or his family, but I knew he missed both. I worried that living here wasn't working for him. We could move to New York, but I would miss Aunt Julie and Dev too much. I guess that's how Hunter felt about Laura and Thomas and even Leo, though he wouldn't admit it.

"Late again, Michaela," said Tricia, raising her eyebrows at me when I walked into our office.

"Yes, sorry. My alarm didn't go off..." She pursed her lips and placed her hand under her chin.

Hunter's right, I should stop making lame excuses.

"What can I say, we're newlyweds." I shrugged my shoulders and sat down at my computer. Before I settled into work, however, there was something else I wanted to say.

"Tricia, I want to apologize again for what Adam said to you at the wedding."

"Why?" she asked, shrugging her shoulders. "I don't have time for a guy that can't mind his manners. No, thank you. I'm glad he was upfront about not being interested because neither am I."

"You're right."

"Of course, I am. Besides, Dev's boyfriend has a bestie, and we're hanging out tonight."

"Oh, you and Dev are hanging out tonight? Friday night?" I asked.

"Yes, why?"

"Are you watching TV or something?" *Don't say Buffy.*

"Why would we do that? No, we're checking out the new bar that opened on Queen Street."

"Oh, that's good," I said, relieved and disappointed in myself for being jealous.

Later that morning, I came up with an excuse to speak to Dev.

"Hey, were you able to order those boxes for the lipsticks we're sending out next week?" I asked him, even though he'd told me yesterday he would order them today. So I wasn't surprised when he stopped working and looked at me like I'd lost my mind.

"Has loving Hunter already got your brain messed up?" he asked. "I said I would order them today. That was only yesterday." He resumed tying a red ribbon on a different set of press kits going out today.

"That's right, it slipped my mind," I said, and then casually, "So, season two episode six of *Buffy* tonight?"

"Tonight?" he asked me, surprised.

"Yeah, it's Friday night," I responded, picking up a piece of ribbon and twirling it between my fingers.

"Sorry, Michaela, but I made plans tonight. I didn't think you and Hunter wanted a third wheel only days after your wedding."

I frowned and my face flushed.

"Oh my God, you did still want to watch *Buffy* tonight, didn't you?" asked Dev. "Is everything all right between you and Hunter?"

"Yes, everything's fine. I just thought everything would stay the same, that's all. I don't want to lose my best friend because I got married."

"You are not going to lose me, Michaela, ever."

I smiled. "Thank you for being so considerate. I don't know why I'm being emotional. I think I'm just worried about Hunter being unhappy here. I get this feeling from him."

"It's only been a few days. Give him, and yourself, some time to adjust."

"You're right," I said but looked down at the desk.

Dev watched me closely. "Would you be willing to move to New York?" he asked.

"I don't know," I said.

"Why? What's holding you back?"

"Because I would miss you and Aunt Julie," I answered truthfully. "I know it's selfish of me when he's given up his own family to be with me."

"You can't stay somewhere to make others happy. If they truly love you, which Julie and I do, we will love you no matter where you live. Talk to Hunter."

I grinned because that's exactly what I would have said to him if the tables were turned. "Thanks Dev, I promise I'll talk to him tonight."

My phone buzzed in my hand. I turned it over and saw Hunter's number. "Give me a sec, Dev," I said, and he continued tying his press kits.

"Hunter? Hi..."

"Michaela, I'm sorry but I have to go."

"What?" I panicked.

"I have to go back to New York."

"Why?"

"Those calls were from Thomas and Laura. There's been a coup at the kingdom."

"A what?"

"My aunt Elenora has imprisoned my father and claimed the throne. I have to go now. I'll call you from the airport."

"Don't go without me. I'm leaving work now and coming straight home. Promise me you won't leave!" I shouted.

"I promise. But, Michaela, you've got to hurry."

"I will." Then I turned to Dev. "I have to go. Tell Suzanne, uh, tell her...oh, I don't know. Tell her I went to New York!"

"Is everything all right?" he asked.

"I don't know, Dev," I said, afraid of what this all meant.

"Be careful. I'll handle Suzanne. You take care of yourself."

I leaned forward, gave Dev a big hug, and raced out the door before Hunter could leave without me.

When I reached our apartment building, Hunter was standing outside. He held my suitcase beside him.

"I hope you don't mind that I packed a few things for you and didn't wait," he said as he lifted the red suitcase into the trunk of the car.

"Not at all," I said and sat down in the passenger seat. "What happened?" I asked when he pulled out onto the street.

"Thomas and Laura both called while I was in the shower. I tried Laura first, but she didn't answer. When I rang Thomas, he sounded out of breath. He said there were armed manticores stationed at the dungeons, the courtroom, and the mansion. He said he waited a day before calling me because he thought they could handle it on their own, but they haven't. Elenora's stronghold is impenetrable."

"Why is she doing this?"

"Because Elenora has been hungry for power since the day my father took the throne and not her. I wouldn't be surprised if she's been planning this coup for decades."

"Why now?" I asked, but the answer came to me as soon as the words left my mouth. Before Hunter could say it.

"Because I left," he whispered. "And gave her son a claim to the throne."

"Leo wouldn't be behind this," I said and shook my head.

"Thomas says he isn't, but it doesn't matter. That's not how it looks to the rest of the Manticore Kingdom. My father looks weak, having both his children renounce the throne while Elenora and her son are the loyal manticores. I might as well have handed her the throne myself."

"This is not your fault, Hunter," I said, but my voice lost conviction when guilt pierced its sharp nails on my heart.

Twenty-One

Hunter

The sun had set by the time we arrived in New York. Laura had picked us up from the airport, and we now sat in her apartment with Thomas.

"How many manticores does she have command of?" I asked Thomas.

"It's hard to tell, but there are at least fifty stationed at each site."

I nodded. "Where is Davis?"

"He's with Elenora," Laura said. "I don't know how involved he was in her plan to take over the throne, but he is definitely involved now. He has chosen his side."

"And Leo?" I asked.

"He will be joining us shortly," said Thomas.

A tremor of unease shot through me. "I hate to ask you this, but how sure are you that Leo is innocent in all of this?"

"He knew nothing," said Laura. "I was with him when it happened. We were eating breakfast with Father when Elenora and Davis walked in with an army of manticores behind them. He looked as shocked and betrayed as the rest of us. Perhaps even more."

My nostrils flared and my body shook, then the door to Laura's apartment opened. Leo walked in. His eyes stared into mine. Dark circles stained the skin underneath them and I knew he hadn't slept in days.

"So, the prodigal son returns," he snarled the words at me.

"Leo, don't start," warned Laura.

"Why not?" Leo asked. "He decides when he wants to be a part of the kingdom and when he wants to walk away?"

"I called him back here," said Laura. "We need his help."

"No, we need hers," Leo said and looked at Michaela. "She's the powerful weapon, isn't she?"

A growl rose in my chest instinctively, needing to protect Michaela from Leo's wrath.

"It's fine, Hunter," said Michaela. "And he's right. What can I do to help?"

"Stay out of it," I told her, afraid she'll get hurt.

"No," she replied, unsurprisingly. "I am a part of this family now, and I am willing to do whatever it takes to get your father back on the throne."

"Why would you do that for him when he didn't care about saving you?" I knew my words stung, but I couldn't stop them from firing out of my mouth.

"Because if that's what all of you in this room want, then that's who I'm doing this for," she said.

Laura squeezed Michaela's hand, and I knew I had lost this battle.

"Now, what do you need me to do?" Michaela repeated.

"Can you control the minds of Elenora's manticore army like you did those security guards at your trial?" asked Thomas.

"Yes, I can do that again," she assured him.

"That's not going to work," I warned them.

"Hunter, you have to let me be a part of this," she said, her eyes pleading and her hand waving me off.

"I realize that, regardless of how I feel about you fighting, you will anyway. I accept that," I explained. "However, Elenora is going to anticipate this move. She's seen what you can do and will be prepared for it."

"You're right," said Laura. "What do you suggest, then?"

I walked toward the window, organizing my thoughts as a plan formed in my mind.

"We need to come up with a strategy that does not involve Michaela," I said, "At least not at first."

"Why?" asked Leo.

"Because Elenora will try to take Michaela out before we can take control of her army. We keep Michaela hidden until it is too late for the manticore army to do anything about it."

"Fine, then what?" Leo put both hands on his hips. "Fight those manticores ourselves?"

"Yes," said Hunter. "With an army of our own. She will not expect that."

Everyone was quiet for a moment, but then Laura spoke first. "It is going to be a bloodbath," she said looking down.

"Yes," Hunter agreed. "But we didn't start this war, she did. Those lives will not be on my conscience."

Laura looked at her brother. "Yes, they will, Hunter. Don't deny it." Then she looked away. "We will learn to justify it, though."

"I will not stand back and watch her take something that does not belong to her. If we do, chaos will reign. Anyone who sits on that throne will always have to worry about when the next ambitious manticore will start an uprising. No, we must show them that this type of treason will not go unpunished."

Leo pushed away from the table and walked out onto the balcony. He knew what I meant. He knew what sort of punishment traitors received in our kingdom. I hoped he would find the strength to see this through; otherwise, he and I couldn't move forward.

"Who do we know that is loyal to the king?" I asked Laura and Thomas.

"My understanding is that most are. Those that are opposed have already joined Elenora's army," said Thomas.

"They support him, but will they die for him?" I asked.

"I don't know," said Thomas, shaking his head.

"Thomas and Laura, you both need to start recruiting today. We meet with those willing to fight with us tonight at midnight at this underground location." I wrote down the address of an abandoned warehouse I'd come across while hunting Jenkins. "Make sure it is still empty first. Michaela and I need to check on something in the meantime."

"What about me?" asked Leo, walking back inside.

"You need to find out what your mother's next move will be. Then meet us at midnight at this warehouse on the East Side."

"Consider it done," he said and left.

"Let's go," I said to Michaela, and she grabbed her coat.

"Where are we going?" she asked me when we were inside the elevator heading down to the parking garage.

"To my family home."

"Aren't you worried Elenora will be there?"

"I'm counting on it," I whispered and stared straight ahead.

When we reached my father's home, the front porch lights were on but many of the windows were dark. I wasn't certain if Elenora was inside, but I wasn't planning to use the front door anyway. I drove past the house and down a hill toward the creek.

"Didn't we just pass the house?" Michaela asked.

"Yes. But we are entering through a different door."

I parked my car on the shoulder of the road and walked down to the creek with Michaela beside me.

Belatedly, I glanced down at her shoes and was relieved to see she wore a pair of sneakers. This was going to get messy.

I walked up to the rusty grate that blocked the passageway and ripped it off.

"Is this the exit to the tunnel that John used?" Michaela asked.

"Yes," I responded. "I need to see if the door is still open on the inside. This will be our way into the house."

Michaela nodded and followed me into the dark tunnel. I had forgotten how dark it was inside there until Michaela turned on the flashlight from her phone.

"Oh God," she cried when she saw the rat carcasses, but she held on to the phone.

"Don't look down," I said. "Or up, for that matter," I muttered when I spotted the spiders crawling along the dirt ceiling.

When we stood at the entrance door, I heard voices. I held my finger to my mouth, and Michaela nodded in understanding. I pushed aside the cover of the peephole and saw Elenora seated at the desk. This was the reason I'd raced over after Leo had left. I hoped to catch him speaking to his mother, and it sounded like I'd made it just in time.

***

"Mother, I see you've made yourself comfortable here," Leo said when he walked into the room.

"I have," responded Elenora, sitting at the writing desk next to the window. She didn't look up from the book she was scrawling in.

"Funny, I expected you to take King Marsel's room," he said.

"It is Uncle Marsel now," she reminded him, and then closed the book. She stared at her son. "His old room reeks of John's death and the failed assassination attempt. It does not suit me. This one is fit for a queen."

"Yes, it is," Leo said, his eyes surveying the room.

"Why have you come, Leo?" asked Elenora.

Leo circled the room, picking up a photo sitting on the dresser. "This one belongs to you. I remember it from when I was a kid. It's a picture of you and your father."

"Yes, he meant a lot to me. We were very close."

"Is that why you are doing this?"

"By this, you mean assuming command?"

"I mean, usurping the throne."

She stood from the table and walked up to Leo, taking the photo in her own hands. “I followed my father wherever he went. By the time I was four or five years old, I would sneak into his study whenever he held meetings. I hid under his desk or behind the curtain and listened to manticores plead with him. I grew up wanting to read about policies, not princesses. When I got older, he appointed me to the King's Council. Everything I did was for the kingdom. I even married the King's General. We were the only ones privy to the king's decisions. He trusted me that much.” The wood frame creaked in Elenora's grip.

“I never cultivated, studied or did anything that was not related to the kingdom,” she continued. “I worked harder than anyone else, knew the old ways, and helped create the new ones. Yet, when the time came, Marsel was the one to take the throne. Not me. Marsel was not as prepared as I was, as experienced, or even cared as much as I did for the kingdom. He took it upon himself as a duty, whereas for me this kingdom was my life. I did not usurp the throne, Leo, I only reclaimed it. Took what deserved to be mine.”

“You claim to know the policies, and yet the most basic one that decries the eldest to become ruler, you choose to ignore?”

“Two minutes, Leo. That's all that separated me from the throne. Two minutes. I stayed quiet at first, allowing Marsel the opportunity to prove himself, but time and time again he only proved that he was more interested in humans than he was in manticores. Why should we continue to hide?”

“Marsel wants us to assimilate into society.”

“Assimilate by denying who we are, by pretending to be something we are not? I cannot live like that. Manticores should not have to live like that.”

“Then persuade the king otherwise. Don't just take what doesn't belong to you.”

“But it does belong to me!” she shouted. “It does not belong to someone who does not appreciate who we are and what we are capable of."

"What would you have us do? What is your plan?"

She narrowed her eyes and examined her son. Then, she walked back and sat at the desk again.

"What is it that you want, mother?" he repeated.

"Why have you come, Leo?" she asked him again and sighed this time. "Have you come to join me or to thwart me? Tell me now, so at least I know where you stand. You ask me of my plans, then tell me yours."

"How can I decide when I do not know where this will all lead?"

Leo walked up to her and stood over the desk. "What is your plan?"

Elenora's face was blank, but her hands twitched. She held on to the edge of the desk, her knuckles whitening. "To dominate," she whispered. "To lead not just manticores but all occupants of this earth."

"That is a bold endeavor. How will you accomplish that?"

"One city at a time."

"There have been others in the past who tried and failed."

"No manticore has ever tried it, but I will, and I will not fail," she said without hesitation. "Now tell me, son, where do your loyalties lie?"

Leo looked at the adjoining door and then to his mother. "My loyalty is with the king," he said, looking straight into her eyes.

"You will fight against your own mother?"

"You made it so when you imprisoned your brother, the king."

"Then you have made your choice," she said. She waved him off and picked up her pen again. "Leave now, before I decide to reunite you with your uncle."

Leo took one last look at her before quitting the room.

Twenty-Two

Hunter

"What time is it?" I asked Michaela while we waited in the dark abandoned warehouse.

"It's 11:32 p.m.," she said. "There's still time."

I paced the concrete floor and then walked over to the window. A thin, opaque plastic covered it and sealed off the wind howling outside.

"What if they don't come?" I asked, voicing my worst fear aloud for the first time.

"They will," said Michaela, looking down at her phone. "There's still time."

A new plan began to form in my mind—one that involved just myself, Laura, Leo, and Thomas. Two of us could sneak into the dungeons and release my father, while the other two pounced on Elenora and arrested her. I hadn't figured out what to do about the manticore army yet, but that would come. I had to think of another way.

"Laura and Thomas are coming," Michaela said, peeking through the front door. A few minutes later, they walked into the warehouse. Just like Michaela and I, they wore boots, dark clothing and were armed with assault rifles.

"You are alone?" I asked, disheartened to know I was right. "The others did not want to join us?"

"No," Laura said. "We are not alone." She pointed to the window where at least a dozen manticores marched toward the warehouse.

Relief like I had never felt before washed over me. "Thank God," I whispered, not wanting to show my earlier doubts.

When Laura opened the door to let the manticores in, I turned to Michaela and embraced her. "It's going to be all right," I assured her. "We've got at least a dozen manticores on our side. I can make this work with a dozen."

Michaela rubbed my back, and I released another breath of relief.

"That's good," she said. "What can you do with a hundred?"

I whipped my head around and saw more manticores filing into the warehouse. In a matter of minutes, they'd filled the entire room. Emotion rose in my chest and clogged my throat. I tried to swallow it down, not wanting to show it, but I was overwhelmed by the number of manticores willing to put their lives down for my father to reclaim the throne.

I leaped onto a steel table and addressed the crowd. "Manticores of the kingdom, welcome." I inhaled a deep breath and continued, "Your loyalty humbles me."

A few nods and murmurs came from the crowd. "I have asked you here tonight to defend your king and your kingdom. The throne was held by its true king, and no manticore can simply take it. The ascension to the throne has always been awarded to the first-born heir, and until our people decide they no longer wish it to be so, then we shall defend it. Tradition is our bond, our kingdom is our strength, and preserving its ruler is our duty. No manticore shall take it from us!" I shouted, and the king's army roared back its agreement.

"I know I left you," I began, and a few manticores looked down, uncomfortable with my admission. "But I have not abandoned you. I stand with you today, and I will lead this army and defend our king until my last breath. I swear it." A louder murmur came from the crowd.

I turned to Laura. "Have you told them the plan?"

"Yes, I have."

"What about weapons? We cannot lead an army defenseless. Where is Leo?"

"I'm here," Leo called from behind me. When I turned around, he opened the back door and motioned with his head for me to follow him. When we were outside, he walked over to a white van and opened the back door. Inside the van, there were hundreds of weapons: guns, rifles, grenades.

"So, your contact came through?" I asked. When Leo had found me after meeting with his mother, he assured me he could secure the weaponry.

"That politician from Texas owed me, and I called in my favor," he said

"I don't even want to know what you did to be owed something like this."

"It's better that you don't," he agreed.

"Then we are all set," I said and turned to Laura. "All right. You and Thomas take half the army and fight your way inside the kingdom to release the king." I passed her the grenades. "Leo, Michaela, and I will go to the mansion and take on Elenora and her army. The remaining soldiers will come with us. Once the king is free, meet us at the house. It will be easier to secure the king in a smaller location until we have everything under control."

Laura walked toward the center of the crowd, dividing it in two.

"All right, everyone to my left, come with me. The rest of you, follow Hunter. It is now 12:01 a.m. Synchronize your clocks. This all begins in one hour."

"The witching hour," Michaela said beside me.

"Yes," I replied without looking at her, afraid of what I would see in her eyes.

"It's true, then?"

"Yes. Our abilities tend to be strongest between midnight and four in the morning." I finally turned to look at her face and saw her staring ahead in thought.

"Are you afraid, Michaela?" I asked. "It's natural to be afraid, especially before battle."

"Yes, I'm afraid," she whispered. "I'm afraid of what I will see. Afraid of someone I love getting hurt. But mostly afraid that I will lose another piece of me tonight. A piece of my humanity."

"You don't have to come. You can stay here. I will not judge you for it. In fact, it would make me feel better."

She smiled and looked at me. "I'm sorry to disappoint you, Hunter, but I'm not going to let you fight this battle alone. I know who I am now. I have to embrace both sides of myself."

"Perhaps you don't have to lose a part of yourself to make room for another. Perhaps you simply add to who you are."

"I like that," she said and smiled. It quickly turned into a frown.

"What is it?"

"I have an idea. I'm not sure it will work, but I think it's worth a try." She climbed onto the steel table and surveyed the manticores around her. Her mouth moved, and Latin tumbled from her lips. "*Ut haec verba, et proteget te in nocte*," she repeated twice.

The manticores watched her but no one said a word. She nodded her head and leapt down from the table.

"What did you do?" I asked.

"That was a protection chant I learned from the books. It shields humans from supernatural influences. I figured it would be worth a try on manticores."

I opened my arms and she walked right into them. I held her

tightly, praying she would be unharmed in the chaos. "Promise me you will stay out of the fighting," I said.

"You know I cannot promise you that," she responded.

I knew, but I had to try. "Promise me that if things go badly and we are losing, you will leave and find safety."

"I promise to be safe," she said, and all I could do was hold her tighter and kiss the top of her head.

"I swear to protect you with my life," I whispered in her ear. "I am here for my kingdom, but I will never turn my back on you either."

"I know that," she said. "I will never doubt it again. But I also understand that you cannot turn your back on your people. This kingdom is a part of you, and I understand it needs to be a part of our future too."

"Thank you," I said, and my chest tightened with emotion again. "Let's go and fight for our future." I held her hand in mine as we walked out into the starless night.

Cars peeled out of the lot, and I drove around them to reach the front of the line. Before we arrived at my father's street, I turned into the tennis court park nearby and watched about ten cars follow me in. When everyone got out of their cars and I had their attention, I gave my final instructions. "The house is not too far from here. It is about a fifteen minute walk taking that pathway," I pointed to my right where a footpath led to some trees and then the road to my father's home. "Michaela, Leo and I will enter the house first. You wait quietly outside. When Leo and I are ready and in position, Michaela will wave this red flag from the top window on the southwest side of the house." I held up the flag. "This will be your signal to rush in."

I organized the manticores into groups of two and gave each group an entry point into the house. Some would enter through the front doors while others would have to crash through the windows. I knew where the guards were stationed; Michaela and I had observed most of them in our reconnaissance visit earlier.

"If we take control of these guards, we can secure the house. Be careful and always stick with a partner. Most of the guards are stationed alone, so you will have the advantage of numbers if you stick together. Am I clear?"

They all nodded.

"They've never fought together before," said Michaela. "How will they know how to fight?"

"It is in us to hunt and fight. We do not need to train for that. It is life without a fight that we need to learn."

I checked my watch. We were twenty minutes away from the hour Laura had set for us to begin. It was just enough time for our manticore army to walk over to the house and for Michaela, Leo, and I to enter through the passageway.

"Manticores, are you ready?" I asked them.

They nodded again, but I didn't need obedience right now. I needed confidence, strength, certainty that they would win.

"You were born for this. Do you hear me?" I shouted. Standing in the middle of the parking lot, I turned my head to look each of them in the eye. "You were born to protect and root out any predator looking to take your place. King Marsel is the true and lawful king. The others are going to set him free now and we will fight anyone who defends the traitors. We will ensure the usurper is punished! Now, manticores, I ask you again... Are. You. Ready?"

"Yes!" They roared, and I roared back. The growl reverberated through my chest and stretched my throat as it violently pushed through me. My instincts kicked in, and I felt my fangs lengthen and venom drip in my mouth. I hummed from its sweet taste. My heartbeat accelerated and I saw nothing but a path of destruction before me.

"Now!" I roared and pointed in the direction of the pathway.

They turned and ran like the hunters they were born to be. I raced in the opposite direction. Michaela and Leo followed closely behind me, their footsteps pounding the ground, as I led them toward the passageway.

Twenty-Three

Hunter

I did not impede my anger, instead I sharpened it. My bloodlust peaked and I felt its heat on my skin. The animal in me broke free, and my body wanted nothing more than to feel the flesh of another manticore between my teeth.

When we reached the inside entrance, I did not hear any voices or movement on the other side. The plan was for Michaela to wait in the tunnel for fifteen minutes while Leo and I searched for Elenora. I waited for Leo to walk up beside me. One look at his face and I knew his instincts had risen to the surface, as well. His eyes glowed with the need to attack.

I nodded once, signaling the countdown had begun. When I nodded a second time, his hand clenched his rifle. I held mine up in position and then nodded a third time. I allowed myself one breath before I pulled my leg up and kicked the door open. It broke off the hinges. Two guards abruptly stood up and reached for their weapons. Not wanting to use my weapon and alert the other guards, I rushed toward the one closest to me and rammed my shoulder into his stomach. I crashed down on top of him. A swift hit to the temple with the end of my rifle and he was out cold.

I stood up and saw Leo manage to take care of his guy, too, without firing a bullet. He grabbed the guards' weapons and threw them into the tunnel and out of reach. I caught a glimpse of Michaela, and she exhaled a breath of relief when she saw we were all right. I hoped to make fast work of the others before it was time for her to leave the tunnel and signal our army.

"This way," I said to Leo and stepped toward the dressing room that led to the king's chambers.

"My mother won't be in there," said Leo.

"I'm counting on that." I told him. "We need to secure it, otherwise they can come at us from behind."

We walked up to the dressing room door. I did not kick it down this time but instead slowly turned the handle. Leo rushed in first, gun at the ready. The room sat empty. I walked over to the door leading into the king's chamber and pressed my ear to it. I heard two guards talking and laughing. I pointed two fingers at Leo and nodded once before I kicked open the doors. The guards sat at a table, playing cards. When we stormed in, they shot up and overturned the table. The action delayed them from reaching their guns, which were left on the other side of the room. These guards were young and inexperienced and quickly rushed toward us unarmed.

"Don't kill them," I said to Leo. I grabbed one of the boys, wrapped my arms around his windpipe and squeezed until he passed out. Leo did the same, and they both fell to the ground next to their playing cards.

"Where do you think she is?" I asked Leo. "It's one in the morning."

"I don't know," he said, and lines creased his forehead. He was worried and so was I. We were sure Elenora would be at the mansion tonight.

We tiptoed down the carpeted hallway. The house was still. We did not hear the other guards, but I could smell their manticore scent. The house was full of them, I just couldn't see them yet. Leo and I had five minutes before Michaela and the others were set to join us. I considered heading back to the passageway and telling her to give us more time. We were not ready yet, we still hadn't found

Elenora. But I would only lose time, and I would not convince her to stay anyway. It had already taken a great deal of effort to convince her to give me just fifteen minutes.

Leo and I slowly climbed down the stairs, guns at the ready. When I reached the bottom step and turned toward the study, I saw them. Elenora and Davis stood in the hallway, arms crossed, with at least fifty armed manticores around them.

"Did you really think I would not prepare for something like this?" asked Elenora. "I've been prepared my entire life."

"How did you know we would come tonight?" I asked.

"I smelled your scent in the passageway earlier. Just like John, you don't know how to cover your tracks."

"Were you the one helping him?"

"I did not help him. He did my bidding. He was incompetent at it too."

"How long have you been planning to steal the throne?"

"It is mine. I cannot steal what belongs to me."

"We both know that is not true."

"Do we? The midwife who delivered Marsel and I is dead. Perhaps she was mistaken, and I was the one born first. There is no one alive to dispute it. My claim to the throne is legitimate."

"Enough. It's over, Elenora. Give yourself up now, and I will spare you your life," I told her and took a step closer, my weapon aimed at her heart.

She laughed with bold amusement. "How is it over for me, when you are the ones outnumbered?"

I shook my head. She'd anticipated my loyalty to the king, and even her son's, but she had not imagined others would support her brother as ruler over her. When the front door and all the windows on the first floor came crashing down around us, Elenora's wide eyes and open mouth confirmed my earlier suspicions. The loud crash deafened me for a moment. When the ringing in my ears stopped, all

I heard were the angry shouts of battle. Elenora stood before me, her face pale and her eyes growing with each manticore that rushed in. She had not anticipated the pride of the pack. But her shock quickly gave way to anger. I saw the moment she herself turned into a deadly predator. She crouched low and sneered at me.

One of Elenora's manticores caught me off guard and pulled me up off my feet from behind. He squeezed my chest until my ribs felt like they would crack. I drove my elbow into his stomach, releasing myself from his hold. I grabbed his head and smashed my knee under his chin, knocking him out and onto the ground. Another guard ran straight for me, and I crouched low and lifted him by his legs over my head. We were all armed—Elenora's manticores and ours—but our instinct cared not to pull a trigger, it urged us to kill with our bare hands. I'd never felt further from being human than in that moment. The bloodlust rushed through my veins, and I roared. I wanted to tear every manticore in front of me limb from limb.

Elenora used her guards as shields as they fought, but she kept her eyes trained on me. She pushed one of the largest guards toward me. He had a long black beard, kohled eyes, and fists the size of my head. I planted my feet on the floor and held my ground, but his full force as he charged was unstoppable. I landed hard on my back. The wind knocked out of me, I couldn't catch my breath. The guard didn't wait for me to regain my strength; instead he took advantage and landed a punch to my ribs and then a jab to my face. Tiny specks of light danced in front of my eyes, and I shook them off. When I could see clearly again, the guard's teeth were bared and coming straight for my neck. I raised my hand to stop him. Undeterred, he sank his teeth into my forearm.

"Fuck!" I shouted, anticipating the pain. But I didn't feel anything. No soreness, no tingling, nothing. Even a simple bite from a manticore should have hurt. The confusion must have shown on my face because my opponent's eyebrows creased and he looked down at my arm. I used the distraction to raise my hands above my head, fold them together, and bring them crashing down on his chest. The force of my hit unsteadied the guard, and I pushed him off me. I didn't hesitate; I plunged my teeth into his shoulder and he roared out in agony, writhing on the floor in pain.

Although it was difficult to be certain, I thought I heard a noise coming from upstairs. Then I smelled her sandalwood scent. *Michaela.* Whether Elenora smelled her too, or read my reaction, our eyes locked, and a smile spread across her maniacal face. *No! Don't touch her!*

Elenora raced toward the stairs and reached them before I did. She climbed to the top of the staircase and raced for my mother's room. When she reached the doorway and found the room empty, she curled her hands into fists and roared until the house shook.

"Where is she?" she yelled when she saw me approach.

An immense sense of relief washed over me when I recognized Michaela wasn't there. Then panic set in when I realized I didn't know where she was either. Elenora checked the passageway. When she found the tunnel empty, she rushed to open the door to the dressing room. I followed her, hoping to reach Michaela before she did. When she walked past the young guards on the floor and paid them no mind, I felt vindicated in our decision to attack tonight. She did not deserve to lead our people.

When we did not find Michaela in the king's chamber, we both ran out into the hallway toward the staircase. But before we could reach it, we stopped and stared at the scene before us—Elenora with jubilant glee and I with utter horror. Downstairs, the battle had come to an end. No one moved because Elenora's army had their rifles aimed at the hearts of our fighters.

"It's strange, my love," Davis said. "I always thought humans were cowards for using machinery to win their battles, but now I see the strategy has merit."

"You see, Hunter, it is over. For you," said Elenora gliding down the staircase.

"Shall we tie them up and bring them to justice?" asked Davis, enjoying his win.

Elenora reached the bottom floor and walked over to Leo, who had a gun aimed at his chest. Elenora stood in front of him and said, "I gave you the opportunity to choose the right side, but you turned your back on me, your mother."

"You are going to chastise me for my lack of familial bond? Besides, you ceased being my mother the moment you betrayed your king," said Leo.

"Well then, that will make my next move easier to defend," she said and walked back to the staircase and stood on the third step.

"Kill them," she ordered her army in a steady voice.

I panicked, but Davis stopped them before I could. "Wait. Certainly not our son, Elenora. Leo, move away."

"All of them," said Elenora. "Now!"

"No!" shouted Davis, but in a second it would be too late. I wouldn't make it in time, not to stop all of them, not to stop the blood bath Laura had warned this would be.

At least, I had to try to save one. I hopped over the staircase and came crashing to the ground next to Leo. I took him down with me and covered his body, waiting for the shooting to begin. But it never did. Instead, I heard the loud clanks of rifles hitting the marble floor and then the manticores' screams. I looked up and saw the soldiers standing in front of me wither to the ground, shouting in pain. I stood and watched in amazement as each member of Elenora's army bellowed in agony, their backs arching, their necks outstretched. I could see their desperate veins throbbing in their necks, while our fighters stood back and watched in horror. Elenora stood still, just as shocked as I was, but I didn't hesitate to grab her wrists and bind them behind her back while Leo did the same to his father, who was crying out in agony.

When they were both restrained, I looked around and that's when I saw her. She stood at the top of the stairs now and made her way down. Her violet eyes blazed, and her brown curls swirled around her head. Her red mouth moved but I couldn't hear her words. She made a fist with her right hand and then slammed it down at her side. All at once, the manticores stopped screaming and fell to the ground.

I walked over to the guard closest to me and put my finger to her throat. A steady and strong pulse beat against her vein.

"They'll sleep for the next twelve hours," Michaela said, and I could only nod in amazement.

"I held off for as long as I could, but when Elenora gave the order, I had to act before it was too late," she said.

I laughed, and it sounded a bit hysterical even to my ears. "Thank you," I said.

"What took you so long," Leo muttered behind me.

"Our soldiers weren't affected. We didn't feel anything," I said.

"No. I'm relieved the protection chant worked."

"Me too." I cringed. "Actually, I think it protected me from another manticore's bite, as well." Michaela raised her eyebrows at my wound. I imagined she was just as impressed with herself as I was.

"And Elenora? Why didn't she go down?" I asked.

"She was upstairs when I laid the groundwork for the elaborate chant. When she returned, I didn't include her, figuring the king would want her conscious when he arrived."

I stared at Elenora. Her breathing was ragged, and her wild eyes glared at us. Yes, I preferred her conscious so she could witness every moment of her downfall.

"What do we do now?" Michaela asked.

"Now we wait for Laura, and then take these two to stand before the king," I explained.

I reached for my wife and brought her body close to mine. I brushed her curls away from her face and saw that her eyes had returned to their usual glimmer.

"I was so scared," she said.

"You were scared?" I scoffed and pulled away to look at her. "First, I thought I would lose you, then I thought I would lose everyone."

"I didn't want to kill them." Her gaze moved down to the bodies around us. "I didn't want to have that on my conscience," she explained. "So, I made them believe they were experiencing the worst pain they could imagine. I made them feel as though every bone in their body was breaking at once."

"Ouch," Leo said, wincing at the same time as I did.

"Was that you?" asked one of our manticores. "You did that?"

I had forgotten about our fighters and that they would not know about Michaela's powers.

"Yes," she said.

"What are you?" one female fighter asked, stepping closer to Michaela.

My instinct hollered to protect her.

"I am a Shed," she said, and the fighter's brow creased.

"What is that?" she asked.

"I promise to explain everything soon," I said. "Just not right now. All you need to know is that Michaela is my wife."

"Your wife?" another manticore called from the back. "Is she the reason why you left?"

"No," I said. "My reasons are my own."

The manticores crowded around us, and I heard them asking questions. *What is a Shed? Can she hurt us? It looks like she can. Can she kill us?*

My eyes caught Elenora's, and I saw her smile while she stood awaiting her punishment.

We didn't have to wait long for Laura to meet us. I heard her car just a few minutes later.

Twenty-Four

Michaela

A crowd of manticores circled around us, and I grabbed Hunter's hand. He squeezed my fingers and led us toward the front entrance. The doors were open. I stood there next to Hunter as we watched his father emerge from Laura's car. The king's steps were measured, and he looked every inch a ruler despite having been locked in a cell for three days. When he reached us, he stopped and inhaled a deep breath.

"Hunter, I'm glad to see you," he said. His eyes moved in my direction, but he did not acknowledge me.

"Father," Hunter said and used his body to block the entryway. "Michaela is my wife now, and your daughter-in-law."

"I heard," he said. "Now step aside so I may confront my treasonous twin."

Hunter stayed put for a minute, staring at his father, but then he stepped back and allowed the king to proceed inside his home.

The crowd that had circled us earlier now dispersed to allow their king to pass.

There was a hum in the room, and I suspected it was the sound of barely controlled growls. I was unsure from whom the sound came.

"Elenora, what have you done?" he asked when he reached her. Despite having her hands restrained behind her back, Elenora stood proudly.

"What I should have done decades ago, Marsel," she spat.

The king shook his head. "I don't understand. Our father gave you a place on his council. I then supported you as a leading member of this family. Why wasn't that enough for you?"

"Those roles were just platitudes, crumbs thrown my way to stave off my hunger, but they did not work. I could not be satisfied watching you kneel at the feet of humanity and beg for a position in society when we should be the ones dominating it. No, that was never going to be enough for me, Marsel."

"If it were just me you betrayed, I could have forgiven you, but you betrayed the kingdom—pitted manticore against manticore." He looked around the room, as though only now seeing the bodies scattered on the floor.

"These dead soldiers are on you," he said.

"They are not dead, you fool," sneered Elenora.

The king turned to look at me, and I saw the question in his eyes. He wanted to know if this was my doing. I nodded once to confirm his suspicions.

"Well, you are fortunate no one has died today. Perhaps I will be lenient with you after all—"

"Oh, for the love of Hades, Marsel! Listen to yourself. You stand before a manticore that has dethroned you, locked you in a cell, and taken possession of your home and kingdom—and yet you talk of leniency! How could you? What sort of manticore are you?"

She spat on the ground and took one step forward. "I thought it would make a difference. I thought if she died, it would spur you to be the king you needed to be. I thought avenging her death would be the catalyst to finally making you the kind of leader we needed, but you continued to be weak. You gave me no choice but to take control of the kingdom myself!"

"What do you mean if she died? Who are you referring to?" he asked, clearly confused.

But I was shocked by the clarity of it all.

"My God, it was her," said Hunter beside me, and then to Elenora, "You were the reason my mother went to see Lucia."

Elenora's eyes fluttered toward Hunter. "Your mother's meek nature was a terrible influence on my brother," she said. "And Lucia was beginning to sway him toward assimilating their laws and neglecting ours. Lucia did not want to come to New York to protect her family, yet your father had no problem inviting a killer to our home. It could not be endured. By sending the queen to Lucia, I knew I could kill two birds with one stone."

Hunter let go of my hand and I saw a flash of his teeth as he reached his hand out for Elenora. I grabbed his waist and held on tightly.

"I'm going to kill you," he growled.

"Ah, I always had hope for you, Hunter," she said proudly.

"How did you get my mother to go?" he bit out. "What lie did you tell her, because I never understood why she got on that plane and told no one else about it."

"It was you. You were the key," said Elenora.

"Me?"

"Yes. You were away with James, and I used your absence to create the framework of my lie. I told your mother that Lucia had called looking for your father but spoke to me in his absence. I lied again when I said that Lucia was holding Hunter hostage in her home. I said that Lucia had discovered evidence of Hunter killing a human, and she would mete out her justice as she saw fit. She'd threatened to kill Hunter that night if the king did not come to Toronto to defend his son. None of this was true obviously, but that didn't matter. All that mattered was that your mother believed every word."

A grin spread across Elenora's face. "She was frantic. She asked me what to do. I insisted I'd tried to get ahold of Marsel, but he was not responding, and I had no idea when he would return. She begged me to call Lucia so that she could explain the situation, but I said that wouldn't work. The only option was for her to go to Toronto herself and plead for Hunter's life. I told her I would send Marsel after her as soon as I got ahold of him. Of course, I never did."

"You sent her to her death," Hunter snarled.

"She was a soldier who died for the cause."

"Don't you dare. You lied and used her. And then you used my father's grief to murder three innocent people on a plane."

"Lucia had to die. She had killed manticores, robbing us of our own justice. She could not continue to interfere in manticore business."

My hold on Hunter tightened as I clenched his shirt between my fists. I felt his arms circle around me. He turned me toward him. A sob escaped from my mouth, and he pulled my face into his chest. He held me there as another sob racked through my body. I shook and couldn't stop. The senselessness and selfishness of Elenora's manipulation buried me. So many innocent people had died because Elenora felt they were nuisances to her.

"You killed her," the king said softly behind me. "It was you all along."

"I did what I had to do," said Elenora.

"All these years, I tried to justify my actions by blaming Lucia when it was you—you were responsible for everything."

"I did it for the kingdom and its future."

"No, Elenora," said the king. "You did it for yourself. You have always only cared about yourself. You claim you wanted to do what was best for the kingdom, and yet you acted all alone, on your own advice, your own impulses. A ruler makes decisions based on what's best for the people. You've always done what's best for you."

"You're wrong. You hide behind the people because you do not have the courage to make the tough decisions. You want to kill me now, don't you? But you can't bring yourself to do it."

"I do want to kill you," the king said, and his voice shook. "I want to throttle you with my bare hands."

"Then do it, Marsel, if you dare," she said.

When the king did not move closer, I breathed a sigh of relief.

"You are just as weak as she was," Elenora sneered.

My eyes caught a flash of movement, and I felt a breeze when Marsel launched himself across the room toward Elenora. He circled his hands around her throat and squeezed. Elenora wore a smile on her face that looked grotesque as she gasped for breath. But the look on Marsel's face frightened me more. Tears fell from his eyes, and his body trembled. He didn't want to kill her, it was clear on his face, but he couldn't let her go unpunished.

"Stop him," I said to Hunter, but he ignored me.

I turned to Leo. His forehead creased and his eyes were glossy. He, too, looked as conflicted as Marsel.

"Do something," I shouted at Leo, and that seemed to move him into action.

But when Leo took a step forward, Marsel shouted, "Stay back!"

Leo froze at this command. But I was not affected.

"King Marsel, don't do this," I pleaded. "You will regret it."

But my words had no effect. I could see Elenora's body slacken, and she no longer struggled against the king's grip.

"Michaela, can you do something?" Leo begged me.

"What can I do?" I said, frantic now. I could probably force the king's mind to let her go, but that would not stop him from trying again. Then he would be furious with me. As much as I hated Elenora, I knew the king would never reconcile murdering her, and Leo would never forgive it. "Wait!" I shouted and the king turned to stare at me. I knew he had loosened his grip when Elenora coughed but he didn't let go.

I recalled the neutralizing chant, but I was afraid of what had happened with Jenkins the last time I tried it. I grabbed onto the amethyst necklace that had belonged to my mother, and I focused on cleaning the energy in the room. Then I narrowed my focus on Elenora. I tried the first few words of the chant, but they still fell awkwardly from my lips.

Then I tried chanting them in English: *Poison behold! Listen to my voice. You are no longer needed, no longer wanted, no longer necessary. I claim thine fire and water thee down. Make thee as timid as a brook. I take this death and bring you a new life.*

The words spilled out without hesitation. I said them again, louder this time. A breeze rushed through my hair, and I felt the now familiar zing of energy flow through me. I opened my eyes and saw Elenora's body violently shaking. The king let her go and took a step back. Elenora put her own hands at her throat and tore at her skin as though she needed to rip it off. Her body convulsed and she dropped onto her knees to the floor. She retched but nothing came out. Her arms wrapped around her middle as though she was in excruciating pain. While kneeling, she continued to retch, but nothing but tortured sounds rushed out.

"What's happening?" asked the king. Hunter turned to me for an answer.

"I believe she is losing her venom. I said a chant to neutralize it, but it's never been successful before so I'm not sure what is happening exactly."

After a few minutes, Elenora's body stilled, and she collapsed onto the floor. Leo knelt next to her and checked her pulse. "She's still alive."

"Arrest her and Davis," said the king. Leo picked up his mother—one arm under her neck and the other under her knees—and carried her outside. Hunter walked up to his uncle and shook him but he didn't awaken. I placed my hand on Davis's forehead and reversed the chant. His eyes fluttered open. Groggy but able to walk, Davis surrendered without a word.

I turned to see the other manticores in the king's army stare at me, probably unsure what to make of me. I didn't know what to say to reassure them, so I said nothing.

"We need to talk," King Marsel said to me. "Meet me in the courtroom chamber. I will be there after I get Elenora and Davis settled in their new cell."

He walked out of the house with Leo trailing behind him.

"Laura, can you take Davis?" Hunter asked as he pushed his uncle toward the door.

"No problem," she responded, and then to me said, "Thank you."

I nodded once, unsure if what I had done would save or hurt my chances of being accepted by Hunter's people. They'd witnessed a lot tonight, and even I couldn't say what exactly had happened.

Twenty-Five

Michaela

Hunter held my hand while he drove us toward Central Park and the hidden kingdom.

"You were incredible back there," he said. "When I saw you on the staircase, you looked like an avenging goddess. A light blazed from within your eyes and glowed from your skin. Then, when you focused and nailed that neutralizing chant, it was nothing anyone on this earth had seen before."

"What will this mean for us? Will your people be afraid of me?" I asked.

"Perhaps at first, but then they will get to know you, and they will fall in love with you just as I have," he assured me.

"I hope you're right. Right now, I feel nothing but wariness and fear from them," I said.

Hunter parked in the underground lot, and we stepped inside the elevator. He reached for my hand again, and I squeezed a little tighter.

When the elevator landed on the bottom floor, Hunter led me down a familiar hallway, and I shuddered at the memory of being in the dungeons not too long ago. When we entered the cold hallway, I saw Leo sitting on the floor outside of the cells. His back leaned against the stone wall. He stared at his parents. My heart broke from the pained look on his face. His eyes were bloodshot red.

"How is she?" I asked.

"She looks to be resting," he said, not taking his eyes off his mother.

Davis cradled his wife in his arms. "I was unaware of her role in the queen's death," he said. "Tonight, I didn't know she intended to murder those manticores. I've been to war. I know soldiers die in battle, but we do not kill them when they are defenseless."

"You will have to explain yourself to the king and beg for his mercy," Leo said, his head resting back against the bars. His eyes closed. "And hope that he believes you."

"Can you forgive me?" Davis asked his son.

"I don't know." Leo sighed and dropped his head to his knees.

"She is moving," Hunter said beside me just as I saw Elenora open her eyes.

Her eyelids fluttered until she focused on the cement ceiling above her.

"Davis? What happened?" she whispered, her voice sounding hoarse.

"Elenora, how do you feel?" Davis asked, checking her neck.

She swallowed and winced. "My throat and stomach hurt," she said and raised her fingers to her neck. She had scratches there from her own nails, and bruises from the king's hands. "Marsel," she whispered. "He tried to kill me but then I blacked out. I don't remember anything else."

"Do you remember me?" I asked and stepped forward. Elenora turned her head toward me and narrowed her eyes. That's when I noticed them.

"Your eyes," I said, surprised.

Davis placed his hand on Elenora's cheek and turned her head to face him. He peered into her eyes, and his mouth opened. His own eyes grew bigger.

"What is it, Davis?" she asked when she saw the horrified look on his face. For the first time, I heard fear in her voice.

"They are blue," Davis said steadily and tried to smile. "A beautiful blue."

"Blue? But that can't be. Mine have always been amber." And then to me she sneered, "What have you done?"

She pushed Davis away but didn't seem to have the strength to support herself yet. She fell to the ground on her hands and knees. She panted there for a breath or two and then pushed up to stand on shaky legs. Elenora kept one hand on the stone wall for balance.

"I am going to kill you," she said, and she bared her teeth. But the motion looked strange. She looked like a child pretending to be a lion and not quite convincing me of her ferociousness. She sucked in a deep breath and let out a piercing scream. Her face contorted in anger, but her eyes remained the same shade of blue. She pressed her fingers to her mouth, rubbing against her front teeth.

"What is this?" she said, and then stretched her hands in front of her face inspecting her short nails. They had not transformed despite her fury.

"You did this to me?" she shouted.

"Yes," I said calmly, despite my growing unease. "I neutralized your venom. It appears by doing so, I've taken away your ability to trigger your instincts, as well. The venom must have controlled your response. Now that the venom is gone, so are your instincts."

She shook her head and grabbed her ears, as though she could not stand to listen to another word I had to say. She released an angry sob and fell to her knees on the ground. Her body shook violently.

"I am nothing without my venom, without my instincts, nothing. I wish you would have let Marsel kill me," she cried.

"You are not nothing, Mother," Leo said, raising himself up. "You are human."

Hunter steered me away from Elenora's sobs, which had now

grown louder. Becoming human to her must be a fate worse than death.

He led me up the stairs and toward the courtroom. But instead of going to the large doors that I'd entered the last time I was on trial, Hunter opened a smaller door right beside the courtroom. Inside, the king sat at a desk looking up at a portrait of his late wife.

"You may leave us, Hunter," the king ordered without looking at us.

"I'm not sure that's a good idea," Hunter said, putting his hand at the small of my back.

"I will not harm her, I assure you. I just want to talk," he replied, finally turning his head to look at his son.

Hunter turned to me. "Do you feel comfortable with me leaving? I will stay if you want me to."

"Maybe wait outside the door, just in case," I said with a smile, but really only half joking. He smiled and leaned over to kiss my cheek. He stepped outside, leaving the door slightly ajar.

"I could insist that he shut it, but he probably could still hear us even if I did," said the king. "Please, sit down." He motioned to a chair in front of the desk. I took a seat on the leather-upholstered chair and waited for his next words.

"When I look into my son's eyes, I see my own reflected back at me," he said.

"Yes, your eyes are very similar," I said, trying to keep the conversation light.

"I'm not referring to their color but their intensity. I see how much he loves you, and in his eyes, I see the love I felt for my wife reflected back at me. I didn't want to see it when I still blamed your mother for taking her from me." He glanced at my face and shook his head. "You look so much like her. I could not stand to even look at you."

I winced at his words, knowing that my mere presence caused him such disgust.

"But I learned a lot today. I now know why my wife left without telling me, and why she pursued Lucia. I understand she did it because she thought she was doing the right thing to save her son. But I also learned something else today. I was not the only one who lost someone they loved because of that fateful day. Drowning in self-pity, I didn't think about how my vengeance would hurt Lucia's daughter. My grief shielded me from facing the truth of what I did. Elenora may have orchestrated the events, but I played my part, for which I am truly sorry. My decision not only ended three lives but hurt those left behind to grieve them. I—more than anyone else—should know how much that hurts. But I wasn't thinking. I was only suffering, and I let my misery guide me to make one of the worst decisions of my life. I regretted the order almost immediately. The subconscious shame I felt at having made that murderous decision fueled me to seek rehabilitation and leniency instead of execution. I never wanted to feel responsible for taking a life again. I could not carry it on my conscience. The burden was too heavy already."

I felt the king's pain in his voice, and it ripped in my heart. I knew what grief could do to a person. A tear fell down my cheek, and I wiped it away. I did not want to cry or feel sympathy for him. I wanted to be angry with him.

"You didn't have to kill them. You could have listened to her. You could have believed her," I said, frustrated that only now he saw the pain his actions caused.

"I know. I could now imagine that conversation in my head. I imagine picking up the phone, speaking to Lucia and listening to what she had to say. At the time, I couldn't imagine any words that would explain what she had done."

"But that's the thing, you didn't have to imagine it. You should have just listened to her," I cried.

"I am so sorry, Michaela," he said, and I caught him wiping his own eyes. "I cannot take back what I did, and I am ashamed of my actions. I am reminded of them every time I look at you, but I can only beg you for forgiveness."

The tears fell uncontrollably now. I didn't bother to wipe them away. I could barely see through my watery eyes. I closed them tightly to regain control and forced a breath through my constricted chest. I held on to my amethyst necklace and pictured my mother and father.

"As much as I want to, hating you will not bring them back," I said. "Blaming you does not make me feel better either. I've learned that nothing takes the pain away. I've just gotten better at living with it. But I will forgive you, because if you feel half the pain that I do having lost a loved one, I know you have been punished enough. I forgive you because I want to have a life with your son. I forgive you because I want to finally let go of this pain and just remember my parents' life without focusing on their death."

I made no effort to stop crying. It was noisy and messy, and I didn't care because it was real. I had held sadness and regret in my heart for so long. I suspected there was more to their death, but I didn't want to look into it. Now that I knew everything, I could finally grieve them properly.

I hadn't heard Hunter come in. He strode across the room, picked me up off the chair, and held me tightly in his arms. He didn't let go until I stopped crying and wiped away my tears.

"She is done paying the price for another's sin, and frankly so are you," said Hunter to his father.

The king nodded once and walked over to us. He extended his hand and Hunter shook it. He turned to me with the same gesture. I studied his steady hand and then pressed my palm to it. He placed his other hand over mine for a moment and then released it with a smile.

"Are you all right?" the king asked me.

"Yes," I said and smiled weakly. "Are you?"

"I will be."

"We need to discuss what we're going to do about Elenora," I said. "And what we will tell the kingdom about me." As much as I wanted to curl back into Hunter's arms, we had to figure this out immediately.

"What are your thoughts? The both of you," said the king.

Hunter frowned and tilted his head. "Well, Michaela's chant neutralized Elenora's venom and she no longer has her instincts to summon her fangs or claws. She has rendered her powerless against us," said Hunter.

The king raised his eyebrows at me, and I thought he looked proud.

"I'm impressed. I never knew this was even possible," he said. "Knowing Elenora, I don't think we could have given her a worse punishment. She will be banned from the kingdom and sent to live on her own. I do not want to see her ever again."

Hunter nodded at this. "What about Michaela?"

The king turned to me. "What would you have us reveal about you?"

"The truth," I said. "Your people do not deserve lies and if I am ever to live among them and gain their trust, they must know the truth about me."

"Fine. You will tell them yourself on Saturday when they are all gathered together," said the king.

"What's happening on Saturday?" asked Hunter before I could.

"Your wedding reception, of course," said the king, with a wide smile this time.

Hunter returned his smile and shook his father's hand. "Thank you," he said.

I panicked, picturing hundreds of angry manticores staring at me.

Twenty-Six

Michaela

The next morning, I woke up to breakfast in bed.

"I was worried this was only a Toronto thing." I grinned.

"No, it's a Hunter thing." He smirked and prowled up onto the bed. I giggled but let him kiss my neck.

"So, what's the plan for today?" I asked.

"I was hoping we could visit someone special to me." He sat next to me and took a bite of my toast.

"Sure, why not?" I scooped up my mug of coffee before he could grab it. "I'll be in a room filled with manticores on Saturday. Why not start making friends now?"

I took my time, enjoying breakfast while Hunter put on a suit jacket, getting himself ready to leave for the kingdom. I wasn't too keen on heading back there again today, but Hunter dressed quickly and kept glancing at his watch, so I reluctantly dragged myself out of bed.

Hunter drove and we arrived at Central Park in no time. We took the elevator down and greeted the two security guards stationed at the doors. Hunter led me past what looked to be a library. There were several walls and rows of books and tables where manticores worked on their laptops. We turned to our left after the library and walked through a corridor that expanded into a larger foyer. The walls here were paneled in dark wood and the floors laid in a herringbone design. The floors were a lighter shade of oak than the walls. It reminded me of boarding schools I'd seen on television.

Several of the rooms we passed were filled with students—some looked to be as young as thirteen and others in their twenties. A group of students walked toward us. They noticed Hunter first and then stared at me. I imagined they could tell I wasn't a manticore, probably wondering what a human was doing down there. That got me thinking.

I stopped Hunter before he knocked on a door.

"Could you tell I wasn't a manticore when we first met?" I asked him.

"Yes," he said, looking confused.

Perhaps this wasn't the right time, but I continued. "Could you tell there was something not fully human about me?" I asked.

"No," he said. "You had a unique scent, and I was drawn to it, but I think that was just my attraction to you. No one else has mentioned anything to me."

"Huh, so these students and the manticores on Saturday will only know that I'm not a manticore?" I asked, to be certain.

"Yes," he assured me.

"Okay, go ahead and knock. I just wanted to clear that up."

He smiled and knocked lightly on the door.

"Come in," said a male voice on the other side.

Hunter opened the door. An attractive man, with brown and gold eyes and black hair, sat behind a desk. He wore glasses and a grey sports jacket. The kind with patches on the elbows. He looked exactly as I would imagine a boarding-school professor looking like.

"Professor Wallace," said Hunter, smiling. "I'd like to introduce you to my wife, Michaela."

A grin spread over the professor's face, and he extended his hand forward.

"Pleased to meet you, Michaela," he said.

"You, as well," I said and shook his hand.

"I had heard a rumor about your marriage. I am happy to see it's true." Professor Wallace's warm gaze met mine. "If her violet eyes mean what I think they do, she is also The Shed you were protecting."

"You know about me?" I asked.

"Professor Wallace is the one who deciphered the book I brought back with me. I came to him the day I left you in my bedroom," said Hunter, and I recalled that morning with a smirk.

My smile made the professor blush, and I found it endearing. "I am very impressed with your knowledge in ancient languages, Professor," I told him.

"The myth of The Sheds is something I've pursued for many years," he responded.

"Do you still believe it's a myth?" I asked, and a smile tugged at my lips.

"Absolutely, just as manticores are a myth," he said with a wink.

"While we appreciate your discretion, Professor," Hunter began. "Michaela is going to tell the kingdom the truth of who she is on Saturday."

His eyebrows pulled closely together. "May I ask, why?"

His concern made me falter for a minute, and I wondered if we were doing the right thing. "Because your people deserve to know the truth," I said.

"Michaela, your people have kept it a secret from us for centuries. Perhaps there is a reason for this. Perhaps it is for the best," Professor Wallace replied.

I considered his words, but I could not imagine living my life in secret, hiding who I was. "I truly believe people fear what they don't know," I explained. "If manticores see that Sheds are nothing to fear, they will accept me."

"Manticores are dominant by nature," said the professor. "They will see you as a weapon to ascend them to power."

"Elenora already tried it and failed," I assured him. Hunter grimaced at the reminder.

"I heard that your father escaped and took back the throne last night. Is it true?" the professor asked, sounding relieved by the news.

"Yes, it is true. We left him in his courtroom chambers last night."

"That's wonderful. How did you accomplish it?" Then, as though he just realized the force necessary to overtake the throne, he asked, "Were many manticores lost in the battle?"

"Not one," said Hunter proudly and smiled at me.

"I was able to immobilize Elenora's army," I explained. "Hunter's fighters then brought them to the dungeons and secured them in cells."

"The king will decide what he will do with them," said Hunter.

"And Elenora?" asked Professor Wallace.

Hunter blew out a breath. "Michaela neutralized her venom. She no longer has it, and it seems she's also lost the ability to call on her instincts. She appears to be..." And he stopped. He struggled against a smile and lost. "She appears to be human now."

The professor raised his eyebrows at this but then frowned. "I have never heard of such a thing. I didn't even know it was possible."

"It is," I said.

The professor sat back at his desk. He tapped his finger on his lips for a few seconds. He finally looked up at me.

"Michaela, since you want to share your truth with the kingdom, would you consider guest-lecturing here at the school?"

I must have looked confused because he explained. "I told Hunter that we never shared our suspicions about The Sheds to our students, or any manticore, because we did not want to start a hunt that could harm innocent lives. But, if you would come and explain to everyone who you are and what you do, I think it would show manticores that you are a friend and not our enemy."

"Don't you think my marriage would be enough?" asked Hunter sardonically.

"No," said the professor without any mirth. "Others can say she's manipulated you or put you under a spell. This way, they can see for themselves, the kind of person she truly is."

I didn't know how I felt about that. I didn't want to be some sort of poster child for a cause, but at the same time, I did understand Professor Wallace's point.

"I will think about it," I said, and he nodded in acceptance.

"We also came here to personally invite you to a reception my father is hosting for us on Saturday. Every manticore in the kingdom will be invited, but I wanted you to hear it from me first."

"Thank you, Hunter. I will be there," he said. "It looks like I should prepare for a lengthy discussion on Monday from the students following the reception. I'm sure they'll have a lot of questions."

I smiled and wished him a good day. Hunter shook the professor's hand and then held on to mine as we walked out of the office. I considered the professor's offer, and my thoughts must have shown on my face.

"You look like you have a lot on your mind," said Hunter.

"It's fine. Professor Wallace just gave me one more thing to think about." I waved off his concerns, but ideas swarmed in my head.

He walked me over to a bench close to the professor's door.

"What is it, Michaela?" he asked.

"Are you happy, Hunter?"

"Of course, I am. Why would you ask that?"

"I mean, are you happy in Toronto? Do you miss this?" I glanced around at the students and hallways around us. "This isn't just your old high school. This is who you are. These are your people. When we moved to Toronto, I didn't realize everything you were leaving behind."

Hunter was quiet. He wasn't denying anything I had said.

"When my father wouldn't accept you, Michaela, I told him I would leave everything behind for you. I did it, happily, with no regrets. I missed the kingdom, but I am happy with you," he said.

"Now that your father does accept me, where is it you want to be?"

He inhaled a deep breath but didn't respond. It was answer enough for me.

"I think we should move to New York," I blurted out and watched his face carefully. He kept it blank, of course.

"You do?" he asked evenly. I detected no emotion.

"I do. I cannot go back to the same job and pretend that I have not changed. It feels like I'm trying to be something I'm not. I am not that person anymore."

"What will you do here in New York? If I know you, Michaela, you will not be happy here staying idle."

I smiled because he was absolutely right. "I think I'll start my own PR company. I always knew that would be my plan down the road. I'll start small, maybe just a client or two, and see how it goes."

"Nothing you do is small. I learned that long ago." He chuckled.

I swatted his arm, but my smile grew somber. "It will be hard to say goodbye to Dev and Aunt Julie."

He nodded.

"But I feel like this is the right decision for us."

"We will find a way, Michaela," he said to me. Having my words repeated back to me made me smile.

"We will find a way," I agreed and wrapped my arms around his neck. He nuzzled my ear, and a growl vibrated against my chest.

"Let's get out of here," he said. "And back into our bed."

"Are you tired?" I asked, teasing him.

"Absolutely not," he said.

Twenty-Seven

Michaela

Hunter placed his hand on my knee, and it stopped trembling. It had been shaking since we got in the car. Honestly, I'd been nervous since we returned to Toronto a couple of days ago. I feared telling my aunt I was moving to New York—for good.

"Are you sure you still want to do this?" Hunter asked.

I bit the hangnail that was no longer there and chewed on my skin.

"Yes," I said without any conviction.

He let out a sigh. "I'm worried about you, Michaela. I've never seen you this nervous."

"Moving out on my own was one thing," I explained. "But leaving Aunt Julie to move to New York...I don't know. It feels like I'm abandoning her."

"Why don't you ask your aunt if she wants to come live with us in New York?"

"You would be okay with that?"

"Of course, I can get her an apartment in my building."

"Yes," I said, feeling better. "I would love that."

By the time Hunter pulled into the driveway, I was calm enough to face my aunt.

When she answered the door, I stepped back from the look on her face. Her eyes were red and swollen, her hands shook, and she was sniffling when she asked us to come in.

"Aunt Julie, are you okay?" Stepping into the home, I didn't take my eyes off her. "What happened?"

"Oh, Michaela," she began, but another sob broke. She reached for a tissue in her pocket and shook her head, unable to finish her sentence.

I glanced at Hunter, terrified. What could have made Aunt Julie cry like this? Hunter placed a hand on my aunt's arm and walked her to the couch.

"I'm so sorry," she said when she sat down. "I told myself I wouldn't cry anymore, but I can't seem to stop."

"It's all right," soothed Hunter. "Take your time. Tell us what happened whenever you're ready."

She looked at him and patted his knee. "Thank you." Then she turned her smile onto me. "Michaela..."

I sat next to her and ignored the panic rising in my chest. I swallowed it down, but a lump had formed in my throat.

"There's something I have to tell you," Aunt Julie began. I nodded, encouraging her to continue. "I received an unexpected visitor today." She smiled but then dropped her head down and let out another loud sob. I looked up at Hunter, but he stared back just as clueless as me.

"Julie, you're going to give the poor girl a heart attack. I couldn't wait any longer," said a voice from behind me. When I turned, an older woman walked toward us from the kitchen. She wore a blue floral printed wrap dress and beige sensible heels. Her violet eyes gazed into mine.

"My God," I whispered and stood up from the couch on shaky legs. I stared at the woman, with certainty now. "Grandma?" I asked.

"I prefer *Nonna*, but I can live with Grandma." She smiled.

I stood there, staring at the woman in front of me. I couldn't believe what I was seeing with my own eyes.

"Where have you been?" I demanded, and she flinched.

"Michaela!" Aunt Julie admonished me. But my grandmother raised her hand to stop her.

"Why don't I make us some coffee?" said Aunt Julie. "Mama, please take a seat." She stood from the couch, but my grandmother placed a hand on Aunt Julie's arm and stopped her from leaving the room. She patted the couch and my aunt sat down.

"I have been away," said my grandmother. "Staying away, but always nearby."

"Why?" I asked.

"I wanted no part of the life your mother had chosen. I did not want them to call on me. I wanted no part in killing anyone or anything, regardless of what they were."

"But you didn't just leave my mother, you left Aunt Julie and me too."

"I couldn't see how I could keep a relationship with you and keep myself hidden from them," she said. "Your mother made the decision to join them, not me. I blame her for dividing our family."

I winced from the accusation. I was not ready to place blame on my mother yet.

"You could have come back ages ago, when Aunt Julie needed a mother and I needed a grandmother." My heart raced and my voice rose. I was angry with her for abandoning us.

"Nicholas knew about your mother. I thought it was just a matter of time until he came looking for you and convinced you to take up her role."

"My mother never told Nicholas about me. She never told me anything about The Sheds." At this the older woman tilted her head. She looked surprised.

"So, you see? Your own fears proved to be baseless. You had nothing to worry about, while we had nothing to hold on to but each other."

"Michaela, wait," said Aunt Julie. "We cannot blame her—"

"Maybe you can't, but I sure can," I said to my aunt.

"I understand why you left your small village," I continued and saw her eyes widen. "Yes, Signora Tassone told me everything. I had to travel seven thousand kilometres to discover this information from a complete stranger instead of my own family. But I understood why you fled and didn't tell anyone where you went. I even admired your morals—not wanting to kill manticores—but what I could not understand is why you never came back."

"I was afraid," she said. "I was scared what would happen if the same manticores that killed your mother decided to come after me. I thought the curse had skipped you."

"Curse?" I asked, startled.

"Yes, Michaela. For me, being born this way was a curse. My life was not my own. I was told whom I had to marry and what my life's purpose was meant to be. I did not want any of it. I made sure your mother was aware of our lineage but kept her hidden from those who chased me, until she sought them out. All I did was undone by her penchant for power."

"I don't think she sought power, but instead felt a responsibility to do something with the gifts she was born with. I do not agree with everything she did, but at least she did something. She did not run away from who she was."

"I am not running now," she said, and I saw her straighten her spine a little.

"What do you want?" I asked, still angry with her. "Now that Nicholas has me, you are free to come out of hiding?"

She pursed her lips, like she wanted to yell at me but held back.

"Don't hold your tongue on my account," I said. "If you have something to say, then say it."

"Fine," she said. "You think you know everything? You think because you heard a version from Anna Maria that you know me? Well, you don't know me, Michaela. I left my entire family, my home, and everything I knew for a country I knew nothing about, not even the language. I protected my children with my own life and kept a quiet life so that they could continue to live as normally as possible. I was scared, so I ran. I am sorry that I did not come back after Lucia and Marco were killed. I live with that regret every day. Most days I convinced myself it was best that I stayed away, that it would be easier for you if you never knew me. But then I selfishly missed you and fantasized about us being a family again."

I did not soften my face, even when hers contorted in pain. I was still too angry with her. "Where is my grandfather?"

"He died shortly after we moved away. I've been on my own this entire time," she said.

Aunt Julie let out a little sob, but I turned away because I didn't want to hear it. I did not want to feel sorry for the woman who'd left us. Her loneliness was her own doing.

"You know—" I laughed without any humor "—I had an easier time forgiving the manticore king for killing my parents than trying to find forgiveness for you. At least he did it to serve justice for his family. You abandoned us to save yourself."

"Murder is never justified," my grandmother said. "Even if you think you are doing it to avenge another life. It only brings misery. I did not leave just for myself. If I'd come back and Nicholas found me there with you, he would have set a course for your life."

"Nicholas is not this villain you believe him to be. I never had a chance to meet his father, but he took my giving up the cause much better than I would have imagined. Perhaps if you were just honest with what you wanted..."

"You don't think I was honest with his father?" she said. "Of course, I told him I wanted no part of it. I told him every day, and every day he tried to convince me that this was my purpose in life. That I am nothing if not a manticore slayer. That as a descendent of Shed, I was born to pick up this sword and die on it if I must.

He didn't care about me. I was a weapon and nothing else to him. I do not expect you to forgive me, Michaela. At least not today. But I did not want to leave this world without letting you know that I am alive. I do love my family, and I am sorry for the mistakes that I have made."

Her chest heaved from her words, and she glared at me. I suddenly saw the resemblance between us. For years, I wished for my family back. When I'd made that wish, I imagined it would be my parents standing in the living room today. Instead, I got a furious grandmother. I nodded, coming to a decision. "There is one way you can prove to me that you care about me and not yourself. That you are willing to risk your own fears to be the supportive grandmother you say you want to be."

Her face softened, and a hint of a smile grew on her lips. "Anything," she said. "I'll say anything."

"Not say, be," I told her. "Be at my wedding reception on Saturday."

"Absolutely." She laughed. "I would love nothing more than to celebrate your wedding."

"But you already had a wedding," said Aunt Julie, tilting her head.

"Yes, but my father-in-law would like to host another one with Hunter's side. It will be in a ballroom in New York, and the room will be full of hundreds of manticores."

My grandmother's face fell, and she gasped for a gulp of air. I stood and walked out the door. I didn't want to see fear on her face or hear any excuse from her lips. I would never forgive her if I did.

"I'll send you both a plane ticket," I called from outside. Hunter shook his head when he climbed into the car.

"You know, sometimes you scare me," he laughed. "I hope I never get on your bad side."

"Well, it's been a tough week," I said to him. "And I'm late."

"We're not going anywhere, how can you be late?" He chuckled again.

"That's not the kind of late I am referring to."

And then he stopped laughing. I couldn't help but smile.

Twenty-Eight

Hunter

Michaela insisted it was normal for her to be late, and I wanted to believe her, but I couldn't help the unease that ran through me. This wouldn't be an average pregnancy, since there was nothing average about either of us. She'd dropped this bomb a few days ago, but I hadn't stopped thinking about it since. She, however, refused to talk about it.

We packed up her apartment in Toronto and headed back to New York. We'd landed at JFK only yesterday, but I'd wasted no time getting us settled. I wanted her to be happy here.

"Thomas, has the lawyer given you the keys yet?" I asked when he picked up the phone.

"Yes, I have them in my hands now," he confirmed.

"Great, I'll meet you there," I said and ended the call.

Michaela had scheduled a meeting with a former client this morning. She also wasn't wasting time getting her business started. I'd offered to pick her up from her meeting since I would be in the neighbourhood. But that wasn't exactly true. I couldn't wait to surprise her.

She stood outside of Savor restaurant with her client. I recalled his name was Gabriel. I'd met him the first time I kissed Michaela at James's apartment. Michaela stretched out her hand, and Gabriel stared at it with a smile and then leaned in to kiss her cheek. He reached over and kissed the other cheek. Both of his hands gripped the tops of her arms, but then slowly slid down to hold her hands. Michaela pulled away awkwardly. A growl rumbled in my chest. She noticed my car and walked over. I had ten seconds to control myself. I breathed in deeply, filling my lungs with air, and held my breath for three seconds. I exhaled and did it again. A smile spread across Michaela's face as she approached the car.

"Hi, Hunter," Michaela said when she got in. "Have you been waiting long?"

"Are you okay?" I asked her but didn't take my eyes off the bastard.

"Yes, that was uncomfortable," she said. Then noticing my hands balled into fits, she said. "I will handle it."

"Just say the word and I'll take care of it," I told her, my fingers now gripping the steering wheel, imagining it was his neck.

"Hunter, I said I'll handle it." She sighed. "I appreciate you wanting to help, but I've dealt with his type before. I'll take care of it."

"You promise you'll come to me if he doesn't back off?" I asked, and when she hesitated, I added, "Michaela, I won't kill him."

I couldn't give her my word that I wouldn't hurt him, but the bastard would live.

"Fine. I promise," she said while applying lipstick using the sun-visor mirror. "Where are we going? You said you had a surprise. I'm not sure I'm up for one right now."

"I think you'll like this one."

I drove to the address I had researched and saw Thomas standing outside. He walked over to my side of the car. I rolled down the window, and he handed me an envelope.

"Everything looks to be in order," he said.

"Thanks, Thomas," I responded.

"Hi, Thomas!" Michaela greeted him from the passenger seat. She leaned over me to speak to Thomas. "We'll see you at the reception tomorrow night?"

"I wouldn't miss it for the world." He chuckled. "I'll see you both tomorrow."

I walked Michaela to the front of the building. I subtly waved off the doorman to open the door for her. This building looked very different from mine. It reminded me of the Plaza Hotel when it first opened on October 1, 1907. It had tall, white, wood-paneled walls, chandeliers dripping with glass, and a shiny oak floor that extended throughout the hallway. It had old-world charm but with modern technology.

"Wow, this place is stunning," she said. "What are we doing here?"

"There's a section I wanted to take a look at. I thought it could work well for a new partner I've taken on, but I wanted your opinion on it first."

"Sure, sounds like fun," she said and held the elevator for me as I got in. The elevator doors were gilded and gold. The tinted mirrored walls made the space feel more homelike rather than businesslike. I pressed the button for the penthouse level.

Michaela smiled. "I like this space already," she said.

When we reached the top floor, there was only one door in the entire hallway; however, it wasn't the one I needed. I turned right and saw another door with the same number written on the envelope that Thomas had handed to me earlier: 1603.

"This is it," I said and unlocked the door with the key inside the envelope. The room inside was nearly an exact replica of the foyer downstairs, down to the shiny wood floors and crystal chandeliers. There wasn't any furniture inside, but a table was set up on the balcony. I smiled knowing Thomas had followed my instructions to the letter.

Michaela turned, her eyes seeming to take a snapshot of everything in the room. "This place is as beautiful as the lobby," she said.

"That's rarely the case." She laughed. "What sort of development is this for?"

I ignored her question and peered at the kitchen with its white cabinets and huge marble island. I guided her toward one of the bedrooms and saw that a new carpet had been laid, and chandeliers hung inside these rooms, as well. I held Michaela's hand as I toured the apartment. The penthouse was more than three thousand square feet, including three bedrooms and an office.

"Let's go see the terrace," I said, curious what this part of the penthouse looked like. I had noticed the table and chairs, but I hadn't seen how big it was. It extended the entire length of the family room and wrapped around the building. A free-standing hammock swayed in the breeze, and a daybed was nestled in the corner. It was perfect.

I walked back to the table and unpacked the basket.

"Oh, Hunter, is that picnic for us?" Michaela asked, bringing both of her hands to her face.

"It is. I thought I would surprise you with dinner under the stars, just like our first date," I said and uncorked the wine. I poured her a glass and offered it to her.

"To us," I said.

She smiled and tilted her head to the side, examining the drink.

"Do you like it, Michaela?" I asked her, hoping she'd say yes.

"Mmm, it's very good. Is it Chardonnay?" I didn't know if she was being deliberately obtuse or if it really hadn't dawned on her yet.

"Yes, it's Chardonnay. But that's not what I meant," I said. "Do you like the apartment?"

"Of course, what's not to like?" she said. "I mean, it's out of some modern-day fairy tale."

"Good, because this fairy tale is yours," I told her, and my heart raced, anticipating her joy.

"What?" She looked genuinely confused, and for a minute I panicked, worried this wasn't a good idea.

"I bought this place for us," I said and then rushed to explain. "In Toronto, the apartment was yours, and I felt like I'd simply moved in with you. When we decided to move to New York, I worried you'd feel the same way I did. So, I wanted us to move into a place that we could call ours—together."

When she still didn't respond, I felt like such a pompous ass. I thought surprising her would be romantic, and now I realized it was inconsiderate.

"It doesn't have to be this place if you don't like it. We can choose something together, whenever you're ready."

She walked back into the apartment, wineglass in hand. She went into the kitchen and put the wineglass on top of the island. She moved from the fridge to the stove to the island, opening up drawers. She picked up her wineglass again and walked toward the largest bedroom. I followed her, trying to decipher any facial expression, but she was a blank slate. She peeked inside the walk-in closet and then entered the ensuite. She slipped off her heels and stepped into the claw-foot tub in the center of the bathroom. With her arm stretched out of the tub, still holding her wineglass, she said, "I can live here."

She gave me a radiant smile, and I was lost. I walked up to her, grabbed her glass of wine, and set it on the floor. I swung one leg and then the other into the tub until I sat facing her. I pulled her hips forward until she straddled me.

"Hunter." She laughed as she tried to get her balance. I waited for her to grab onto both sides of the tub, and then I unbuttoned her blouse. Her skirt had already ridden up to her hips, and I leaned in to kiss the sensitive spot at her neck. Her sandalwood fragrance—which was uniquely Michaela—hit me full force, and I couldn't be patient any longer. I ripped the blouse, and the buttons pinged on the marble floor. Her panties were next. I unbuttoned my clothes.

"Hunter," she said again, only this time it sounded like a plea. "I haven't read this part in any fairy tales."

"Then you've been reading the wrong ones," I said.

Twenty-Nine

Michaela

Hunter and I had spent last night familiarizing ourselves with every room in our new penthouse. Today, I was in his old apartment getting ready for our second wedding reception. I'd decided to wear my wedding dress again because, really, any woman given the opportunity to slip on her gown again would take it.

But this time, my palms were sweaty, and my stomach churned. Unlike the first reception, tonight I felt on display, as though I would be the entertainment. However, I appreciated the gesture the king had offered us. It was his way of welcoming me into the family and the kingdom.

"Would you like me to pin up your veil?" Laura asked. She'd arrived earlier to help me dress. Aunt Julie's plane had been delayed and hadn't landed until an hour ago. I told my aunt to go straight to her hotel room and freshen up, not to worry about me. Laura sweetly offered her assistance.

"I don't think I'm going to wear that tonight," I said, making this last-minute decision.

"In that case, this gift will be perfect," she replied.

"What gift?" I asked as I watched Laura leave the room then walk back in with a medium-sized black jewelry box.

"The one my father has sent for you," she said. "Open it."

I lifted the lid and gasped when I saw what was inside.

"Oh, wow, is that a tiara?" I asked, as Laura pulled the headpiece out. The tiny diamonds sparkled in the light and the large amethyst in the center shined brightly.

"This belonged to my mother," said Laura. "But my father added the amethyst for you."

I felt out of breath, as though I had the wind knocked out of me. The king's generosity overwhelmed me. I placed a hand over my heart.

"But Laura, this should go to you."

"I have several pieces from my mother, but this crown belongs to you. As Hunter's wife, you will rule alongside him when his time comes."

The closest I imagined myself to becoming a ruler was owning my own company. The thought of being responsible for thousands of manticores was more than a bit daunting. "Let's hope they will accept a Shed as their future queen."

"They'll love you," she said and squeezed my hands.

Laura drove us to the reception at the Manhattan hotel. We were a little early, but I preferred to have a few minutes to myself. I wanted to calm my nerves before I had to go out there and greet everyone.

The ballroom was enormous; it could seat thousands in here at once. I hoped there would not be that many. Candelabras sat on every dinner table, and at least a half dozen candles were lit on each one. It was all very romantic and reminded me of a fairy tale.

Hunter paced at the back of the room. He'd put on the same black tuxedo he'd worn in Toronto. The suit fit his broad shoulders perfectly. James had surely had something to do with that. Whenever I saw Hunter's handsome face, I couldn't believe he was mine.

When he noticed me in the room, he reached me in seconds and pulled me into his arms. His lips found my ear and he whispered, "I missed you," before sealing the words with a kiss. When I pulled away from him, he finally noted the crown on my head.

"Your father gave this to me as a wedding present," I said. "It was your mother's."

"I recognize it," he said. "She wore it on special occasions. But it looks different."

"He added an amethyst to it."

"It's perfect," he whispered, and then I heard someone say from afar, "It is."

King Marsel strode into the ballroom. He looked younger than his years and the healthiest I'd ever seen him.

"Thank you," I said when he reached us.

"Wear the crown proudly, my dear," he said. "It suits you."

Laura walked over to us, her phone still next to her ear. "Are you guys ready? The guests have started to arrive."

Hunter looked at me expectantly. I took a deep breath, felt the weight of the crown on my head, and said "Yes, I'm ready."

Hunter led me to the ballroom doors. He stood to my left and the king was on my right. Hunter squeezed my hand as Laura used both of hers to push the doors wide open.

A crowd had formed in the lobby. The first guests approached cautiously, until the king extended his hand and they rushed eagerly to accept it.

"Thank you for coming, Mr. and Mrs. Jackson," said the king. The couple looked surprised that the king had remembered their name, and then jubilant smiles spread across their faces. "Let me introduce you to my daughter-in-law, Michaela."

I put my hand forward and they shook it vigorously. I had to pull my hand back, as I worried Mrs. Jackson's enthusiasm may dislocate my elbow.

The king proceeded to the next group of manticores and then the next. Surprisingly, he knew most by name, and their love for their king was apparent in their elation to shake his hand. Whether they were truly happy to welcome me, or simply couldn't stop smiling from being singled out by their king, I felt no tension in the room.

Not long after thinking this, however, a strange sensation came over me. I tensed and turned to see the king stiffen beside me.

"Here comes Davis," he said. "Michaela, are you up to greeting him?"

"I am if you are," I said.

"Davis," the king said and stretched out his hand. I offered mine, as well. Davis looked horrible. His eyes had dark shadows sunken below them. His skin was weathered and blotchy.

"What did you do to him?" asked Hunter after Davis walked off.

"I may have used some questionable methods. However, many were Davis's own ideas."

"Do you believe his remorse?" asked Hunter.

"I do," said the king. "And...I asked Leo to keep a close eye on him, just in case."

Hunter smiled beside me, but the feeling of unease remained long after Davis left. A few minutes later, I felt as though thousands of tiny ants were crawling up my skin. I turned and saw a man staring at me. He had brown eyes and blonde hair.

"Who's that?" I asked Hunter, just as the man approached us.

"Tommy Ross, thank you for coming," the king said formally without any joviality.

"I wouldn't miss this for the world," he said and then winked at me.

I extended my hand and he turned it over. He placed his wet lips on my knuckles. I couldn't help but wipe my hand on my dress when his sweaty palm finally released mine.

"I don't like that man," I said to Hunter when he left.

"The feeling is mutual," Hunter said.

Fortunately, Leo was next, and that put me in a better mood until I saw that he was alone. "Where's Scarlet?" I asked.

"She couldn't make it," he said, distracted. "You look beautiful, Michaela. If you weren't already married, I'd snatch you up myself."

"All right, Leo, save your charm for another woman," said Hunter. "One that's not my wife."

The last guests walked through our receiving line. I strained my neck, trying to catch a glimpse of my aunt Julie, but I didn't see her.

"Don't worry," said Hunter. "She'll come."

I nodded because I couldn't get past the lump in my throat. It wasn't Aunt Julie I worried wouldn't show up. I didn't ask her when she landed if she'd come alone. I didn't want to know if that was the case.

When there was no one left in line, the king turned to me and said, "Shall we take our seats?"

He offered me his arm and walked me over to our table. The head table sat on a small platform with four chairs laid out in a row. Laura already sat at the chair farthest right, waiting for us.

The waiters had poured a glass of champagne for every guest, and the king grabbed his glass and lifted it up high. Before he could speak, the ballroom doors swung open, and two petite ladies surveyed the room.

"Aunt Julie," I said and then whispered "*Nonna*." The word seemed foreign on my lips. I couldn't believe she'd come! Tears filled my eyes. I pushed myself away from the table and raced across the empty dance floor to greet them.

"You came," I said breathlessly when I reached them.

"We were held up at Customs. Your grandmother thought bringing fresh cheese in her luggage was a good idea."

I laughed at the absurdity of that statement and hugged my aunt Julie. I turned to embrace my grandmother next. "Thank you," I whispered, and she held me tightly.

I released her but held her hand. It trembled in mine. I squeezed and turned to face the crowd. Hundreds of manticores stared at us.

"Are you all right?" I whispered to my grandmother. Then another thought dawned on me. "Have you ever met a manticore before?"

"Only your husband," she said with a smile.

I turned to address the guests, "Everyone," I said as loud as I could. "This is my aunt Julie and my grandmother Ramona."

A murmur grew among the guests, and I worried someone would say something unpleasant. But then I heard clapping. It came from Leo. He casually leaned back in his chair. Soon, others joined him until everyone was clapping. My aunt Julie and my grandmother smiled, but they looked more like grimaces. They were uncomfortable with the attention, but at least it was welcoming rather than intimidating.

I walked them both to Leo's table. I had already seated my aunt Julie there and left an extra seat just in case.

"Ladies," Leo said when we arrived. He stood to pull out the seat next to him. "The pleasure of your company is all mine."

"Thank you," I whispered in his ear and patted his shoulder before heading back to my table.

"Is everything all right?" Hunter asked when I returned.

"Yes, everything is great," I said, happy my grandmother had come. She'd come for me. I didn't imagine this was a small feat for her, and the gesture truly soothed a piece of my heart that I had closed off many years ago. I was confident we would pave a path forward after this.

After I sat, the king rose again, champagne glass in hand, and addressed the room. "May I have your attention, please."

The chatter in the room hushed until not a single voice could be heard.

"Thank you for joining me today to welcome Hunter's wife, my new daughter-in-law, Michaela, to our family. Many of you have just met Michaela for the first time tonight, but I hope you will take the time to get to know her in the coming weeks, as she and Hunter have decided to move back to New York City."

The guests cheered and many turned to look at each other with big smiles on their faces.

"While many of you have only just met her, I am sure you have all heard of her by now," the king said, and the guests quieted down again. "She is not like us, and some may say she shouldn't be marrying my son. But Michaela has more courage, strength, and love than anyone in this room. I stand here before you today because of her. She not only saved my life, but she saved my soul. She has forgiven my past and vowed to start a future with Hunter. I am proud to call her *daughter*."

I caught a tear that fell down my cheek and quickly wiped it away before it destroyed my new title as a courageous warrior. I guess I was still the same Michaela, and that made me smile.

I stood to thank the king, and then he passed the microphone to me. I hadn't expected that and hadn't prepared a speech. "Um," I said to a frighteningly quiet room. "Thank you all for coming today, and thank you to King Marsel for his kind words and this beautiful reception."

I pushed a piece of hair that had escaped my pins behind my ear. I turned and saw Hunter shake his head at his father, but the king was beaming at me. I didn't want to let him down.

"When I met Hunter, I didn't know who he was or where he came from. I didn't care. I fell in love with him the moment I met him. We had several obstacles to overcome. Some you've already heard about and others we battled in private." I turned to smile at Hunter. "I would do anything to protect him and the people he loves, and that includes all of you." I paused and inhaled a deep breath. "I join you today not as one of your own, but I hope as your partner—and if you'll have me, your leader one day. I will do whatever's in my power to keep you safe."

This time, a man I didn't recognize began the applause, and the king joined in emphatically. Tommy Ross rose from his chair and left the room. My grandmother, whose eyes shined brightly from the tears gathering in them, sat with her hands clasped to her mouth. I wiped a tear from my own eyes when I realized how far we'd all come.

I sat next to Hunter, and he squeezed my hand and kissed my lips. "I'm the luckiest man in the world," he said.

I felt pretty damn lucky myself right then.

***

The rest of the evening continued as a fairy tale, with me dancing with my Prince Charming and officially becoming a princess myself.

The reception began to dwindle around midnight, even though Leo had told me a manticore celebration usually went well into the early morning hours. "We thought it best to go easy on you for your first time," Leo said, wagging his eyebrows at me. I laughed. Hunter did not.

"I'm warning you for the last time," Hunter said, and Leo shoved him on the shoulder. Hunter fought to hide a smile.

"It was a beautiful reception, Michaela," said Aunt Julie.

"You look wonderful in that dress," said Ramona. "I'm sorry I missed it the first time."

"That's all right, I'm just glad you're here now."

"Ramona Shedly?" a voice called from behind us. Shocked I recognized that voice, I turned to see Nicholas walking into the room. My grandmother looked at me confused, her eyebrows pulling together.

"I didn't invite him," I said when her eyebrows shot up.

"Nicholas Giannis?" she said when she faced him.

"Yes," he said with a smile. "You look exactly like the picture my father had of you."

"Your father kept a picture of me?" she asked skeptically.

"In his office, even after he married. He said he didn't want to put it away. It was a sore spot with my mother, as you can imagine," Nicholas said with a wry smile.

"What are you doing here, Nicholas?" I asked.

"Please pardon my intrusion," he said, lifting his hands up in front of him. "I waited until everyone left because I wasn't exactly comfortable entering a room full of manticores, and..."

"Shh..." said Hunter looking around to ensure none of the wait-staff heard him.

"Sorry," he said, raising his hands again. "Forgot about your rule. Anyway, I heard that you had resurfaced, and I wanted to see you for myself."

"Who told you?" she asked.

"My grandson Adam has been keeping a close eye on Michaela. He saw you when she came to visit last week."

That little revelation caught me off guard. Hunter, as well.

"You can tell Adam that Michaela no longer needs anyone watching over her," said Hunter. "I will—"

"I can take care of myself," I said to them both.

"I've told him that," said Nicholas. "I guess he's just having a hard time with it."

"I can make it easier for him," Hunter muttered under his breath.

"I'm sorry to show up like this but I wanted to meet you, Ramona. I have prayed for so many years, hoping you were still alive. My father and I both. He is no longer with us, but I know he would be happy to know you're all right."

"Thank you, Nicholas," said Ramona. "I owe your father an apology for running out on him. I hope he forgave me."

"He forgave you," said Nicholas. "But he never forgot you."

My grandmother was taken aback by this declaration. Perhaps she never thought the man who wanted to marry her had actually loved her. Maybe she'd been wrong about him.

"I know it's late now, but can I come see you tomorrow?" asked Nicholas.

"Yes," said my grandmother. "Let's have lunch tomorrow. I would like that very much."

Thirty

Epilogue

Michaela

I screamed until my lungs burned. The pain encompassed my entire body, so I could no longer tell where it came from. I was sweating, exhausted, and overwhelmed.

"I can't take any more," I panted to Hunter, who looked more tortured than I did.

"You don't have to, Michaela," he said for the tenth time. "You don't have to be a warrior right now. Don't try to be a hero...please...I beg you...just take the epidural."

I'd been offered the needle hours ago, but one look at the sheer length of it and I'd screamed at the physician to get the hell away from me with that thing. I would rather take on a room full of bloodthirsty manticores than have him stick that in me.

Another contraction came on, and I gripped Hunter's hand to distract me from my pain. His face contorted but he didn't make a sound. *Smart man.* He knew better than to complain about his poor little hand when my entire body felt like it was being ripped open.

"I see the head," the physician said.

"Thank God," I said, breathless.

"Just a few more pushes, Michaela," he called out.

"Yeah, well easy for you to say, Doc, from where you're standing."

I sucked in a deep breath and pushed down on my pelvis with everything I had.

"That's it, keep going," he said, and I inhaled again and gave it one last big push.

"You're doing great, Michaela!" shouted the physician, and then I heard silence.

"Is the baby all right?" I panicked and pushed Hunter toward our child. He rushed over to the physician, who held the baby in his arms. Then I heard the blessed sound of a baby's cry.

"Oh, thank God," I said, and my throat clogged with a new emotion—fierce, protective love.

"It's a girl," said the physician.

"A girl," I whispered. A baby girl. I squeezed my eyes shut and let the tears roll down my face.

My day had started in the most ordinary way. I woke up a little more swollen than usual but felt pretty good. Hunter drove me to the kingdom where I'd worked as a guest lecturer for the past six months. I'd taken Professor Wallace up on his offer. Since the academy had decided to teach their students about Sheds, I wanted to be the one to oversee it. I'd even asked Nicholas if he would guest lecture with me. He was thrilled to be a part of it. As I had expected and experienced myself, he was a natural teacher.

The students were reserved at first. I'd expected that, of course, but I thought they were less nervous about me being a Shed than they were about being taught by their future queen. In time, however, they'd started to ask questions enthusiastically and even asked if I could demonstrate a few of my powers. I regret to say, I may have shown off a little in front of them. It was worth it, though. The students came to class eager for their next lesson.

After my morning classes, I'd spent the rest of the afternoon working on a client's product launch. At the end of the day, I felt tired but satisfied. My life was not at all as I had imagined it would be a year ago. It was so much better, and none of it would have been possible if I hadn't opened my eyes to the possibility of there being more than what I saw in front of them.

I heard angry snorts coming from my baby and I opened my eyes. Hunter rocked her in his arms. He looked down at her like she had just performed the greatest of feats, instead of waving two angry fists at him.

"Hunter," I called.

"She's perfect," he responded.

"She's hungry," I replied and stretched out my arms. Hunter placed her in them. I cradled her to my breast and watched her root.

"What are we going to name her?" I asked. We'd been thinking of names for the past month and had plenty we agreed on if it were a boy, but the girl's name always eluded us.

"What about the one from the story?" said Hunter.

I smiled, recalling it. "Yes, that's perfect."

"Michaela, your aunt and grandmother are outside," he said. His amber eyes on me. "Are you okay if they come in now?"

I'd kicked everyone out of the room when I knew I was in labour. I'd wanted it to be just Hunter and me.

"Yes, tell them to come in."

Hunter walked across the room and opened the door. A few minutes later, my aunt and grandmother walked in. My aunt cried as soon as she saw me, but my grandmother was more stoic.

I looked down at my precious little girl and saw she had already stopped feeding. She had fallen asleep.

"Michaela, sweetie, how are you feeling?" asked Aunt Julie.

"Tired," I said but smiled. "Tired and happy."

"Oh, we're so happy too." She leaned over to look at my precious bundle. "Hunter told us you have a baby girl."

"Yes," I said and hesitated before I revealed the next part. But I knew I was right. A few moments ago, when her eyes had locked with mine, I'd seen my own reflected back at me. "She has violet eyes."

I heard my grandmother's quick intake of breath. I couldn't tell if she was happy or worried.

"May I hold her?" she asked.

I nodded and gently lifted my daughter from my breast. Her mouth was slightly open, as though she'd fallen asleep midsuckle.

"Have you given her a name yet?" asked my grandmother, as she adjusted the baby in the crook of her arm and settled the blanket snuggly around the infant's neck.

"Violet," I said.

"Oh?"

"We named her after the original one," I said and waited to see if my grandmother knew what I meant by that. She nodded and walked away, holding Violet and rocking her gently in her arms.

"That is a good name, little one," she said, cooing to the baby. My eyes felt heavy, but I fought to keep them open. My grandmother's voice sounded far away but she was only a few feet away from me, standing in front of my window. The curtains were open, and night closed in on us. I closed my eyes but listened to the sound of my grandmother's voice.

"There once was a young and beautiful woman with raven black hair and purple eyes, but it was not her striking features that earned her the attention of the villagers around her, it was her song. She had a voice like that of a songbird and she sang wherever she went. Her voice would bring joy to the sorrowful, it would soothe the sick, and on rare occasions make your heart leap so high you could hardly breathe. Yes, she was that wonderful, that powerful.

"Her parents named her Violet, after the unusual color of her eyes that she inherited from her mother. But unlike her mother, who kept to herself, Violet wanted to share her gifts with others. She knew they were too special to keep secret. One day, as she made her way through her village to visit a friend sick in her bed, Violet came across a ferocious beast. The beast had long nails and sharp fangs, but what made him truly terrifying was his anger. He roared and gnashed his teeth at Violet.

"Everyone in the village ran away to hide and escape the beast. But Violet did not run away. She did not hide, instead she sang. She sang using words no one could later describe. She sang until the beast's' roars could no longer be heard. She sang until he took in his last breath and fell to the ground with a loud thump next to Violet's feet. It was said after that day, the villagers were never again plagued with beasts. They said Violet had slayed the beast with her song and eyes gifted by the gods."

I smiled, pleased that my grandmother knew the story but not surprised. There was a lot she still needed to share with me, but now she could share it with my daughter too.

Before I closed my eyes, I saw my grandmother turn Violet toward the window, her little face on display for the outside world to see. A flash of lightning lit up the sky, and a radiant shade of purple glowed along the horizon. A sigh of contentment rushed through my lips, and I fell asleep dreaming of ancient gods, little girls, and a dazzling violet sky.

The Story Continues...

Stay tuned for the third book in the VIOLET SKY Paranormal Romance series.

To stay in the know on book release dates, bonus materials, promotions and more, sign up for Eve Marian's newsletter at www.evemarian.com.

Acknowledgements

A huge thank you to:

My husband and children, who motivated me throughout this entire process.

To my alpha readers, Gilda and Lauren, who yelled at me to hurry up and finish the second book. I cannot express how your unwavering support and generosity means to me. You gave your time freely and enthusiastically. Thank you!

To my editor, Katie, for her polite questions that always made my story stronger.

To my critique partners Anuja, Nita, Jayme and Nadja for their encouragement and brilliant writing suggestions.

To everyone who purchased the first book, or sent an encouraging message on my social media channel—I cannot thank you enough! You are the reason I keep writing.

Thank you.

About the Author

Eve Marian is a former journalist and public relations executive. She lives in a suburb of Toronto with her husband, two children, and clever cat named Chase.

To follow Eve Marian on social media or to stay up to date on the latest releases, visit www.evemarian.com.

www.ingramcontent.com/pod-product-compliance
Lightning Source LLC
Chambersburg PA
CBHW030339310726
48979CB00001B/101

* 9 7 8 1 7 7 7 8 0 1 3 7 3 *